Follow the
Dove

Follow the Dove

Catherine M. Byrne

Matador
5 Weir Road
Kibworth Beauchamp
Leicester LE8 0LQ, UK
Tel: (+44) 116 279 2299
Fax: (+44) 116 279 2277
Email: books@troubador.co.uk
Web: www.troubador.co.uk/matador

ISBN 978 1848768 062

British Library Cataloguing in Publication Data.
A catalogue record for this book is available from the British Library.

Typeset in 10.5pt Book Antiqua by Troubador Publishing Ltd, Leicester, UK

Matador is an imprint of Troubador Publishing Ltd

Chapter 1

The first time she saw him Isa forgot to breathe.

He was standing in the warehouse doorway of the recently established Floating Shops of Kirkwall, gazing in her direction. Low in the sky, the sun slid over his blond hair. For a moment, her limbs refused to move. She mentally made a note of the date, knowing she would always remember this day – May 16th, 1899.

'Get a move on girl. You're not paid to stand about gawking.' Samuel Lierstock the overseer, a big-set man, his skin mottled and unhealthy, white wisps of hair clinging to his scalp, strode into view.

Isa jumped and spun around. Wiping her brow, she scuttled back to the shelf and dragged down another bolt of cloth. She placed it in the packing case and smoothed the surface with her fingers until Lierstock walked away. By now, other workers blocked her view of the door. Once the way was clear, she found herself looking into the eyes of the stranger. Well aware of her own attractiveness, she tilted her head, tucked a black curl under her scarf and allowed a smile to tug the corners of her lips. Small and wiry she might be, but she had a complexion that glowed with health and the energy of a fireball. She turned back to her work, face burning at her own daring.

'Who is he?' she whispered to Bella, her workmate and friend.

Bella, twenty-six, a fair sized woman, married with three bairns, had taken Isa under her wing from the first day she started at the warehouse. Without asking, she knew whom Isa meant.

'Davie Reid. One of the Raumsey lot. Ye keep yer eyes off the likes of him.'

'Why?'

'Ye're fifteen. Yer mam would go mad. Those lads come here

1

to sell the whisky they make on that wee island of theirs and they're one step in front of the excise man. Now, there's still ten bales to be packed.'

Already Isa felt as if this day had gone on forever. Her muscles ached; her dress stuck to her back, and she had eaten her bread and dripping sandwiches ages ago. Speed made her clumsy. She pulled at a roll of cloth. It slipped from her grasp, hit the floor and rolled open.

'Careful,' whispered Bella, 'ye don't want to anger Leirstock anymore the day.'

With ragged breath, Isa re-arranged the material. This was a good job, better than being a fisher lassie – gutting and packing herring – or leaving home to go into service on the other side, as the islanders called mainland Scotland. However, she could not concentrate. All she thought of was Davie Reid's eyes. She glanced sideways at the doorway, disappointed to find him gone.

After the bell had gone to signify the end of the shift, the warehouse workers walked home together past the built up area along the sea front. Weary to the bone, they still found enough energy to giggle and tease each other. A wind had whipped up and a few drops of rain splattered against their faces. Isa pulled her shawl tighter around her shoulders and fell behind the others.

'Doubt if the ships'll get out tomorrow.' Bella stopped to look up at a sky that pressed downward like a wad of grey cotton wool.

Isa bit her lower lip, stopping a smile. Bad weather could be in her favour. A Raumsey yole would never manage across the Pentland Firth before the storm broke. She asked, 'can we not watch the floating shops being loaded?' They often did this, marvelling at the stock of groceries, meats, shoes and clothes lining the shelves of the large sailing vessels, ready to be ferried to smaller islands.

'Na, I've got to go tend to me bairns. Ye'd best get off and all.' Above their heads, the sky had become prematurely dark as a storm swept from the north. Oil lamps and candles were already beginning to glow through windows.

'Aye, I'll see ye the morn,' answered Isa. Albert Street and home lay before her, but Isa's steps were slow.

'Mind, no dallying. I see the mischief in yer brown eyes,' Bella called after her. Once her friend disappeared through her own front door Isa changed direction and ran for the harbour. Here the wind blew fiercer, beating waves into a frenzy of foam that rushed towards the pier, breaking over and around the concrete walls and shooting skyward. Men were busy hauling their boats across the cobbles to a point well above high tide mark, since the small harbour was not adequate to protect them.

Abe Olyphant, a friend of Isa's father, stared from beneath the peak of his cap and chewed his pipe in the side of his mouth. Eyes watering, with either the wind or regret that he could no longer assist the younger men, he leaned against a pile of creels.

'Stay back there.' He caught Isa by the arm. His hands were aged and gnarled, but his grip was strong.

'I wasn't going right down.' Peering past him, she spotted only local boats, masts swaying. 'Where's the Raumsey yole?'

'The Raumsey lads? Na lass, they don't tie up here. Sail takes too long, see. They berth across at Scapa Bay and bring the stuff over by horse and cart. And they'll be staying the night wi' me.' He pointed at two men she had not seen before. Both tall and bonny, one was as dark as the other was fair. 'The Reid brothers,' said Abe.

She longed to ask the whereabouts of the young lad but if she showed too much interest, Abe might tell her parents. Not that she worried about her dad, but her mam seemed a bit strange recently, as if her mind was on other things. There was little point in upsetting her further. However, Davie Reid would soon be gone. She had to see him again. She just had to. The crush she'd had on a local boy faded like sea mists in the heat of a summer sun. Her brain raced around the possibilities of where Davie might be. Maggie-Jean's shop was the most likely option.

'Ye'll no doubt be having something fine for yer tea?' she probed.

'We'll be having a bit of cod, since yer asking.'

3

'Should I fetch ye some tatties to go with the cod?'

'The Raumsey lad's away for them.'

She kissed the old man on the cheek, and giggled at his surprise. 'Ye'll not be telling me ma' and dad, will ye?' Her head cocked to one side and she grinned.

'Maybe I will and maybe I'll not. Get away home and stop yer nonsense.' In spite of his expression, she heard amusement in his voice. With another giggle and a glance towards the boats, she hitched up her skirts, now sodden around the hem, and hurried back along the street. She leaned forward against the strength of the wind as rain began in earnest, battering her face in its fury. At last, she slipped into the shelter of the shop entrance. Salt encrusted the glass of the upper door so that she was unable to make out individual shapes in the interior. Not knowing if she had missed Davie Reid, Isa wished she had money and an excuse to go inside the shop.

Her shawl was thin and wet. With a shiver, she shoved her hands under her armpits. The door handle turned and the bell jangled above her head. She jumped back, leaned against the wall and took a measured breath, but only an old woman appearred bringing with her a blast of warm, paraffin-scented air.

'What ye doing here lassie, on a night like this?' she asked.

'I'm getting shopping for me ma'.'

'Will ye give me a hand first?'

'I'm in a hurry.' Isa would normally have helped, but for now she jumped from one foot to the other, hugging her body, her eyes already back on the door.

'There's little respect nowadays.' Lop-sided with the weight of her bag, the woman sniffed and toiled into the storm,

Above her head, the bell jangled again. Nerves caused her to stumble and in her efforts to right herself her foot caught in her skirt hem and she pitched forward. At the same time the door opened. Someone grasped her by the arms. Once she regained her balance, she looked up and into the face of Davie Reid. All she could manage was a stuttering attempt at apology which sounded like nothing at all.

'Are ye all right?' he asked, his eyes trapping hers.

Taller than she by at least a foot, his eyes were as blue as the sea in summer, his cheeks and nose, red. Wet strands of hair stuck to his skin, he smelt of damp clothes and salt air. His breathing was ragged. His hands burned into her flesh. A mole below his right eye did nothing to detract from his attractiveness.

'I . . . I . . . tripped.' In spite of the storm raging around them, water running from her hair down the back of her neck and the wet material of her skirt clinging to her legs, she felt safe and warm.

'Were ye going into the shop?' His grin was wide, exposing a chipped tooth. In the dying daylight he appeared more handsome than ever. What in Orkney they called a 'bonnie chiel.'

With her eyes on his lips, she shook her head. 'I'm . . . I'm going home.' Did he believe her? She had been standing in a shop doorway – waiting.

'Better pick the tatties up.' He leaned forward and reached towards the ground, brushing against her as he did so. For the first time she became conscious of the empty straw basket and the potatoes scattered around their feet.

'I made ye drop them. I'm sorry.' She hunched down, hands scrabbling, feeling more of a clumsy idiot than ever.

'It's fine, I'll do it.' His fingers covered hers and she recoiled as if stabbed.

Straightening up she noticed a flush on his face. Surprised, she realised he too was shy. She rubbed her wet hands down the sides of her dress. The fabric, soaked by rain, did nothing to dry them. She nodded towards the road. 'I'll have to go.'

He retrieved the last potato. 'I'd better go with ye, for ye might trip again. Where do ye live?'

'Top of the street.'

Once out of the lee, the gale pushed them together. Simultaneously they gave a short embarrassed laugh. He placed an arm across her shoulders, tentatively at first then with more confidence, and they struggled uphill past rows of terraced houses to where she lived. Never having had a boy's arm around her before, she became aware of his strength and of the extra pressure of his body each time he drew a breath. Everything else vanished from her mind. She wished she could ask him in but this was impossible. Her parents wouldn't be happy to know she'd been alone in the company of a boy not known to them. Ambitious for her girls, her mother harboured an inner terror of one of them having a child before she wed, and as she said, 'ruin her life'.

'Ye're safe,' he said at last. 'I'd best go help with the boats before they swamp.' He let her go and the warm places where his arm and body had been, remained.

'Th . . . thank ye.' Her mouth dry, her mind searched for something clever to say. She needed to keep him, to hear his voice one more time.

He hesitated then spoke too quickly. 'I'll be back before the weather breaks. I'll see ye then.'

'Yes.' Her hands twisted together and she breathed in, terrified least she sounded too eager.

'I don't know your name,' he said.

'Isa Muirison.'

'Goodnight, Isa Muirison.'

Darkness swallowed him up, and the space where he had been left an emptiness in her soul. Taking control of herself, she walked through the doorway and into the reality of her life.

The murmured voices Isa heard as she climbed the stairs fell silent when she opened the door. A tense atmosphere hung in the air. Her mother's eyes were wearier than usual, the plains of her face seemed to droop and her mouth pursed in a line of displeasure. She bunched a cloth in her hands. Curled up in the only armchair, Annie, her sister, bent her head low over a piece of needlework. Sandy, her father, sat at the table, smoke billowing around him, his face animated. Surprisingly, he smiled at her. Isa had imagined her parents' concern or even anger at her late return.

'We've something to tell ye, lass.' He removed the pipe from his mouth. Martha, her mother, turned to the kitchen range. Cleaning the stove was a chore she performed with zest when agitated and tonight the stove shone like new.

'What?' Isa's eyes flitted from one face to the other.

'We're emigrating to Canada.' As if he expected her to be pleased, he grinned.

'Canada?' The word stuck in her throat.

'We're selling the boat, the house, everything. The passage is assisted so it'll not cost us much.' Leaning back, he drew on his pipe.

'Canada . . . when?' Isa stared at her mother in dismay.

'Boat sails at the end of the month.' A martyred sigh escaped Martha's lips.

'Ye can't want to leave . . .'

Her mother's slim shoulders rose and fell. 'It's nothing to do with me. When does anyone ever listen to me?' Isa was well aware of Martha's belief that it was a woman's duty to obey her man regardless of her own wishes, then punish him with her sour attitude and silence.

'Dad?' She turned to her father.

'Next year we'll be in the twentieth century. A time of change. Canada needs willing workers.' His face lost its vitality. 'Say ye're pleased, lassie.'

'No, I'm not pleased. We can't go to Canada – we can't. It's too sudden.'

Was it so sudden? Since he left the navy eight years ago Dad had been restless, always telling them stories of the places he had visited, especially Canada. And he was so impulsive. It was just like him to make up his mind and expect everyone else to share his enthusiasm.

'Annie?' Isa appealed to the older girl.

'We always talked about going across the sea one day.' Annie coughed and pressed her hanky to her mouth.

'We were wee then. Well, I'm not going!' Isa rose and ran to the room she shared with her sister, banging the door behind her.

'If I'd spoken to my folk like that I'd have gotten the back of a hand. But she has a point. Ye shouldn't have sprung this on her, Sandy.' Her mother's raised voice carried through the wall.

Her father, quieter, calmer, far more immovable, had made up his mind.

Isa's knuckles pressed against the sill until they turned white, and the window misted with her breathing.

How dare *he* decide *her* future! What *she* thought never mattered.

For a long time she stood watching the mad dance of the ocean and the white capped waves glinting in the moonlight. Cloud formations seemed less dense as the wind tossed them to shreds and dragged them about the sky. The storm was losing ferocity and there was every chance of it blowing itself out by morning. Somewhere in this town was a boy who made her experience new and disturbing feelings and come first light he would be gone. By the time he returned she would be half way across the Atlantic Ocean.

'Someday I'll take ye over the sea,' Dad use to say and the promise had been so exciting – once.

With the money saved during his sailing days, Dad bought a herring boat and moved them all to Kirkwall from their home in Shapinsay. They thought that would be the end of it.

'For God's sake,' he had told his unhappy wife, 'Kirkwall's not the back end of the world. And what's here for the lassies? Marrying poor crofters or fishermen. Ye've always said ye wanted better for them.'

'Aye, I do, but will ye settle then?' Mam had asked. 'We'll be over to the other side next.'

Money had been tight for the first few years. Then the herring swam into his nets, so he had said, and his gamble paid off. Isa knew Mam had always looked forward to getting a proper house and moving from this flat beside the grocers where she had managed to get a few hours' work a week.

This was not a move to a bigger house, nor to the mainland – it *was* to the other side of the world.

'Isa?' Annie came into the room. 'It might not be that bad.'

'I'm not going!' Isa said, yet knowing in her heart that she had no option. 'And what about ye – what about Luke?'

'Ach – I don't love him – not really.'

Isa chewed on the edge of her lip and looked at her sister's face. Annie, the good one, the sensible one, her mother's favourite. 'How do ye know when it is love?'

'I know it's not Luke.' She sat down on the bed. 'Is that what's wrong? Have ye met a lad?'

'Yes.'

'Who – when?'

'Today. One of the Raumsey boys.'

'Today? Then it's nothing. Isa, your dress, there's mud on the skirt.'

A vivid memory of rubbing her earth-covered hands down the sides of her dress flashed through her mind and with it the emotion of the moment. Tears pooled in her eyes and trickled down her cheek.

'Awe, come on. It mightn't be that bad.'

Isa gulped. 'I'll never clap eyes on him again.'

Annie took her sister's face in both her hands, wiped the tears away with her thumbs and gave short laugh. 'Was it not the lad from the lighthouse last week?'

'That's different. And what's more, I like Kirkwall. I like working for the floating shops. And ye like the clothes shop – ye're that good with a needle.' She did not add that Annie was not strong enough for anything more physical. 'If we both tell him we'll not go – he'll maybe listen.'

The older girl gave an unhappy laugh. Annie was six years old when Isa was born, and because their mam had been ill for some time after, became more like a little mother. Then came another baby, a boy that died, and Martha had never been quite the same again.

'Ye know he won't. And ye shouldn't upset Mam.'

'Aye, well, *ye'll* never need the back of her hand will ye?'

'I think we should accept things. And ye'd best come through for yer tea. There's black pudding and tatties.' Annie coughed, a deep, tearing cough, and pressed her fist to her chest. 'I'll go and see if Mam's got any camphor.'

Annie's bouts of bronchitis were getting worse.

'I'm not hungry,' Isa said, looking away.

Later that night, when Sandy Muirison opened the bedroom door his youngest daughter, wrapped in a blanket, stared out of the window.

'The storm's dying.' He touched her hair.

She jerked her head away. Her dreams had taken flight in these last few minutes and she resented the intrusion. She had imagined herself on the ship, watching Scotland vanish in the mist, when she heard a voice at her elbow. 'I couldna' let ye go without seeing ye again.'

Davie Reid stood behind her. He was coming with them to a big new future. They would have all the time in the world during the long sail to get to know each other.

'Mam's put yer tea in the oven.' Her father's hand remained in the air where her head had been. When there was no answer, he gave a deep sigh and dropped his hand. 'Ye'll love Canada. Wait and see.' Whether she would or not, there was little she could do about it; there was little any of them could do.

Chapter 2

Davie, Jamsie and Jack Reid pitted the *Silver Dawn* against the swell. The storm had ended, but the sea was still rough, leaving little time for thinking. The boat was one of the smaller yoles – no more than sixteen feet, but the brothers were skilled seamen and the breeze blew fair. On reaching the lee of two skerries, they furled the sails and checked their creels for lobster and crab. Three of the creels had been torn from the attached buoys and flung adrift but the other six yielded a good catch.

'Ye're awfully quiet there, Davie,' shouted Jamsie above the sound of the sea booming and echoing from the cliff wall. He pushed his cap back on his head and his curls, damp with spray, stuck to his forehead.

Without replying Davie used his sleeve to wipe the spray from his face, the material rough and wet against his skin. With stiff fingers, he tied string around the pincers of the last lobster and tossed it into the box at the bottom of the boat to scrabble among its mates.

Davie, his mind full of the lassie he'd walked home through the storm, began baiting the creels from a basket of small slippery fish. How could he ever forget those large brown eyes in the heart shaped face, the black curls springing in the wind and the way her cheeks flushed when he smiled at her? And she had agreed to see him again.

After he left her he ran down the road, the tiredness of the day lifting from him. Chrissie Adams, the lass he was expected to marry, never made the blood pound in his veins like Isa Muirison had – Isa, such a slim little madam she'd been like a bird beneath his arm.

'Get the sail up,' Jamsie shouted. His brothers stood, pocketing their pipes, the movement causing the boat to rock. Without losing balance they grabbed an oar each and pulled the yole out of the lee. Davie unfurled the brown sail, experiencing the familiar surge of excitement as the wind filled it. Beneath them the sea swelled – the boat rose, pitched forward and descended into the trough, water slapping over the sides. The boys yanked in the oars. Jamsie grabbed the rudder and turned the prow to face the next wave.

Raumsey was near enough to make out the blurry details of Scartongarth, the croft house where they lived. Davie rubbed his fingers together, already imagining the warmth of the peat fire. He could not see Bess, the family collie, but knew she waited on the beach. Long before the boat became visible, she would run up and down, barking. Mam would hear her and get the soup pan on.

It was impossible to sail directly home. Instead, they had to manoeuvre between the treacherous waters of the Swelkie to the north and the Boars to the south where opposing currents met, causing swirling cauldrons of foam and whirlpools. The men who sailed the Pentland Firth knew how to use the tides to their advantage. By sailing with the flow, they made good time. Less than an hour later they beached the boat, lashed the rope to the iron winch and, taking turns on the handle, dragged the yole over sand and shingle, up the grassy embankment, clear of the highest tides.

Chrissie came running down the incline to meet them, cheeks flushed, skirts hitched up, and her voice excited and loud. 'Your mam was that worried when the storm broke yesterday – but I told her, my Davie will know better than to put to sea the night.'

Davie winced at her using the word 'my' before his name and busied himself with the ropes.

'What I wouldn't give to have a lassie like that run to me,' Jamsie laughed, punching his brother lightly on the shoulder. 'Get yourself off – we'll finish here.'

'I'll do my bit.' Davie did not look up; hoping Chrissie would chose not to wait in the cold. She fell silent, and he sensed her hurt. Wait she did, and not being one to stay quiet for long, was soon entertaining the lads with island gossip. Once the men tied the final knot, they submerged the boxes of lobsters into the sea to keep them alive. With the ropes secured, they began the short walk home.

'Come on, Jacky,' called Jamsie. 'Leave the lovers alone'

Davie would have preferred to go with his brothers but Chrissie demanded attention. She was a bonny lass with her round, fresh face and dimpled cheeks. Her corn-coloured hair fell loose across her shoulders, strands lifting in the wind. She walked beside him towards Scartongarth.

'The box social's on this night. I was scared ye wouldn't get home in time.' She slipped her arm through his and leaned against him. Her cloying touch filled him with a need to escape. These socials could be fun, but tonight Davie had no desire to bid for a box of baking and handcrafts in order to walk the supposedly anonymous owner home.

'Chrissie,' he began, but she held up her hand, stopping him.

'Wait til I tell ye about Tam.' She laughed at some memory.

'What?'

'Ye know he's that keen on Lizzy? Well, he tried to sneak into her loft, to find out the colour of the ribbon on her box.' She took a spasm of laughter, doubling over and clutching her stomach.

Her joviality was catching, and in spite of himself, Davie laughed with her.

'On Sunday – and he'd just come from the Kirk.'

'Ye mean he went up in yon loft in his best suit? The window's missing. Must be full of bird's shite.'

Chrissie sucked in a long breath. 'He took the suit off. When he came down the lads had taken his clothes. He'd to walk home in his drawers and semmit.'

'On the Sabbath?'

They laughed together. Why couldn't it be like this– the pair of them being good friends and sharing a laugh? Why did she have to demand so much more?

She pressed her mouth against his ear and whispered. 'I know we're not supposed to tell, but my box has blue ribbons.'

'I don't think I'll be going to the social.'

'What?' She stopped, jerked his arm and spun him around to face her.

'It's been a hell of a trip – I'm tired. I need to eat, wash and go straight to my bed.'

Disbelief replaced the laughter. 'But . . . But I've been looking forward to this night for months.' Guiltily he bent down to kiss her lips, finding them cold and slightly salty. 'I'll see ye in the morn,' he said, disentangling the arms that went round his neck.

'Davie, what *is* wrong?'

He hugged her gently. Hurting Chrissie was the last thing he wanted. 'Why don't *ye* go? Mind though, I wouldn't want another lad to walk ye home.' Without understanding why, he knew this to be true. He took her hands and placed them by her sides, kissed her cold cheek and went indoors. His brothers and father were already sitting at the table, tucking into bowls of rabbit stew and potatoes.

'I'm right glad to see ye,' said his mother, Tyna, setting down another dish. 'Where's Chrissie? Is she not coming in?'

'I'm tired out the night Mam. I told her I'd meet her in the morn.'

'Don't ye dare go making a fool of that lassie.'

'I'll not do that. She told me about Tam,' he said, keen to change the topic.

'That Tam! They say his drawers and semmit had never seen soap and water in months.'

Laughter filled the small kitchen. Tyna wiped her brow and turned her attention back to her youngest son. 'But I'm worried about ye.'

'Leave the lad be, Tyna,' said his father; 'No doubt they had a heavy night at old Abe's.' He winked at Davie.

'Aye, that's it.' Davie began to eat his stew, grateful there would be no more questions. In truth Jack, Jamsie and Abe had passed out with tiredness and a bellyful of whisky long before he went to sleep himself. He wrinkled his nose at the memory of the smells in Abe's room; the peat fire, the steaming stockinged feet, the damp old dog and the whisky breath all mixed together with the odour of boiled cod.

'Or maybe... he's got an eye for a Kirkwall lassie,' his brother Jack said.

'When did we have time for the lassies?' Davie snapped.

'Ye'd better not,' said his mother. 'Yon Chrissie's the one for ye, Davie. She's a hard worker and she'll make a fine wife.'

'And she's got fine broad hips to shelter ye from the wind when ye're at the lambing,' said Jamsie, mimicking his mother's tone. He ducked, holding his hands up as she threatened him with the ladle. 'Well, I hope ye've got plenty hot water on for a wash Mam because I'm not too tired for the dancing. What about ye Jack?'

'Aye, it'll be a good night. Who knows, maybe I'll bid for Chrissie's box. She makes a tasty bit of cake. Sure ye don't want to come, Davie?'

'Stop teasing the lad,' his mother swatted him with a dishcloth. 'Chrissie'll not be going without Davie. It's about time ye got a lass of your own.'

'No lass would look at a sour bugger like Jack,' muttered Davie.

'At least I'm not like ye – still tied to mammy's apron strings and scared to move unless big Chrissie tells ye.'

Davie made an effort to still the familiar knotting of his stomach. His brother's touchiness and bouts of temper were growing worse. He glanced at his mother and noticed something in her eyes, something like distress or even fear. She slapped her hand on the table. 'Will ye two stop yer carry on. Chrissie and Mary-Jane are both fine lassies.'

Jamsie had been courting Mary-Jane Adams for over five years. At twenty-nine, he was the oldest son and heir to the croft and boat. When he married his bride would come and live here – and there was little enough room. Jamsie and Mary-Jane were waiting for one or both younger boys to move on. Jack had never had a steady girl, so his mother's hopes centred on Davie and his lass, Chrissie, who Tyna loved like a daughter.

Jamsie pushed Jack's shoulder. 'Aye, come on,' he said. 'Leave the lad be.' Something about Jamsie would calm stormy waters, so his granny used to say. He was the only one who got through to Jack these days.

Much later, his brothers gone and parents bedded, Davie, stared at the wooden beams of his attic bedroom. He tried in vain to clear his mind of all thoughts so sleep would claim him. Eventually he gave up and went outside to where the thunder of the ocean filled the air.

The shoreline before him curved into a horseshoe shape. Shelved cliffs formed a natural harbour, but inadequate for the fishermen's needs. In the distance lay the Skerries, ominous rocks in a river of moon-cast silver. On a calm night like this, the unearthly cries of the seals were extra loud, as if they mourned for something beyond their reach.

He lowered himself onto the stone bench and looked beyond the slow sweep of the lighthouse beam towards the larger islands to the north. And Davie thought of Isa Muirison.

He had to see her again – but how? The next shipment of whisky went as far as St Margaret's Hope, a long sail from Kirkwall. Even if it were possible, what was the point in courting the lassie? He had nothing to offer her.

He always planned to join the navy or get a berth on a drifter and chase the herring, where the real money lay. In his father's day, men found extra employment guiding large vessels round the islands, but since the building of the lighthouses, the pilots of the Pentland Firth were less in demand.

Davie pulled a mouth organ from his jacket pocket, banged it a few times on the palm of his hand and raised the instrument to his lips. As he played a haunting melody he closed his eyes and gave himself up to the music

Bess' sharp bark broke the spell. The long grass rustled and Chrissie materialised out of the darkness.

His family wanted him to marry this girl, thus inheriting the croft and boat she owned. She lived alone with her widowed grandmother. Yet even before meeting Isa the reality of marrying Chrissie had filled him with a nameless dread.

Pushing the instrument back in his pocket, he glared at her. 'What are ye doing here?'

'I went to the dance but I missed ye.' She slid onto the seat, pressing her body alongside his. Her breasts were warm and full against his arm. Her face tilted upwards, her lips inches from his. In the moonlight a tear quivered in the corner of one eye.

He wanted to tell her to go away – go back to her friends and leave him alone. But in spite of himself he felt the heat rise in his loins, and he raised a shaking finger to touch the softness of her skin. How could he tell her that he loved and desired her – but he yearned for something more?

He moved away but she grabbed his hand, pressing it to her breast. 'I'll let ye – ye've tried often enough.' Reaching down she placed nervous fingers on his crotch.

'Chrissie.' Her name wrenched from him like a low groan. 'Please don't.' Why was she doing this now?

'Don't ye want me anymore?' She unlaced the front of her dress and allowed her full breasts to spring free. Her skin, milky and soft, held Davie's gaze.

'Want ye . . . ah. . .' His voice trailed to a stop. A heat filled him up.

'I will . . . if ye want.'

Groaning, Davie cupped a breast in his palm, finding it both softer and heavier than he imagined. A shudder shot through him. He lowered his head seeking a nipple with his mouth. She jumped slightly, and laced her fingers between his. 'Come to the barn.'

Something told him to stop, but his body took on a mind of its own and he followed her. Together they fell on the straw, hands and mouths hungry.

When it was over he rolled away and stared at the moonlight through the open barn door. Chrissie moulded herself against him, her bodice open, her skirts around her waist, her naked thigh across his. 'We'll have to marry now, won't we? I'm nineteen already, same age as my mother when she birthed me.'

He closed his eyes as ice water ran to his bowels. What had he done?

Chapter 3

A gentle June wind blew from the sea, stirring the dust on the streets of Kirkwall. The sun shone through errant cloud and birds sang in the sparse trees. None of these things was of any interest this Sunday morning, for the Muirison family had had no sleep the night before. Isa's father entered the kitchen and ran his hand over a stubbled chin making a rasping sound.

'I've put the passage back till next spring. There are no available berths until then.' Sandy Muirison sank into his chair and his body seemed to collapse around him. Annie's cough had grown worse and she was not fit to travel. The previous night her temperature had spiralled out of control.

Martha came from the bedroom carrying a rolled up towel. She swayed, grabbing the edge of the table for support. The cloth slipped out of her fingers and fell to the floor, the folds separating and spreading. Stains like a red splintered rose dotted the material. She cried out, dropped to her knees and scrabbled at the towel.

'Annie's coughing blood,' Isa gasped. 'Why haven't ye sent for the doctor?'

'No, no doctor!' Martha sobbed.

Isa understood. They were terrified of tuberculosis. Tubercular cases were taken from their families and left to die among strangers in a sanatorium. 'Ye weren't going to tell me. Why? Why does no one tell me anything?' she cried.

'It's her throat – raw with the cough,' Sandy explained – too quickly. 'When we get to Canada the dry air'll put her right – ye'll see.'

Martha's chin trembled. The corners of her mouth gave the slightest twitch. Her pupils darkened for a second and she blinked several times. She took a slow controlled breath. 'It will, won't it?' she asked her husband.

'It really will.' He covered his wife's hands with his.

'Go to the Kirk,' Martha said to Isa. 'Please. It'll look bad if none of us puts in an appearance.'

'No, I don't want to ...'

'Yer mam is right. Ye need to get out of the house lass,' said her father.

Isa studied the black centre of her thumbnail, bruised when a box in the warehouse had landed on her finger a week ago. Now the dark colour faded and radiated, turning yellow at the edges. She died inside.

'Just go.' Irritation flared in her mother's voice. 'Every thing's fine. All fine.'

Isa lifted her head and met her father's eye.

'Ye don't have to, Isa.' Sandy turned to his wife. 'I'm sure the good Lord will forgive us for missing the service this once.'

Isa needed to strike out at someone to release the pain building inside her. 'I'll not stay where I'm not wanted,' she shouted. She ran to the bedroom, shutting the door a little too hard. 'I'm sorry,' she mouthed, when Annie moaned in her sleep. Afraid to get too close in case she inhaled the poison robbing Annie of her vitality, afraid in case the spectre of death hovered over the bed, Isa snuck from the room.

The kirk bells rang at eleven o'clock. Isa had hour and a half to spare. Outside the house, she breathed the fresh, clean air into her lungs. A straggling weed grew where the wall met the pavement. Annie is going to be all right, she told herself repeatedly. The nervous energy started in her legs, travelled up her body and into her arms. Gathering up her skirts, she ran through the streets and out to the countryside.

She ran because she was young and strong and the life's blood surged in her veins. She ran because she wanted to escape from her sister's illness and the possible consequences. She ran because if she did not her body would explode into a million pieces.

The good folk of Kirkwall stared at her with disapproval – such behaviour on the Sabbath was unheard of. She did not stop until she reached the shores of Scapa Flow, more than a mile from her home. Time and time again she returned to this place. As usual, she scanned the horizon for the sail that never appeared, knowing there was little chance it would today. Boats did not go to sea on a Sunday, but maybe – just maybe.

What a bad girl she had become, she thought, and buried her face in her hands. Her sister fought for every breath, and here she was thinking about the lad from Raumsey. Even her parents hadn't wanted her around. The blowy air dried the trickles of tears to cold ribbons against her cheeks. She should be at the kirk. She had to make a pact with the Lord.

Running was not so easy this time. Her feet seemed heavy and each breath seared her lungs as the landscape rose before her. 'Please, please God,' she gasped, the blood pounding in her ears, 'I'll not do anything wrong ever again – just let Annie live.'

Shapinsay kirk had been nothing compared to St Magnus Cathedral in Kirkwall. The high arched ceilings, stained glass windows, carvings and space gave such an air of reverence that within these walls Isa felt small and insignificant. In this holy place a promise made to the Lord was absolute.

She crept into the back row as the minister began to speak. He stopped and waited until she settled. Eyes of the congregation turned and stared, both curious and critical. Without caring, she bowed her head and clasped her hands, speaking to the Lord in her heart.

He must have listened to her, because Annie's fever broke in the night. Overcome with relief Isa lay awake beside her sister, talking for hours. They talked of the past and the pranks they had played, they talked of the future and Canada where Annie would grow fit and strong, of the young men they would marry and the children they would have. When she realised the other girl was asleep, Isa shut her mouth and snuggled down beneath the covers. Sandy's explanation of the blood-stained towel had to be right, she thought. Fuelled by her own faith, Isa allowed herself to be swept away on a wave of improbable hope.

From then on she tried to be true to her promise. She spent

most of her spare time helping her mother, because Annie's cough did not improve.

In spite of everything, Scapa Bay still drew Isa back to its shores, the longing for Davie Reid so severe it was almost tangible.

Chapter 4

In the middle of July, a large merchant steamer sailed into a thick bank of fog and smashed against a rock-stack near the tiny island of Swona, south of mainland Orkney.

The islanders salvaged the cargo and set it out on the grass on top of the cliff. With a surplus of goods, the population decided to hold a sale. The news spread throughout the islands.

The big boss, Robert Gardiner himself said anyone wishing to, would be free to go provided they worked extra hours in the evenings. Excitement raced through the warehouse. The *North Isle Steamer* was providing a ferry service to and from the sale. Isa's stomach flipped over because Davie Reid was bound to be there. However, her euphoria was short lived. Her father did not see the point when they expected to be gone in a couple of months.

'Tell them we're all going, they can't refuse then,' said her friend Bella the next day.

'They don't care what *I* want – all they care about is Annie.' Isa blinked back the hot sting of tears.

'Och, lass, don't say that. They're worried sick and ye can't blame them.'

'I'm going. I don't care what they say.'

'Ye do need a day off, and yer folks aren't that bad. Don't let them guess the real reason though,' Bella said, as together they gathered their belongings.

'There is no real reason. I want to go and I will.'

'Ye'd be better not having a confrontation.'

Isa hung her head as they made their way home. In spite of her brave words, if her dad or mam forbade her she knew she would not be going.

As she entered the house, her parents immediately fell into the state of silence that often coincided with her arrival. She took a deep breath and said, 'Robert Gardiner is giving us the day off tomorrow. The girls are all going to the sale.' Her eyes flitted from one face to the other.

'Aye,' said her father, 'and ye'll be wanting to go too.'

His mouth fought a smile. A twinkle bounced in his eyes. This had to be a good sign.

She twined her hands together. 'Please. I just want to look.'

'Ye could do with a break,' Martha said.

'If Annie needs me . . .' Isa started, praying this was not so.

'If she's fine tomorrow, ye can go.'

Isa took a deep breath not daring to hope. 'How is she the day?'

'Ask her yerself.' Sandy removed the pipe from his mouth and pointed with the stem towards the door. Isa needed no second telling. Annie, wrapped in a blanket, sat in her chair.

'Ye're better.' Isa dropped to her knees beside her sister.

'I want to smell the sea. Would ye open the window? Mam won't. She thinks I'll catch a chill.'

What did her mother know? Annie wanted fresh air and that is what she would have. Isa pushed the casement all the way up, welcoming the sea-scented blast into the cloying odour of the sickroom.

'I wish ye could come to Swona too,' she said.

'Ye're going then. I thought ye would.'

'Ye know about it?'

'It was me who asked mam and dad to let ye go. Just tell me about it when ye get back.' Annie gave a faint smile. 'Now help me to bed, I'm fair worn out.'

Easing her out of the chair, Isa was shocked to discover how light and fragile her sister had become, as if nothing but bones lay beneath the clothes.

'Read to me.' Annie settled back on her pillows and pressed the ever-ready towel to her lips. Isa was glad to. She loved books, where every hero became Davie Reid, and every heroine became herself. When the other girl's breathing took on a deep, even rhythm, Isa blew out the candle.

For a long time after she settled in bed, Isa lay staring into the dark, one minute excited about the trip, the next worried in case Annie took a turn for the worse.

Annie had a good night. Isa's spirits soared as she left the house. Bella let out a whoop when she met her friend heading towards the pier in the morning. 'They let ye come, then.'

Isa laughed, 'I told ye I would come anyway.' She grabbed the older girl's arms and danced her round in a circle. The sky was fresh and clear and the sea, a deep crinkled blue with white ruffles on the wave tops, spread before them.

The sail seemed to take forever, until at last the shores of Swona appeared out of the mists. Isa grasped the rail, her hair blowing back from her face, her eyes straining at the distance. 'The other island, over there, is that . . .'

'Aye, that's Raumsey.' Bella poked her in the ribs.

'Ow.' Isa rubbed her side and Bella laughed.

'Don't worry; he's bound to be here.'

'*I* don't care,' Isa turned her head and glanced round the bay. Several vessels from other islands already dotted the inlet and her heart leapt when she recognised *The Silver Dawn*.

The steamer dropped anchor. Small boats ferried the passengers, a few at a time, to the curved pebbled beach sheltered on either side by high rocks. On the top of the brae the crowd had already gathered, eating sandwiches, murmuring and laughing. The abundance of goods for sale amazed everyone. Bales of jute and canvas, furniture, foodstuffs, cooking pots, dishes and hundreds of white lame (pottery) jars of preserves sat haphazardly on the ground.

Isa and her friends ran from one item to the other, touching things the like of which they had never seen in their lives.

'Come and look at this,' shrieked Bella, as she laid a hand on a large ornamental dog with a squashed nose. Isa examined the white china face and the black eyes with their circles of gold. Then she lifted her head, eyes searching the crowd. At last they found the only thing that interested her – the fair curling hair of

Davie Reid. As if he sensed her gaze upon him, he turned, looked quickly, and looked again. It was as if the sun reflected off his face. He came over and stopped in front of her.

The crowd ceased to exist for Isa. Her eyes met his, flitted to the curve of his lips and back to his eyes which seemed to have grown large. She struggled to overcome a desire to reach up, take his face between her hands and kiss his mouth, as she had in her fantasies. She took a deep but shaky breath. 'Grand to see ye,' she said, surprised at her own control.

His face coloured. Taking her arm, he led her away from the others. Neither said a word as they climbed the hill, walked to the edge of the cliff and stood looking out to sea.

'I thought ye'd be back to Kirkwall.' She spoke when she was able.

'I wanted to, but it's not my boat.'

His calloused fingers brushed hers. She turned to face him. His mouth tugged upwards in the slightest of movements, his pupils darkened and he grasped her hands. He bent down and pressed his lips against her mouth. The sudden shaky heat growing in her groin startled her. He drew away, his expression tense and faintly surprised.

'I'll no stay away – by faith, I'll take the boat if I have to steal it.' His fingers traced the outline of her mouth and she giggled. Her sister's illness and the impending trip to Canada receded far into the background. For a while they stood in companionable silence, hands clasped. The sounds around them, the sea sucking and pulling at the shore, the crying of the birds, the booming voice of the auctioneer, the shouts of the bidders, a sudden bark of a dog, the bleating of a worried ewe, all faded into a pleasant blur.

'Hey there.'

The unexpected shout startled them both. One of the men who had been with Davie in Kirkwall, was sprinting up the hill. She sensed the tension in the hand holding hers and heard it in his voice.

'My brother, Jack,' he explained as the man drew alongside.

'If ye've finished here we've to leave. We've bought what we want and we need to catch the tide,' Jack's eyes crawled over Isa. His lips twisted into a smirk.

'I'll be in a minute,' Davie snapped. He turned back to her and placed a hand on her arm. 'I'll have to go.'

She opened her mouth to protest. He kissed her words away.

'I'll see ye soon,' he promised before turning and running down the hill.

The rest of the day passed in a haze and if someone had asked her later about the sale, she would not have been able to remember. She could no longer join in the laughter and joking of her friends. She was impatient to leave, wanting to be alone to relive the moments with Davie over and over. He said he would see her soon – but he had said that before. Had he meant it? If he didn't, by God, she would steal a boat and sail to Raumsey herself.

Back home she made straight for the bedroom, bursting with the need to tell someone her news. Annie sat propped against pillows.

'I'm so happy for ye. I wish I felt like that – just once.' She spoke so quietly Isa had to strain to catch the words.

'Ye will one day.'

Annie did not answer. Fear flickered in her eyes and that was not how it should to be. Her sister would get better and Davie would come to her. Both those things would happen, for no other reason than she willed them. Isa refused to contemplate anything else.

Chapter 5

'Leirstock's been watching ye for the last half hour.'

'What?' Isa almost dropped the bale of satin she carried to the packing case. She glanced around but the overseer was nowhere in sight.

'Oh Bella! Ye gave me a scare,' she laughed.

'And so I should. If ye don't get the dreamy look off yer face and buckle down, ye'll soon be in trouble my girl.'

'I'm sorry, it's just tha . . .' She glanced at the clock on the wall. It was time to go home. 'Oh, ye're daft.' She placed the bale on top of the others and closed the lid of the crate.

'It's just that . . . ye can't get a certain lad off yer mind.' Bella finished the sentence for her.

'It's not that at all.' She dragged the crate to the wall and rubbed her hands down her sides.

'Then ye won't be interested to know he's been standing outside for twenty minutes or more.'

'What – why didn't ye tell me?' She struggled out of her apron, her fingers tripping over themselves.

'And have ye running off and losing yer job. What kind of friend would that be?'

Isa hardly heard her as she ran to the door. It had been almost two months since the day on Swona, yet to Isa, it had seemed like a lifetime.

Davie leant against the opposite wall, hands in his pockets. Their eyes met and he stood upright, his smile unsure.

'Can . . . can we take a walk?' he asked, a glow creeping up his face as the other girls gathered behind Isa, some of them giggling.

She nodded and took a firm hold of her emotions. With a backward icy glance at her workmates, she crossed the road and fell into step beside him.

They strolled up the street, side-by-side, close but not touching. She forced herself to stroll, arms swinging – not too much. Once well away from the others she spoke. 'Ye came back to deliver the whisky.'

He gave a brief self-conscious laugh. 'Aye.'

The weather was warmer this time, the air thick with the smell of heather-bells and brine, the sky full of crying birds, the sea roaring and crashing over the pebbled beach. They left the town and followed the shoreline. Isa wondered why he didn't try to kiss her. What had changed? Had the girls embarrassed him too much? Had he met someone else? The thought was agony.

'Do ye ever wonder what's past the horizon,' he said at last lowering himself onto the ground.

'Canada, I believe. We're going as soon as my sister's well enough.'

'Ye're leaving Orkney?' He grabbed her hand and pulled her down beside him. 'No. Ye can't.'

She did not speak. When their eyes met, her very soul fused with his. He cupped her face in his hands and kissed her lids, her cheek, her lips, and the kiss lasted forever, blotting out all reason as they sank onto the heather.

'Ye can't go,' he whispered when his mouth moved to her ear. He crushed her body to his, moving his hands over and under her clothes, fumbling. She clung to him, giving herself up to the unfamiliar excitement that had taken possession of her.

'I've got no choice,' she muttered against his neck, breathing in his scent, not wanting to remember the pact she made with God. His roughened fingers found the bare skin at the top of her knee making her jump, and bringing her to her senses. Afraid of his urgency, afraid of what he thought of her, afraid of her own reactions she pushed him away.

He sprang to his knees, his eyes dark and unfocused, his breath ragged. 'I won't hurt ye.' He reached for her again. His hand trembled – the way her insides did. A voice in her head told her to stop.

'I've got to go back.' She struggled to her feet and rearranged her dress. 'They'll be worried.'

He stood up and pulling her to him kissed her, gently. As the kiss grew in urgency, she tensed, ready for flight. He drew away.

'I'm sorry,' he told her with a deep sigh, 'It was seeing ye again. I've thought of nothing else for so long. And . . . ye're not really going, are ye?'

She fell against him and held him, pressing her cheek into the rough wool of his jersey.

'My dad says so, but my sister's very ill.'

He tightened his arms. If only they could stay this way forever.

'I'm sorry about your sister, but not if it keeps ye here.'

'I'll have to go now. I'll walk the rest of the way on my own.' She knew her parents would never approve of a poor Raumsey lad who sold illegal whisky, and right now, she did not want to face further arguments. But she couldn't leave it like this – she just couldn't. Before her courage drained, she blurted, 'Are ye staying in Kirkwall the night? We could meet after tea.'

'I'll be waiting by the harbour wall – until the morn' if I have to.'

Somehow she would manage to escape. With an effort she drew away.

'Mind, ye'd better come,' he called after her.

She looked back and waved, her heart flying as high as the sea-maws circling above them.

At the door she smoothed her skirts. Sucking in air, she made an effort to still her heartbeat. She hoped the flush was gone from her cheeks and her eyes did not sparkle too much. There was little chance of her parents noticing the change in her, for as soon as she entered the house the tension hit her like a blast of north wind.

'Where were ye?' Her mother's voice verged on hysterics. 'She's been asking for ye.'

Her father sat at the table. He lifted his eyes and what she saw in them froze her insides.

'What is it – what's wrong?'

'There's been a lot more blood.'

Annie. It couldn't be. She had been on the mend. She was coming to Canada and she was going to get well. Father told them so and his word was law. Isa ran into the bedroom. Doctor Menzies was bending over her sister. He straightened up and held the palm of his hand towards her.

'Annie!' she screamed, but the face as white as the blood-splattered pillow on which it lay, did not move.

The doctor took Isa by the shoulders and forced her into the kitchen. The heat and the strength of his fingers burned through her clothing. 'I don't think *she* should be here,' he said to her parents. Martha rose and ran to the bedroom.

Her mother's sudden loud keening rent the air and filled Isa with a terror too strong to control. She struggled out of the doctor's grip and fought to shove past him. She screamed and punched his chest until he caught her wrists and held her fast.

'They should have come for me sooner,' he muttered, his solid body blocking her entry. Struggling free she ran outside to the back of the building and vomited among the nettles. Her legs became useless. She sank to her knees where she remained for a time.

Three days later, on a slate grey October day when the wind blew hard through the streets of Kirkwall, they laid Annie to rest. After the friends and neighbours left, Martha and Sandy sat on either side of the kitchen table, neither speaking.

'Will I get the tea?' said Isa, craving to make it better – knowing she never could.

'Not now, lass,' said her father. 'I'm trying to get yer mam to lie down. She needs rest.'

'Rest!' Martha shrieked. 'How can ye talk of rest when we've just buried our daughter?'

'We've got to keep going.' Her husband placed his hand over hers but she snatched it away.

'Please Mam,' Isa whispered.

Martha raised her eyes and looked at her youngest child who shrank back at the ferocity of the glare. Without a word, Martha rose and went to the bedroom.

'She wishes I was the one who died.' Isa wrapped her arms around herself.

'Don't mind her, lass. She can't cope with this.' Sandy rose and followed his wife. 'Just give us a bit of time, eh?'

Isa nodded and watched as the door closed, shutting her out from the circle that had once been her family. She set and lit the stove and crouched over it in an effort to get some warmth into her bones. Although she had no appetite, she had earlier prepared a dish of stew now warming in the oven. She waited and waited until her desperate need for her parents sent her knocking on the bedroom door.

'I've got the tea,' she shouted.

'We'll be out in a wee while.' Her father's voice broke and splintered round the edges. She knew he would not, any more than he came out last night or the night before that. Any minute she would wake up and find this had been all some dreadful nightmare. God had broken their pact. She would never go inside a kirk again.

'I'm not going back!' she shouted into the air. The tears came at last, tearing through her body until she ached all over, leaving her drained and as empty as a broken eggshell.

As the days passed Isa's longing for Davie grew. She needed someone to hold her now more than ever. Her parents gave her no comfort. All they cared about was Annie, and Annie was gone.

She continued to walk across to Scapa Bay whenever she could. There she sat on a rock for hours, staring out to sea, thinking of Davie. She wondered how long he waited for her that dreadful night. Had he heard about Annie? Did he believe she hadn't wanted to see him after all? If only she knew of some way to get word to him.

He came back on a Monday. Work was over for the day when she saw him leaning against the wall across from the warehouse, legs crossed at the ankle, hands in his pockets. With a calmness that surprised her, she bade her friends goodbye and walked as fast as she dared towards him.

'Meet me behind the pier,' she whispered, amazed at her own boldness. She hitched up her skirts and ran along the barrier, her curls falling from the pins that held them, the wind cooling her blazing cheeks. By the harbour wall she glanced around to make sure he was following before she climbed over. On the sun-warmed sand at the other side, she fell to her knees. He was beside her in an instant helping her to her feet.

'Thank goodness ye've come,' she whispered as her throat closed. He pressed her hand to his lips. She was aware of the calluses on his fingers, the softness of his mouth, the flutter of his eyelashes, gentle as butterfly wings against her skin.

'My sister died,' she said when she found her voice. 'That's why I didn't come.'

Without a word he folded her in his arms. Giving way to the tears that always hid just beneath the surface, she clung to him.

He held her until the storm passed, stroking her hair and murmuring. He took off his jacket, laid it on the sand then pulled her down beside him. He kissed the salty droplets from her cheeks, her eyes, her lips.

She whispered his name. She did not want to leave the shelter of his arms. She did not want to go back to the cold silent house where nobody cared. And she did not want to go to Canada.

'I love ye, I've been able to think of nothing else.' His breath in her ear was hot and urgent. His hands fumbled among her clothing.

Her heart grew large, filling her chest. On the sandy floor of the cove she held on to him with a new urgency. Each touch and caress brought new wonder. When, to her surprise he drew away, she clung to him.

'No, don't stop,' she pleaded, for every moment with him was precious. All too soon he would be gone and she would slide back into the emptiness.

'Isa, ye don't know what ye're doing to me.' A hand on each shoulder, he gently prised her away from him.

'Ye . . . don't want me.' she gasped covering her face with her hands.

'Want ye . . . of course I want ye.'

She reached up, searching for his lips, moulding her body into his.

This time he responded. 'Are ye sure?' he moaned.

'Yes,' she said. 'Yes!'

Chapter 6

Davie gathered the breakfast plates and stacked them in the enamel basin. Tyna, his mother, opened a drawer in the dresser and poured in the contents of the large porridge pan. The oatmeal would become more solid as it cooled, and slices eaten as a snack throughout the day.

'Thanks Davie,' she said. 'Ye're the only one who helps me.'

She looked so tired these days. He worried that she did too much, yet neither his father nor his brothers seemed to notice.

Davie's brother, Jamsie, rose and grabbed his jacket from the nail on the wood-lined wall. 'We'd better get the top field ploughed,' he said.

'I'll get to it,' said his father, Dan, without looking up. Jamsie hesitated. Davie hoped this would not lead to yet another argument between his father and brother. Dan was having none of the new ideas that filled Jamsie's head.

Jamsie caught the younger boy's eye and he winked, his face easing into a grin. 'I think I may have done something that might *actually* please ye,' he said to his father. 'I've asked Mary-Jane to marry me.'

Tyna almost dropped the porridge pot she was scrubbing. 'It's not afore time,' she gasped.

'Good for ye man.' Davie slapped him on the arm.

'Ye should have done it long ago. Tyna could do with another woman in the house,' Dan muttered rising to his feet and clasping his son's hand. He pumped it once then turned away.

Jack, still eating, lifted his head. 'Where are ye going to sleep? Will ye be giving them yer parlour, Mam?'

Jamsie and his bother Jack shared a bedroom, and Tyna's parlour, as it was jokingly referred to, was the best room and seldom used.

'We can clear out the salt store at the end,' she snapped, talking about a space that had once been part of the house but with its own door. There was a quiver in her voice when she next spoke. 'My, but I'm that happy for ye Jamsie, for the lassie's been waiting far too long. I'll maybe get a wee bit cloth to make a new dress for myself.'

It was good to see the light on her face. Davie did not remember the last time he had seen his mother in something new. He was glad about the wedding for he liked Mary-Jane with her pale blonde hair and large soulful eyes. Yet he wondered how the two women would get on sharing the same kitchen. His mam could be a stubborn old woman when she had a mind to.

'Shouldn't be too long before Davie's room is empty.' Jamsie winked.

'Na, na, not me.'

'An why not?' asked Tyna, 'Chrissie's the one for ye. What's the point in hanging on?'

Jack snorted and cleared his throat.

Davie shot him a look of ice.

'Davie, I've told Chrissie ye'll take her over for her peat the day,' Tyna said.

'What . . .without asking me?'

'You're getting ours anyway and she's not a man to help her. Ye've to sail to the mainland to collect them. How do ye expect a lassie to do that all by herself, eh?'

'I don't mind Mam, it's just . . .'

Jamsie ruffled his brother's hair and laughed. 'A wee while among the peat stacks with Chrissie, eh Davie. Surely ye wouldn't' turn down the chance of that.' He turned to his mother. 'Don't worry about him. That lassie'll have a ring on his finger before the years out. I'll put a wager on it.'

Davie ducked away scowling. He would help Chrissie of course – but only out of a sense of duty.

He glanced at his brother Jack whose dark, glittering eyes watched him, a sardonic sneer on his face.

Davie stood in the boat, lifting the peats from the hold and throwing them onto the quay where Chrissie loaded them into a cart. With each movement of her body, her dress strained over generous curves. Her arms were brown and almost as muscular as a man's and her hands broad and work-coarsened with short bitten nails. Tendrils of hair stuck to the sides of her flushed face. In spite of the biting wind blowing from the sea, she wiped sweat from her brow.

'What's wrong?' Chrissie's eyes focused on him and the adoration in them made him wince.

'Nothing.' Davie, realising he had been staring at her, bent down to lift several peats at once. He cared for her deeply as his best friend, but could hardly stand her displays of affection. Her growing possessiveness irritated him, filling him with the need to flee. Unable to tell her it was over, he acted uninterested in her presence and hoped that she would tire of him.

'Is it because of that night? I know I was brazen but I've never been with anyone else . . .' Her voice trailed off as she scanned his face.

He jumped on the pier and tossed the last armful of peats into the cart. Disturbed by the shift of balance, the horse between the shafts flattened his ears and shuffled his feet. 'No, no. I don't think badly of ye.' He glanced at the sky. The daylight was fading beneath dark layers of cloud.

'Ye've been avoiding me.' She grabbed the horse's bridle to steady him.

'I'm not ready Chrissie.' He turned away.

She spoke hurriedly. 'I've been thinking. My boat's lying ashore and not a man to sail her. And ye don't need more than two men on the *Silver Dawn*.'

He began to shake his head but she raised her hand to stop him. 'The boat needs to be used, and Granny and me, we could do with a fry of fish not begged from another table.'

She studied him, eyes scared, cheeks red, nostrils quivering as she breathed, a bead of sweat trembling on her upper lip.

Something at the back of Davie's mind told him to say no, this was a tender bit of bait, but he also realised something else. This was a chance to master a boat himself, sailing where he wanted whenever he wanted. Maybe it was not too late to go back to Kirkwall this year, for he thought of little else these days. Crossing to the mainland for the peats had not been too bad this morning. He just might be able to make Scapa Bay before November when the weather would break. He just might.

'The use of your boat for the price of a wee bit of fish?' he asked.

A light came on behind Chrissie's eyes. 'Aye, and she'll need maintaining mind. It'll take a bit of work.'

'Ye'll not be thinking' anything else?'

'No, Davie,' she shook her head, but her lips lifted a notch at the corners. 'I'll wait till ye're ready.'

He wanted to say he might never be ready, but instead he nodded and turned his eyes towards the hills of Orkney.

Chapter 7

At this moment, Isa hated Doctor Menzies. He shouldn't have touched her like that. Probing and prodding in her private places. She fought back tears. If her mother had not been in the room she would tell him what she thought of him – aye, she would. Flushed with embarrassment she bit on her lip. Trying to still her shaking hands, she came from behind the screen.

'Sit down,' the doctor ordered. He scribbled on his pad then peered at Isa over his spectacles. She dropped her head and studied the desk where the polished veneer was marred; a white half-moon shape. Someone has set a hot cup there once, she thought. The only sounds in the room were her mother's steady breathing, the slight rustle of paper and the mechanism of the clock on the wall. There was a sudden whir and it struck one.

'Are you aware you're pregnant?' The doctor's voice seemed far away. The air rushed from her lungs. Her fingers, plucking at the material of her skirt, became clumsy and she clasped her hands together in an effort to keep them still. She wanted to be sick.

'But . . . Doctor she can't be!' Her mother leant forward and gripped the desk so hard her knuckles shone white.

'I'm afraid there's no doubt about it.'

Isa could not say a word. Martha's shocked voice continued, 'But she's not yet sixteen.'

A short silence followed before the doctor spoke again. 'I'm sorry Mrs Muirison, but she *is* pregnant.'

The muscles round Isa's abdomen clenched and she placed her hands over her stomach. What were they saying? The word pregnant – it meant having a bairn, didn't it? She was having a bairn. Growing inside her. All because . . . she and Davie . . . but it happened once . . . lasted no time at all . . . how could this be real?

No, it was a dream – another dream like the one where Annie died.

Martha stared at her, face white, eyes like black holes. Isa stopped breathing. Holding onto the desk for support she fought to stand upright. The room swayed. She longed for her mother to hold her but there would be no such comfort. Martha stood stiffly, her hands at her sides, her expression mask-like.

'You know where I am if you need me,' the doctor said, coming around his desk to open the door. The final glare he gave Isa reduced her to less than nothing.

Martha nodded at him once before walking from the building. Outside, the buffeting wind and driving rain matched her mood. Martha gripped Isa above the elbow and dragged her to the harbour and into her father's office. It was thankfully empty. She faced the girl. 'Who's the boy?'

'Nobody Mam. I don't know what ye mean.' She could not hold back the tears any longer. They bubbled up from her heart and spilled down her cheeks. Denial seemed the only course open to her, as if this would make the inevitable less true.

'Ye'll tell me the truth.'

'It is true!'

Martha drew back her hand and slapped her daughter hard across the cheek. The door opened and Sandy came in. 'I saw ye arrive. . .' his voice drained away. Clutching the side of her face, Isa tried to run past him but he grabbed her arm.

'What's this?' His eyes flew from one to the other.

Martha breathed hard. She spluttered rather than spoke; 'she's . . . ex . . . expecting.'

'Expecting?' The word exploded and his mouth fell slack. He grabbed Isa by the shoulders and bent until his face was level with hers. 'Lift your head and look at me lassie.'

She was no more able meet his gaze than stare at a naked sun.

'God help us,' he exclaimed. 'She's no more than a bairn herself. Who did this?' He swung from her and stared at his wife. 'It's one of the Raumsey lads. Abe warned me she had a fancy. God forgive me, I thought no more about it.' He turned back to Isa. 'Tell me the truth, girl.'

All she could do was shake her head and push her chin into her chest so hard her neck ached.

'This . . . is the last straw!' Martha screamed and clapped her hands to her face. Loud wailing noises flowed from her mouth. Isa lifted her head and looked at her mother in horror. The woman's body shook and her eyes shone bright with either anger or madness. Turning, Martha ran out of the door.

Isa had to get out of here, had to run away and keep going until all the pain was behind her. She had never seen her mother in this state and it was all her fault. Her father grabbed her and held her fast.

'Leave yer mam,' he said through clenched teeth. 'She's never cried for Annie. It's got to come out. Tell me the truth now for pity's sake. Is it the boy from Raumsey?"

At last she found her voice. 'He loves me. He'll marry me when he knows.' Would he? Suddenly she was not so sure. He had not come back as he promised. Maybe he had never loved her at all. Maybe no one did. She longed to tell her father how she felt, how alone and shut out from their lives. As she fought to find the words, he shook her so her head snapped forward and back.

'Marry? How can ye marry? We're going to Canada. '

'I don't want to go to Canada. Don't go Dad, please stay here.' She longed for him to put his arms around her and tell her everything was going to be all right. He sucked in a breath and raised his eyes to a space above his head.

'Home, now.' He pointed at the door and spoke not a word until they arrived at the house. Inside he walked to the window, ran his hand over his head and turned to face his daughter. The rage she saw in his eyes terrified her. He punched the flat of his hand with his fist. 'By God, I'll kill him.'

'Please Dad,' Isa appealed through her tears. She hated everything that had happened – everything that was happening, but she couldn't live without Davie now – she just couldn't. Since they had become lovers, her yearning for him had taken over her entire world. Now she was having his bairn and she did not understand why he had not come back. She had never been this lost and afraid in her life. 'Oh, Annie,' she cried in her heart, 'how I need ye now.' A storm of emotion swept over her and she railed at the fate that deprived her of a loving sister.

Her mother's cries echoed through the wall for what seemed like forever. Isa stood, unable to move. Her father paced the floor, before he dropped onto a chair, and covered his face with his hands. Later, she had no memory of when her mother returned or when she herself went to bed. She only remembered lying on top of her quilt, fully clothed, listening to the low murmured voices in the next room. Unable to identify individual words she covered her ears, trying to block out the sound. Sleep would not come. She punched the pillow, used it to cover her face and screamed into the feathered depths.

In the morning her father entered her room without knocking. He appeared old – older than when Annie died. 'We've decided, lass,' he said, his voice resigned. 'What's done's done. We'll go to Canada after the bairn's born and tell folks it's your mam's. She's young enough yet.'

Sheer amazement swallowed all previous emotions she had been experiencing. 'Ye can't!' Her hands became tight fists as she fought for self-control.

Sandy shut the door behind him. 'How many times have ye seen this boy?'

'Often enough to know I want *him*.'

'And if he marries ye what then? Live a life of poverty on an island. Everything I've done has been for ye. Ye and Annie.' His voice broke. He pressed a fist to his mouth and squeezed his eyes shut.

She turned her face to the wall. The choice was between her family and Davie, and whomever she chose, she might never see the other again. She could not bear this.

If only she could speak to Davie but she had no address for him and no way of knowing how many Davie Reids lived on Raumsey. To have a letter fall into the wrong hands was unthinkable.

She lived on hope. Hope that he did love her. Hope that he had not forgotten her. Hope that he would return to Kirkwall before the ship sailed for Canada.

All winter she clung to that hope. All winter she watched the horizon for as many hours as daylight and weather permitted. All winter she longed for him to come to her. And as she longed for him he grew in her imagination. He became taller and broader, his hair became blonder and thicker, his eyes bluer, his smile more ready, his nature excessively kind and loving, his powers to make everything right, absolute. He became the epitome of the perfect male. The pain of missing both him and Annie rolled into one large open void.

Martha, her mother, was no comfort. The woman turned away from the swelling body of her youngest daughter and spent her days weeping and huddling in front of the open stove door until her legs became mottled red. Her shining house became untidy and dust covered.

Isa's consolation came from hugging her expanding waistline and picturing the beautiful boy that grew within her. Because she knew it was going to be a boy. She never contemplated otherwise. A child that would slip from her body with the minimum of pain, who would have Davie's blond hair and blue eyes, who would be chubby and smiling and seldom cry. She imagined herself holding the baby when Davie beached his boat, imagined him running towards them, wonderment and delight in his eyes – gathering them both in his arms. Her fantasy never moved beyond that point.

Christmas and the New Year approached. There would be no celebration in the Muirison home. So acute was the raw pain of Annie's absence coupled with Isa's fall from grace.

Chapter 8

On the island of Raumsey, the festive season began with the children's treat; a concert put on by the school pupils, followed by a dance in the hayloft of the Mains Farm.

Chrissie looked bonnie that night and the more often Davie visited the whisky keg the bonnier she grew. Avoiding her had become difficult these last few weeks. She did not make advances to him but was always around, her body full and ripe and smelling warm and soft and womanly. The satisfied smile on her face told him she had seen the hunger in his eyes.

If only she did not expect so much, he thought when the blood raced through his veins and he longed to reach for her. He recognised this lust as his natural desire for a bonnie lassie and nothing more. The girls had a trick or two to stop themselves from becoming pregnant. He suspected, however, Chrissie would be too quick to trap him with a youngster. Withdrawing didn't always work, so he had heard. Luck had been on his side that night in the barn.

Those thoughts brought the usual heat to his loins. Then he remembered Isa and the way she had clung to him. My God, he hoped the lassie was all right. He knew he shouldn't have touched her – but at the time nothing else seemed to matter.

Determined to stay clear of Chrissie, he began the night dancing with every woman in the hall. By the time the fiddlers and accordionist slowed the tempo from merry jigs to waltzes, he had lost count of how many women he had spun round the floor. Suddenly Chrissie was in his arms, warm, loving and willing. Whisky had dulled his resolution and he allowed her to lead him out into the icy darkness. The moon was full and the snow covered the ground like a crisp white sheet.

Isa sprung to mind again – the girl who could already be

making a new life in Canada. He had wanted so much to go back to Orkney before the bad weather began in earnest, but Chrissie's boat was in worse shape than he had thought. It would take until spring to get her seaworthy and by then Isa would be gone.

Chrissie shivered and hugged him and without warning her lips pressed hot and soft against his own. 'It's warm in the barn,' she whispered. He would have followed her willingly if a bunch of young lads had not spilled down the loft steps laughing and falling, holding onto each other for support.

'Davie,' shouted Tam, his best friend, slapping him on the shoulder. 'We're away to get another keg of whisky. Come on.'

'He doesn't need any more,' protested Chrissie clutching at his sleeve, but the lads' spirits were high and the mood catching.

'Hold on.' Davie disentangled himself and ran after them. 'I'll see ye in the morning,' he called to Chrissie. He knew that whatever the boys had planned, they would not be coming back tonight.

If he had looked back, he would have seen his brother Jack materialize from the darkness to lay a comforting hand on Chrissie's arm.

The next morning Jessie MacKenzie, a neighbour, burst into Scartongarth, her screams echoing up the stairs to where Davie lay in his bed.

'My, Jessie, sit down. Ye're as white as a sheet.' His mother's voice, loud and concerned.

'A pig – a pig in my meal kist! And me with a bad heart,' Jessie gasped.

Davie imagined the grossly overweight woman clutching her chest as she staggered to the nearest chair.

'Sit ye down. I'll get ye a cup of tea.' Tyna's voice grew stern, her mind probably already working out the identity of the culprits.

Davie turned over – a smile tugged at his lips. It had been one hell of a job getting the squealing young pig from the sty to the kist. Nevertheless, high on youthful spirits and whisky, they had laughed until their sides ached. Trust Tam to think up something like this and it not even Halloween.

'*DAVIE!*' His mother's expected voice yelled up the stairs.

He pulled the pillow over his head and wrapped it round his ears, wincing as he moved. Maybe it had not been such a good idea. His brain pounded from too much drink, the pig's trotters left him covered in bruises and Jessie was a bit old for such a prank. Then he remembered the way his body responded to Chrissie, and he decided it had been, after all, a very good idea.

It was not until the day before Christmas Davie was able to make up for his act of devilment. The early air was frigid and the light barely blanched the sky when he broke the ice on the barrels so the animals could drink. Somewhere in the distance he heard a familiar yapping chorus.

'Geese!' His father shouted, running from the croft house. With one hand he held his hastily pulled on trousers. In the other he brandished a rifle. It was unusual to see these birds so late in the year. Occasionally, if they had been disturbed in their winter quarters on one of the larger islands they would take to the air.

'They're coming,' Dan yelled almost throwing the gun at Davie who was by far the best marksman.

Davie caught the weapon and, swinging it skyward, waited until the geese flew overhead. The rifle kicked against his shoulder and the shot rang out, a hollow sound that punctured the air. He gasped as much with surprise as delight when the black and white body tumbled from the sky. Davie ran over the field, jumping ditches, booted feet sliding on icy patches until he came to where it lay. A fine sized bird. A much better Christmas dinner than the side of salted ham planned for the pot. Moreover, there would be enough to give a generous lump to Jessie. Now perhaps his mother would stop her endless carping.

Christmas comprised of a family meal and church. Apart from that, work still had to be done and the day passed much like any other. Gifts, if any, were for children.

The year melted into Hogmanay. The men, armed with a peat, black bun and a bottle of whisky took themselves first-footing. Before the night was over, they would find their way to every door on the island, seldom returning home before dawn.

All during this period Chrissie was a constant visitor in the Reid house. Although Davie was often in her company, he managed to avoid being alone with her. Any spare time he did have, he spent getting the *Christina* seaworthy.

Needing another man to accompany him, Davie enlisted the help of his friend, Tam. As a reluctant winter gave way to spring, they sailed the yole as far as Huna on the mainland of Scotland for her maiden voyage.

Tyna was delighted, seeing Davie's interest in the boat as a sign of the growing closeness between himself and Chrissie.

Chapter 9

That year the chill of winter lay over the islands until well into April. The stacks of peat around the cottage doors were running low and the wind carried spindrift across the land, withering young shoots as soon as they appeared. Nevertheless, eventually spring spread northward and the swelling tides calmed. From the early mornings until the curtain of darkness, fishing yoles and yawls of various sizes dotted the firth.

The month of April found Davie scrutinizing the horizon until the sail of the *Endeavour*, the first of the floating shops, made an appearance. Within minutes he was on the beach pulling the *Christina* into the water.

'I'll get your supplies,' he shouted to his mother who followed him. 'It's too rough for women folk the day. Give me yer linie.' He took the written list and a handful of coins from her hands. People spilled from cottage doorways and flowed towards the shore, carrying baskets and enamel buckets of fish or eggs. The floating shops came not only to sell, but also to buy.

Davie pushed the boat out. He wanted no company today.

Chrissie appeared over the top of the brae and waved but he pretended not to see her. The yole rose on breakers determined to throw the craft back against the shingle, but Davie struggled with the oars until, his muscles burning, he pulled clear of the surf.

As he neared the *Endeavour*, he threw out the line of corks that served as a buffer between the two vessels then tossed a rope to the boatman's outstretched hand.

'How are ye all,' Davie shouted as he leapt aboard the floating shop.

'Grand, and ye?' the Orcadian welcomed him.

Davie handed him the written list and the basket of eggs. 'Are the Muirisons still in Kirkwall?' He had not meant to blurt it out like that. He had intended to slip it into conversation, but it was too late. The boatman's eyes narrowed.

'I'm not sure. Isa hasna' been seen in the warehouse for a few weeks.'

Davie combed his hair with his fingers and stared at the far distance. 'They'll be gone to Canada.'

'Don't think so. I heard a rumour – the lass is in the family way.'

Davie staggered backwards almost losing his balance. Blood pounded in his ears. He fought to regain the breath that had rushed from his body. Before he recovered enough to speak, another boat arrived with Chrissie, Mary-Jane and two other women perched in the hold.

'Why didn't ye wait for me?' shouted Chrissie as she hitched up her skirts and reached for Davie's hand.

He had no answer for her.

'Ye're shaking – and ye're as white as a sheet. What's wrong?' Her eyes screwed down as she studied him. Her words barely registered. Isa having a bairn? God, he would have to go to her. Now.

'We'll be over with the next delivery of whisky on Friday,' he told the boatman.

The Orkadian seemed surprised. 'Is it not a bit choppy yet for yer peedie boats?'

Davie threw back his shoulders and puffed out his chest. 'Never too choppy for a Raumsey lad,' he declared.

The other studied him for a full minute and a knowing smirk spread across his face. He said, 'whatever ye say. I'll let the boys know.'

'Under no circumstances!' Dan Reid banged his fist on the table. 'There's a good run on the cod just now and there is no spare a boat to go to Scapa. If the Kirkwall men are that keen on the whisky let them come and get it.'

'I can sail the *Christina* myself,' Davie snapped, looking at Jamsie for support.

His brother caught his eye and tuned to Dan. 'It's me ye're mad at. There's no need to take it out on the lad.'

'And no wonder ye make me mad. All that fancy journals and books ye're reading. Ye'll not learn how to run a croft through reading.'

'It's common sense. We've not enough grazing and animals are tethered on the grass verges up and down the road. The lambs are still skinny and underfed. Cut back on the livestock and concentrate on the fishing. Herring's where the money is. Especially now the Council's agreed to build a new pier at the north end.' Jamsie shook his head. 'Why don't ye listen?'

'It's not us they're building the pier for. The lighthouse keepers need a place to land their supplies.' Dan's eyes blazed.

'Look Dad,' said Jamsie, 'Whatever the reason things are moving forward. We've got to move with them.'

'I've brought ye all up fine until now. We catch enough herring to last the winter and we've some left over to sell – what more d'ye want man?'

'Sell most of the stock and build a bigger boat.' Jamsie finished his tea and stood up.

Normally Davie wished his brother would let it be. In his present mood Jamsie was not inclined to take his father's side in anything. Today this suited Davie fine.

'And I suppose ye're going to agree with him as usual.' Dan directed his words at Jack who sat at the table, hands around his tea mug.

'The croft's nothing to me and never will be. Why should I even have an opinion? Jack snapped.

'Of course ye should have an opinion. The croft puts food in yer belly and a roof over yer head.'

Jack's eyes grew dark and he opened his mouth to speak but Jamsie held up his hand, silencing him.

'If the lad wants to take the *Christina* to Orkney, I'm about to go as well. And ye come too Jack.' He flung out of the kitchen. Without further words, Jack rose and followed him.

'I'm sorry Dad,' said Davie. 'But the whisky's ready to go.' He hesitated, wanting to tell him the real reason but not knowing how to start. 'Dad,' he began, lifting his hand in appeal but Dan slapped it away. ' I need to tell ye something . . .'

'Get out of here. Go after yer brothers.' Dan pointed his finger at his son's face, his eyes bulging, spit forming at the edges of his lips and settling on his beard. 'Jack always sides with Jamsie but I didn't' think *ye* would take against me. I still own the *Silver Dawn* and the croft – and don't any of ye forget it.'

Davie found his oldest brother labouring with a vengeance on the dyke he was building. It was a good idea – building walls behind which young lambs would find shelter and seedlings could flourish. Yet this too was a waste of time according to his father.

Davie picked up a stone and fitted it into a space. 'Want help?' he asked.

Jamsie nodded. 'Maybe I was a bit quick with the old man,' he said after a while.

'Ye were. He's set in his ways.' Davie reached for another stone. He wanted to say so much more but could not find the words.

'It's not just because of the whisky,' Davie started, wanting to talk about Isa. Jamsie raised his head, his face brightened and the moment slid away.

Mary-Jane walked towards them down the rutted cart track. Sheep scattered before her, some already with lambs in tow. She glided, her head held high, a smile on her lips. She lifted her arm in a half wave.

Jamsie dusted his hands. 'Look at her, Davie, just look at her.' His voice dropped and became indulgent.

Davie looked. Around her shoulders she wore a dun coloured shawl tied at the waist with a man's belt. A threadbare, black skirt covered her legs but did nothing to hide her rough work boots. She was dressed like any other island woman. Yet something about Mary-Jane stood out. Something in the way she moved, something in the soft melodious tones of her voice. Davie could imagine her as a lady of a manor decked out in fine clothes.

'I've been a fool making her wait so long,' continued Jamsie. 'Once I have the running of Scartongarth, I'll make it pay – faith, that I will. Then she'll live the life she deserves.'

Davie turned his back as the couple embraced. His gut churned. His confession, if he was ever to make it, would need to wait.

Chapter 10

Isa lay on her bed, her hands on her belly. The buzz of voices beyond the wall rose to a pitch where she could recognise the words.

'What else can we do Martha? She's determined she's not coming,' said her father.

'She'll have to come. I'll make sure of that.' Hysteria edged into her mother's speech.

'How? I can't reason with her.'

'I'll not leave her. I'll see the boy behind bars first. I hear a delivery of whisky's due.' Martha paced the floor, the steady tramp of her feet echoing through the house. 'A word to the excise man and we'll be free of him right enough.'

'Ye can't do that. They'll all hate us.'

'What difference does it make? We're leaving.'

'We'll find another way.'

'There *is* no other way. God help us, ye've always been too soft with her. Is it not bad enough we've lost one daughter?'

Isa pictured the scene in the kitchen. Her father holding her mother in an effort to placate her. Martha, tearing herself away her voice becoming sharp and hysterical. 'We have to, Sandy, We have to!'

'No no, Martha, settle down now.'

'Then if ye won't – I will.' The sound of a slight scuffle – hurried footsteps – the opening of a door.

'Martha come back here.'

Isa ran into the kitchen. Her father stood in the open doorway.

'Surely she's not going to the excise man?' Isa cried.

'I don't think she will. She just needs to calm down. But ye'd better agree to come with us. I've never seen her like this.'

Isa stood rooted to the spot. Her mam disliked the excise man as much as anyone. She had to be bluffing. 'Don't go to Canada. Not now. Dad, please.'

Sandy raised defeated eyes. He shook his head.

'I've already sold everything and paid for the passage. Your Uncle William has a job for me and a cabin for us.'

A cold panic, all too common these days, surged through her body bringing with it the desire to strike back. 'I wish I was the one who died,' she shouted. 'And I know ye both wish it and all.' Unable to look at the pain on her father's face, she ran into her bedroom,

At last Martha returned. Her eyes met Isa's once and a tremor ran through her body. Something strange glazed those eyes – something far away and desperate that caused Isa to recoil without saying another word.

What's happening to us? she thought. She had been so happy when she heard of a boatload of whisky was due. Foolishly, she had allowed herself to believe that Davie, once he was here, could lift her burdens from her shoulders. Now he might never get the chance. She had to find a way to warn him – and fast.

'I'm going out.' She grabbed her shawl.

'Isa, come back here,' yelled her father but she paid no attention. She had to get Abe, the old fisherman. He would know what to do.

At the harbour she ran from berth to berth and into the sail-shed where several old men sat mending nets.

'Abe,' she shouted, holding onto the doorframe. 'My mam's gone and told the excise man about the whisky.'

'Merciful heavens.' Abe sprung to his feet, the twine and the big wooden needle on his lap falling to the floor. 'She's mad right enough. I'll get word to the shops before the sailing tomorrow and we can only hope they get to the boys in time.'

As dusk fell, Isa stood on the harbour wall staring out to sea at the curtain of rain that blurred the horizon. The cold crept up her bones. If they caught Davie, she would die.

The next morning she left the house at the normal time, but

instead of her job at the warehouse, she went to the harbour. The shops had already set sail. The only thing left was to go to Scapa and wait.

The wind, soft but cold, carried the scent of heather and brine. Sea birds circled, screamed warnings and dived at her when she drew near their nesting grounds. Protecting herself with her hands, she moved to a point where the view of the bay was good. She scanned the horizon for what seemed like hours.

Finally, satisfied her warning had reached them in time she turned to leave. One last look sent her pulse racing. A brown sail appeared in the mists that blended sea and sky together. However, from this distance one boat looked very much like another. She would wait. In the lee of a sun-warmed boulder she settled down, closed her eyes and listened to the constant ebb and flow of the water, as steady as her own heartbeat.

The sound of horse's hooves and trundling wheels made her start and to her horror she realised she had been asleep. Pressing her body against the rock, she edged her way upwards peered over. Old Willie Haw, the man who had come to collect the load, removed his cap and scratched his head. Relief swelled through her at the sight of him. She scrambled over the rock, hitched up her skirts and ran down the hill. 'The excise men are coming. We've got to warn the lads,' she whispered.

Willie's head jerked up. His brown weathered face creased into a thousand tiny lines as he screwed up his eyes. 'The excise men?'

'Abe was going to send a message with the floating shop.'

'It's maybe gone too late lass,' said Willie without panic. He tethered the horse to an upright slab of stone and adjusted his bonnet on his head. 'But it'll not be the first time we've outdone the law.'

They both heard it at the same time – the quick clip-clop of hooves somewhere behind them on the road. The path ran alongside a steep rise, and that rise, along with abundant growths of gorse provided a good cover.

'Oh my, what are we going to do?' Isa hissed.

'First we'll need to get out of here. Come on.' Willie scrambled up the incline and ducked behind the boulder as if he had rehearsed it for weeks. Isa followed.

'Down now.' he ordered, pointing to the ground. Isa needed no second telling and lay as flat as her swelling belly would allow.

'Two of them,' Willie whispered. She raised her head by degrees, daring at last to peek over the rock. The men stopped alongside the horse and cart, then dismounted and walked around. They looked to the left and right, held a hurried discussion then led their horses back along the road. Within minutes they disappeared behind the undergrowth.

'The buggers'll be setting a trap,' Willie whispered and indicated she should stay low. Her heart thudded. Willie seemed prepared to sit here and save his own skin while they caught Davie and threw him in jail. She tensed, ready to climb down and warn him herself. As if reading her mind Willie grabbed her arm, his other hand pointing to the boat rising and falling in the shallows. Two men jumped over the side of the boat and pushed it onto the shingle. Where was Davie? Wasn't Willie going to do anything? She turned to face him. With his pale eyes riveted on hers, he placed a tobacco brown finger to his lips. A sense of total helplessness overtook her as she watched the fishermen unload the cargo.

Then she heard a sound, a falling of stones and a desperate screaming of terns and Davie hoisted himself over the cliff top. Relief swept through her like a rising wave. His eyes opened wide when they met hers but without a sound, he crawled to her side. She set her hand on his back and his warmth ran up her arm. With a brief, grateful smile he turned his attention to the scene below.

Jamsie and Jack filled up the cart as if oblivious to the danger. Once the last keg was in place, they began to lead the horse along the road. The officers of the law appeared as if from nowhere. After a sharp, heated exchange, the excise men ordered Jack and

Jamsie onto the seat in front of the cart. With triumphant grins on their faces, the excise men led the prisoners away.

'What will happen to them?' Isa asked, not caring. All she cared about was Davie, and he was by her side.

'Not a whole lot.' Davie pulled a piece of grass from its sheath and began chewing on it. 'Like last time, Willie?'

'Aye, like last time.'

'Ye stay here,' Davie said in a way that turned her insides to liquid. She did not know what was about to happen. She only knew she could be in serious trouble. They both could. But they were together and nothing else mattered.

'I'll follow you,' she declared, her mouth dry. Yes, she would follow him – follow him to the ends of the earth.

For a second he appeared indecisive, then gave a nod.

With Davie leading, they crept up behind the cart. Isa's heart beat so hard she was afraid it would leap from her chest. Each footstep echoed in her mind.

Jamsie produced a mouth organ from his pocket and began to play a tune. Jack shouted and swore at the excise men. The horse's hooves clomped against the road. The cartwheels shrieked and creaked as they turned. Worried sea-maws cried and yelped. Enough noise to cover the trio's approach.

Time stretched forever in Isa's mind. Davie matched his stride to the speed of the cart. He untied the rope that secured the kegs and passed the first one to Willie. The old man ran with it a little way along the road. He beckoned to Isa. 'Wait a minute, then roll it to the shingle,' he whispered, passing the keg to her. Back he ran to retrieve another.

Every sound amplified in her imagination, she obeyed. Her pregnancy did little to hamper her movements. At any minute she expected the cart to stop and the excise men to come riding along the trail. They would all be caught. She would have to go to jail. She would give birth in a stinking cell. She wanted to be sick. Then the last barrel rolled towards her and her anxiety melted into exhilaration. Once all the kegs were stacked on the beach, Willie showed her a small squat cave – an ideal hiding place.

'I'll sort things here,' he wheezed. 'Ye two get away across the fields to Kirkwall. Ye might be in time to see the excise men's faces when they find the cart empty.'

'Will your brothers be all right?' Isa asked, her voice jerking as they ran hand in hand.

'They'll be fine.'

'Ye've done this before?'

'Not me – but I've heard the story of how my uncle fooled the excise man many years ago. Back then, he walked behind them. When they got to Kirkwall, all they could charge him with was having an empty cart.'

'That's why they made the boys ride up front this time,' she said, understanding. 'Abe did get to warn ye then.'

'We passed the floating shop on the way but it was too late to turn back. Thank God ye were here.' He stopped and pulled her to a standstill. Both flushed and breathless, they stood for a moment, clutching each other's hands. Suddenly serious, he looked at her – really looked at her – his eyes travelling down her body and over the ample shawl hanging from her shoulders. He laid a hand on her belly – on the swelling beneath the material.

'So it's true.' He swallowed, his Adam's apple bouncing in his throat. With a shuddering sigh he rubbed his hand down her cheek. 'It'll be fine.' Something in his voice failed to convince her.

'Why didn't ye come back?'

'I wanted to. I couldn't. The weather – the boat. I shouldn't have touched ye. I'm so so sorry.'

Her blood ran cold. Did he mean he didn't want her? This was not how it was supposed to be. Then his face crumpled. He thrust out his hands, and placing one at either side of her head, gazed into her eyes. 'I'd have swum the Pentland Firth if I'd known, honest to God I would. I'll stand by ye if ye want me, but I've nothing to give ye.'

'*If* I want ye. Don't ye want *me*?'

'Of course I want ye!' He crushed her to him and she let her tears flow freely. For a long time they stood clinging to each other.

'I'll speak to ye the morn,' he eventually whispered into her hair. 'I'll have to go to my brothers now. But don't worry – don't worry.' Then setting her gently but firmly away from him, he turned and ran towards Kirkwall and the harbour.

Back home, the house was as silent as it had been since Annie's death. The kitchen was full of steam and smelling of carbolic. Martha hovered over the stove where she boiled towels in a large iron pan. She twisted round to stare at Isa with bright yet glazed eyes as if she wasn't quite seeing anything.

'You'll be glad to know they didn't get him.' Isa wanted her mother to be relieved. Martha simply turned her attention back to the towels and prodded them listlessly.

'Mam. Say something.' Close to screaming, Isa tried again, but the turn of the woman's back told her more than words.

'Why don't ye understand? Were ye never in love? Ye would never treat Annie like this.' With her nails digging into her palms Isa waited in vain for a reply. Finally, she flounced into the bedroom and threw herself onto the bed. She lay like that, staring upwards to where the plaster was discoloured and beginning to separate. She watched a wood louse crawl across the ceiling. Davie and her bairn were all she had left now. His initial reaction had been disappointing. He was only scared – shocked, same as she had been when she first found out. He would be happy once he got used to the idea, she told herself repeatedly, because she had to believe it.

Chapter 11

In spite of a few shots of whisky, Davie found it impossible to sleep. Oblivious to the biting cold of a rising wind that whistled through the streets of Kirkwall, he sat on the harbour wall, staring at the moon-cast road of silver across the North Sea. The swell was strong with ribbons of spume peppering the surface. Any worries about what the weather might hold did not lie on his mind tonight.

When he discovered he was a prospective father his whole world crashed. He was shaken, dismayed and angry – with himself for being so irresponsible and with Isa for letting it happen. Too late, he had realised how innocent she had been.

Seeing her again on top of the cliff made his heart turn over – the fire of attraction as strong as ever. He did not know how she'd found out about the excise men but she had saved their skins this day. But a bairn. What had he to give a wife and bairn? He picked up a flat stone and made it skim across the water, the force reflecting his anguish.

He stood until the first fragile light of dawn painted the horizon smoky amber and the sea birds welcomed it with loud raucous cries. A solitary figure appeared, moving hesitantly from a side street. Isa. He opened his arms and she ran towards him.

'I haven't slept,' she whispered as he folded her to him.

Looking down at her his heart tore. Her small face was pinched, the end of her nose pink. Dark shadows outlined the plains of her face. 'They're going to take me to Canada. I'll never see ye again and ye'll never see your bairn.'

He closed his eyes against the pain of parting and said, 'it'll maybe be a better life for ye.'

As if slapped, she sprang back, her eyes full of hurt, and he hated himself for his clumsy words.

'I'll have no life without ye.'

'I've nothing to offer.'

'I want nothing but ye.'

He did not answer at once, he couldn't. Her father owned a steam-drifter. They must be well off. How could she understand the harsh realities of his life?

'Even if I took ye with me I would have to leave the island to earn enough to keep us. Ye would be alone among strangers.'

'Ye're making excuses. If ye don't want me be man enough to say it.'

'Oh God, I do want ye.' He did not want to let her go – not now – not ever. Only for her own sake could he set her free. 'I'll get something sorted out. I'll come back.'

'If ye go away I'll never see ye again. Take me with ye *now*!'

'We've nowhere to live...'

'If ye loved me ye would find a way.'

'Isa don't. I *will* come back.'

'Ye won't, ye won't.' She beat at him with her fists. 'Ye know I'll be gone when ye come back. That's what ye want.' She collapsed on her knees, choking on her sobs. Davie pulled her to her feet and pressed her against him, his own tears wet on his cheek.

'Ye're crying too,' she said, cupping his face in her hands and staring at him. She pulled his head down on her shoulder where she cradled it until he had control of his emotions. 'Come with me. Tell me mam and dad ye want to marry me,' she said.

'Aye, aye, we'll do that.' He nodded. Her parents could not be so bad. They loved their daughter. They would know what to do. Pray to God someone would. 'But we'll have to hurry, for the tide'll no wait.'

Isa clasped his hand. 'Together then,' she said. Her eyes took on a new glow. A smile tugged at the corners of her lips.

Martha Muirison stood in her night attire, her hair loose and uncombed, a shawl wrapped around her shoulders. She was tall and slim and Davie could see by the bone structure and delicate lines of her face that she had once been beautiful. A care-worn, despondent expression and dead eyes now sullied any memory of that beauty.

'Mam, this is Davie,' said Isa.

He held out his hand willing it not to tremble but the woman turned her back and began polishing the stove with a ferocity that shook her whole body.

Sandy Muirison, dressed in crumpled work clothes, sat at the table. His curly hair was tousled, grey, and black. Stubble covered his chin. He lifted hostile eyes and removed the pipe from his mouth. 'So ye came back then?'

'Please dad,' Isa whispered.

'Good God girl, we've been worried sick.'

Davie gripped Isa's hand. 'We came . . . to talk,' he said.

'She's only a bairn – my bairn.' Sandy Muirison's free hand bunched into a slow fist, which he brought down hard on the table. His eyes travelled over Davie's face. 'My God, ye're no more than a lad yersel. How old are ye?'

Davie pushed the hair from his forehead with the heel of his hand and took a deep breath. 'Eighteen.'

Tension crackled through the air. Isa's father pulled a chair away from the table and it made a rasping sound as the legs dragged across the linoleum. 'Sit down,' he commanded.

The young lad obeyed, grateful for the solidity of the seat beneath him. Isa fell to her knees by his side, still holding his hand. Sandy Muirison stood up. Although not a big man, in this position he towered above the couple.

'Do ye love her?'

Davie straightened his spine, squared his shoulders, ran his fingers through his hair and stared into the older man's eyes. 'Aye, I do that.'

'Will ye still love her twenty years from now?'

Davie hesitated, but only for a moment. He looked at Isa and knew the answer. Putting an arm around her shoulder he said, 'Aye, and for much longer if God spares us.'

'What future has she got with ye?'

'I've nothing now. I've told her – but I'm not afraid of hard work.'

Sandy shifted his gaze to his daughter, his voice softened. 'Is there anything I can say that will stop ye?'

She shook her head hard enough to make her hair whip round her face.

'Then we'll go and see the minister. We'll not tell him about the bairn. He might not want to give ye a Christian wedding if he knows ye're near six months gone.'

'No Dad I'm leaving now. We'll be married in Raumsey.' The intensity in her voice worried Davie. He meant every word he said, but he wanted time to prepare his family – to prepare himself – to explain to Chrissie. He said, 'maybe yer father's right. Maybe...'

'No,' she snapped, suddenly frighteningly cool and calm. 'If ye leave now I'll never see ye again – if that's what ye want, then go.' She released his hand and stood up.

Sandy looked at his daughter as if he had never seen her before. Martha's shoulders remained still as she too waited for an answer. Davie knew that if he walked out the door he would be walking out of her life forever.

'I'll be good to her,' he said. 'I have my own room and my mother could do with a bit of help on the croft.' That at least was true.

'Then I can't say I'm happy, but I can only wish ye all the best.'

The light on Isa's face was like the sun appearing from behind a cloud to shine on a bleak winter sea.

'Where in the name of the Almighty is that boy?' shouted Jamsie Reid over the melee of a busy harbour. Their glee at outwitting the excise men evaporated as leaden clouds began to ink out the sunlight and the water within the jetty walls took on a solid oil-like appearance.

'Just leave him. It's after ten o'clock. We've already missed the best of the tide,' replied his brother straightening up, then stopping – frozen in motion. 'By God,' he breathed.

Jamsie snapped his head around and let out a *pah* of surprise. Davie was striding along the quayside carrying a small kist balanced on one shoulder. By his side trotted a girl with a black shawl covering her head and shoulders. The rising wind blew her skirts tight against her belly, making her condition all too obvious.

'What is this?' Jamsie demanded as the pair drew alongside. 'Ye can't be taking her on the boat.'

'I've got to Jamsie,' Davie said. 'I wanted to tell ye but...' His voice tapered off and he blinked quickly.

Jamsie realised his brother was near to tears. 'Now I know the reason ye were so hell bent on getting over this early in the season.'

'I'm sorry man, but ye've got to stand by me.'

Jamsie shook his head. 'The way the tide's running it's going to be a long, rough crossing. No place for a woman, especially one in her condition.'

'I'm not going back,' said Isa, jutting out her chin and meeting Jamsie's gaze.

For a long moment he returned her stare, then shrugged. 'There's no time to argue. Ye'll have some explaining to do once we get home Davie, and if ye expect me to back ye up ye can forget it. Ye've played me for a fool.'

Jack laughed, a dark humourless sound that hung in the air. 'Trust ye Davie. What's mam going to think of her blue eyed boy now?'

'Bugger off,' Davie snarled.

Jamsie stepped between them, reached for Isa and helped her aboard the boat. He upturned a couple of fish boxes, fashioned them into a seat and set her kist beside her. Davie pulled the tarpaulin over her.

It would be as well to make the lass as comfortable as possible, for it was going to be a rough sail, Jamsie thought. She must have fallen out with her parents but they would forgive her and take her home. It was the only way. Because once he and Mary-Jane were married, there would be no place for another bride at Scartongarth.

Isa had never been in such a small boat and the makeshift seat pressed into her back. The heavy cover trapped the smell of fish around her. She arranged it over her shoulders, leaving her eyes free to watch Davie. How magnificent he looked; one hand steadying himself against the mast, his head held high, eyes squinting into the oncoming wind, spray plastering his sun-blond hair against the tanned skin of his face. She thought of the ancient Vikings who sailed the firth to plunder and conquer these islands. The moment caught her up in the spirit of adventure. The excitement of it helped to banish the unease she felt at leaving her parents. In spite of everything, she refused to give up on the impossible hope that, at the last minute, they would change their minds and stay in Kirkwall.

'We're about to hit the worst of the weather. Keep covered,' Davie shouted to her. She wanted to reply she was fine but the boat lurched sideways and spray rattled like hail against the tarpaulin. A wall of water grew before them. The yole rose as if plucked by a giant hand. A wave crashed over the side swamping Isa and pitching her backwards. Freezing foam swirled around her body.

Davie was beside her, pulling her upright. 'Are ye all right?' he screamed above the roar.

'Aye.' She chocked back vomit. Jamsie uttered an oath. Jack, shouting something about useless females, threw a pail to Davie. Forcing herself forward she reached for the bucket. 'I *can* bail out,' she said.

With a grateful smile, Davie grabbed a second can. The two of them, frantically trying to empty the boat, made little impact as more and more waves washed over their heads. Her arms and back ached but she concentrated only on repeating the movement, sheer terror fuelling her energy. Scoop up the water, throw it over the side, again and again and again until her mind and her body were numb and she breathed in short painful gasps.

When she believed she had died, gone to hell and was destined to perform this task for all eternity, someone grasped her shoulders and took the bucket from her frozen fingers. She lifted her head. Jamsie's face was inches from her own, his breath hot on her cheek. 'Ye did well, but the worst is past. Davie can manage now.'

Sweat from the heat of exertion dried on her skin to an icy film. The sea crashed, a rough angry grey with gulls buffeted around the sky.

'Get under the tarp,' Davie commanded. 'Ye'll need it in a minute.'

He was away again, once more throwing buckets of water over the side.

Isa coughed and pitched forward as the vomit rose in her throat and joined the swirling foam in the bottom of the boat. By the time they reached calmer waters she was so ill that a strong desire to die replaced the terror in her heart. Only when Raumsey came into view through the dim light of a fading day, did the tears begin to flow.

The boat bumped and shook as it hit the beach. Davie eased the cover from her shoulders and helped her to stand. A fierce chill hit her body and she wasn't sure whose arms carried her ashore, or set her on feet so numb she could hardly walk. She knew the men were around her, all of them, concerned and admiring. Even Jack clapped her shoulder.

'Ye're safe,' Davie whispered. She gave herself up to the strength of his arms as her legs buckled beneath her.

Chapter 12

In the 'parlour' of the Reid household, a small group of family and friends were gathered. Off chance visits, which developed into a bit of a spree. In spite of stiff fingers, Dan still managed a lively reel on his old melodeon.

Chrissie kicked off her boots and lifting her skirts a little, began to dance. Nellie, from two crofts up, sang a song. Davie's friend Tam played the spoons, rattling them in turn on his head, arms and knees. Tyna clapped her hands in time to the beat. Her cheeks glowed and the tot of whisky Mary-Jane had slipped into her tea made her warm and fuzzy. She picked up her violin, easily following the notes Dan played. Mary-Jane smiled at her soon to be mother-in-law. For once, no disapproval showed on the older woman's face.

Tyna was at peace with the world. She could not help noticing Chrissie wore her Sunday dress, and she had spent extra time on her hair. It could only be because the boys were on their way home.

If only Davie was the oldest son. She could share a house with this girl no bother. Mary-Jane was too uppity and had her own ideas. It was as well they built the room on the end when Dan's mother had been alive. Cleared out and cleaned, it would suite the young couple fine. Jack would still be with them for a while of course.

Ah, Jack. All moods and tempers. He was so like... but no, she must not remember the day the black-haired factor with the wild eyes caught her in the barn. She must not remember what he did to her. He left the island afterwards and she never told Dan. She never told anyone. As quickly as the memory surfaced, she banished it to the cupboard in the back of her mind and shut the door. Yet deep within herself, she knew she had never loved Jack.

Then Davie was born – so long after the others. The very thought of him filled her with a sense of indulgence. He and Chrissie – so right for each other. And in them all her hopes and dreams were coming together.

Outside Bess began to bark. Chrissie stopped her dance, patted her hair and smoothed her skirt. 'That'll be the lads.' She ran to the window. 'Yes, I can make out the boat.' She picked up the tray of scones she had brought with her. Placing them beside the hearth, she swung the iron kettle on its hook until it sat over the fire. 'Nothing beats a cup of tea and a warm bannock.' She winked at Tyna.

Tyna winked back. Her Davie was a lucky man.

The outside door opened allowing a blast of cold night air to gust through the house. The familiar sound of men struggling out of oilskins and heavy boots came from the passageway. Jamsie entered first and his eyes did not search out Mary-Jane as they normally did, but instead found Chrissie. He sucked in a breath and glanced over his shoulder. Davie followed, a bedraggled young lassie supported in the hook of his arm.

The room fell silent.

The girl's eyes were dark holes in her face. Black tendrils of hair stuck to her forehead. Her arms hung by her side like limp eels. With an amused smile playing around his mouth, Jack squeezed past them and finding himself a space, leaned against the wall.

'This is Isa – we...we... we're going to be married...' Davie spoke in a rush, his eyes on his mother.

Tyna gasped, glad to be sitting down as the strength rushed from her. Chrissie paled and turned towards the fire. 'Ye'll be needing tea,' she said, her voice sounding strained and hollow.

Tyna struggled to contain her own emotions as she watched Chrissie's shaking hand steady the large kettle and pour the boiling water into the teapot.

'And I've made bier bannocks,' Chrissie said in a small voice.

'That's great, Chrissie. We all love yer baking. ' Jamsie walked over to the dresser and removed several cups.

'Could ...could ye get the tea Mary-Jane? My granny's not well and I'll need to get home.' Chrissie picked up her shawl, wrapped it round her shoulders with slow movements and bade everyone goodnight. Holding her body erect and her head high she seemed to glide across the room and through the doorway. Tyna wondered whether she was the only one to sense the lassie's pain until she looked at Davie and saw the anguish in his eyes.

Maybe it's not too late, she thought.

She turned her attention to the girl who leant against her youngest son. You won't last long, she vowed silently, and then remembered her manners. 'Someone get the lass a chair and some tea. Now then,' she looked at Isa. 'Just how long has this been going on?' She marvelled at the calmness of her voice as her hopes and dreams crashed at her feet.

'Aye lad. Ye've a bit of explaining to do,' said his father as Davie passed a mug to Isa who clasped her hands around it as if she could derive comfort from its warmth.

Isa, confused and exhausted, lifted her eyes. Suddenly everyone seemed to be speaking at once. Voices whirled about her in a haze of white noise, the cup slid from her grasp and she crumpled onto the floor.

Chapter 13

Chrissie reached the brow of the hill. The full force of the gale threatened to hurl her off her feet. Needle-sharp rain stung her face and mingled with tears of rage and humiliation. Although water trickled down her neck and soaked her clothes and the hem of her best skirt dragged along the ground, she had no desire to return home. In the light of a misshapen moon, without any idea of where she headed, she walked down the long empty road that led southwards.

The roar of wind and sea filled her ears. There was no sound of footsteps behind her. When a hand fell on her arm she turned to ice. Her assailant dragged her to the shelter of a barn wall, her strength useless against him.

'Chrissie, Chrissie!' A voice she recognised.

Ceasing her struggling she stared at the face that loomed over hers. 'Jack!' she gasped. 'Ye scared me half to death. What are ye doing?'

'I was worried.'

'Why?'

'We all know how ye feel about Davie.'

'And now we all know how he feels about me! Just go away. Leave me alone.'

'He's a fool.'

'No Jack – me – I'm the fool.' She was crying without control. 'What's wrong with me? Am I not bonny enough?'

'Ye're the bonniest lassie on the island.'

'Not bonny enough for Davie it seems.'

'It's always Davie! Well he's not here and I am.' Jack was close enough for her to feel his hot tobacco breath on her cheek. Fingers like prongs of steel dug into her arms. She tried to move but he held her firm and a new fear prickled her spine. She knew he had always liked her. Surely he wouldn't harm her.

'Anything I can do?' The plains of his face reduced to an eerie mask of light and shadows as clouds scudded past the moon.

'No. Just let me go.'

'I won't hurt you.' But the words burst out as if in anger.

She swallowed, finding her throat constricted. She willed herself to relax, to stay calm.

'There is one thing. Let me go and I'll tell ye.'

Jack relaxed his grip.

'Ye...ye could sail my boat. I don't want Davie to touch it – ever again.'

'Aye I will. And be glad to.'

'Good. I'll see ye the morn.' She made to move but he tightened his grip. Pressing himself against her, his hot lips searched for her own.

'No Jack,' she cried twisting her head.

'Ye don't know what it's like.' He kissed her neck, 'wanting ye.' His body moulded into hers. 'Davie's not worth it.' He searched for her lips again.

She felt his heart beating and the pressure of his erection through her clothes. A desperate rage surged from the pit of her stomach. Using all of her adrenaline fuelled energy, she pushed against him with her arms. At the same time she instinctively pulled her knee upwards.

He stumbled backwards and doubled up, releasing a volley of swearwords.

Free now, she ran into the driving rain. In her haste she tripped and stumbled but regained her balance and ran on. The thunder of her heartbeat diminished the sound of the storm. All she wanted was to be home, to be out of her wet clothes, to fill the tin bath and wash away the horrors of this day.

Her grandmother sat in her basket-chair by the fire. As Chrissie entered, she threw a peat onto the flames. In her ninetieth year her legs no longer had the strength to support her yet her mind was as sharp as ever.

'Ye're late lassie,' she said. If she noticed the state of the girl's clothes, she did not remark on it.

'I was caught in the storm.' Chrissie fell to her knees and held her trembling hands towards the fire, believing she could never be warm again.

The old woman stroked her granddaughter's head. 'My body may be done lassie, but I've seen a lot in my time and heard a lot more. Is it Davie?'

Unable to speak Chrissie stared into the flames.

The old woman opened her arms. 'Come here.'

Chrissie hesitated. They had always been close but without any excess of physical affection. The last time they had held each other Chrissie was thirteen. That day she had come home from school to an ominous silence. 'Where's dad?' she had cried. Her Grandmother was bending over the fire. Wordlessly the old woman stood up and opened her arms. Chrissie knew then the consumption had claimed him and, within a year, he had joined his wife, her mother. Then, as now, she buried her face in the ample folds of her grandmother's skirts. Then, as now, a deathly cold, colder than the winds outside, claimed her body, freezing the tears within her.

Chapter 14

Isa opened her eyes with a start and wondered what had wakened her. Disoriented, she at first imagined herself at home in Kirkwall. Bit by bit she became aware of her surroundings. She was lying in a box bed and the mattress beneath her comfortably moulded into the shape of her body. The only sound was the tick of a clock and the spasmodic gasp of the wind outside.

She swallowed and found her throat sore. The lower part of her rib cage ached. Beside the bed a lamp burned on a small table, the flame flickering to indicate the oil had almost dried up. Dying embers emitted a faint glow from the fireplace. A faded rag rug lay between a pair of winged chairs of cracked brown leather.

Two windows graced the room with floral curtains drawn across. In front of one sat a Singer sewing machine, the same as Annie had owned. A plain wooden dresser with china cups hanging on hooks almost covered the back wall. By the other window was a white-wood table on which sat a large potted geranium. The walls had been lime-washed.

For a few seconds a kaleidoscope of memories whirled through her head before assembling themselves and flooding her conscious mind. Of course – she was on Raumsey. She remembered the nightmare crossing and coming into the hot stuffy house full of people. And nothing more until a burning liquid trickled between her lips causing her to cough and splutter. She had never tasted whisky before but immediately she knew what it was.

She moved and stiffened as a pain shot across her back where it had pressed against the wooden fish-box. Carefully she lifted one aching arm, finding herself in her nightdress and smelling of carbolic. Who had washed and changed her? Where was Davie?

More memories. Hands helping her up – women's hands. A soft voice; 'Let me get yer dress off. Here we go.'

Another voice, sharp and shocked – an old voice. 'My God, she's having' a bairn!'

A sudden fear gripped her and she placed her hands on her stomach. As if sensing her concern the child within her kicked. She gasped with relief.

'This is your family,' she told her baby, stroking the bump that moved beneath her fingers. 'This is where ye belong.' Holding on to that thought she slipped again into a world of oblivion.

Chapter 15

Jamsie was working on the dry-stane dyke with an energy born of anger when he heard someone approach. He looked up into the gentle face of Mary-Jane and his anger subsided a little.

'I could kill that brother of yours,' she said.

'I might just do that for ye.' He turned to empty a barrow-load of rocks onto the ground. 'I don't know where they're going to live. When we get wed the house is ours.'

'What can we do? We can't throw them out.'

'Her folks'll forgive her and take her back. With any luck, Davie'll go with her.'

'Her parents are going to Canada. Davie told yer mam.'

'Well that's bloody fine! How's he going to earn his keep? He'll not be sailing Chrissie's boat any more. And Scartongarth'll never produce enough for us all – not if my father's got anything to do with it.'

'James Reid, ye're not using this as an excuse to get out of marrying me.' She laughed as she spoke but anxiety lurked in her soft grey eyes.

'Ach lass, ye don't have to worry.' The anger fled from him. 'Come on. Half-yoking time.' He put his arm around her and they walked across the field for the mid-morning snack. His mind remained on Davie and Isa. In the brief moment when their eyes met, he understood why this girl had captivated his brother's heart. He had seen behind her fragile beauty to the strength of character beneath. And she had proved her worth last night. For all his blustering talk, he could never turn them out. However, Mary-Jane had been expecting to be the sole mistress of Scartongarth one day.

When Isa woke for the second time the lamp was out and the fire a dead white ash. A ramp of sunlight, dancing with dust motes, streamed through the small window. From somewhere nearby came the smell of frying ham, the sounds of plates clinking and a woman's voice singing a hymn Isa remembered from Sunday school.

Shakily she reached for her shawl that lay over the back of a chair. She needed to relieve herself and guessed a chamber pot would be under the bed, but was afraid to use it in case someone came in. Instead, she made her way along the short passage. The end room was small. A long, white-wood table took up most of the space and a box bed fitted into a space in the back wall. An elderly woman, bent over a black-enamelled stove, straightened up and turned round.

This had to be Tyna Reid. A lot older than Isa's own mother, she carried more weight. She wore her iron-grey hair in a tight bun; her was back straight, her bust large and hanging low on her stomach. She studied Isa with small dark eyes that were simultaneously intelligent and weary.

As if reading the girl's mind she went to the window and pointed. 'The closet's out by the byre. Ye can empty the pot on the dung heap. Hot water's ready and ye can fill the basin for a wash. Ye'd best hurry on now, for the men'll be back for the half-yoking soon.' She cut a slice from a leg of ham which hung from a hook on the rafters. 'Ye'll be needing a good breakfast and all.' The slice of ham hung suspended between her finger and thumb.

'No thank-ye.' Morning sickness was long behind her but today the smell of frying food made Isa nauseous.

'A scrawny wee thing like ye will hardly push a fine bairn into the world. How far gone are ye?'

'Seven months.'

'I wouldn't have thought that.' Tyna turned her back and slapped the ham into the pan where it sizzled and spat. 'Are ye sure it's Davie's?'

Isa gasped. 'Of course it is!' Blood rushed to her face. Snatching up the water jug, she retreated to the 'room' where she had spent the night.

Out on the high field Davie arranged the harrow and clicked his tongue at the Clydesdale. The old horse took the strain. The heavy flat wooden frame began to move along, its pointed spikes raking the ground, breaking and smoothing the clods of earth. Davie wiped his brow and shook his head to banish the sleep from his eyes. Last night he'd tried to explain to his folks. Where his father grudgingly agreed that one wife might be as good as another, his mother gave no such concession. He worried she would take her disappointment out on Isa.

Isa.

Tired of his parents' reprimands, he had spent what was left of the night watching her sleep. She had been restless and cried out from time to time. Only when near to collapse himself had he climbed to the loft to snatch a couple of hour's rest.

When he looked in on her this morning, she'd been sleeping; her dark hair spread over the pillow, one slender arm flung above her head, her hand half curled. Long lashes rested on pale smooth skin. Her lips parted slightly, showing a ridge of small even teeth. He had longed to touch her, to feel the satiny skin beneath his fingers, but had been reluctant to disturb her rest.

The sudden appearance of Chrissie brought him back to the present. She marched along the cart-track that ran by the end of the field, a sack over her shoulder, pieces of drift wood protruding from the top. Davie pulled the horse to a standstill.

He clapped the large animal. It snorted its disapproval, flattening its ears as a tremor ran through the great body.

Davie ran down the furrow and leapt over the flagstone wall. 'Chrissie,' he shouted.

She stopped, turned, stared. Her eyes were puffy, red and empty.

'I've got to explain,' he said.

'There's nothing to explain.' Her skin was pale and blotched, her voice hard and cold.

Shocked by the change in her he said, 'can we not still be friends?'

She gave a bitter laugh. 'Oh no, we can never be friends! Ye will stay away from me Davie Reid. Do ye hear?' She turned and marched up the cart track, the sack of drift-wood bouncing slightly against her hips. As he watched her go, he felt an impenetrable sense of loss. 'I'm so so sorry,' he called after her stiff, retreating back.

Although she finished in the lavatory, Isa, upset by Tyna's words about the parentage of her child, did not immediately return indoors. With her back against the brick wall, she looked round the undulating landscape. A fence of flagstones protected the garden and beyond that stretched grass-land on which cattle and sheep were tethered. At the top of the rise a number of cottages stood in a row.

To her other side the shoreline curved into a bay. Houses of various sizes backed onto the coastline. The tide was far out and the sea was in a somnolent mood, washing across the sandy beach in long, slow, whispering rollers.

Chickens, hungry and complaining, gathered round her feet. Screaming sea birds filled the air above her head and the ever present seals continued their desolate dirge. She saw people too, working on the land and walking along the road. In the neighbouring field she saw Davie talking to a girl and her stomach clenched. For the first time she realised how little she knew about this boy she intended to marry.

Reluctantly she returned to the kitchen where she hesitated and took a deep breath. 'I'm not a bad lassie. I've only ever been with Davie,' she said loudly.

Tyna wiped her hands on her apron and replied, 'that's as maybe, but no decent lassie would lie with a man 'afore she's wed. And ye can't stay here. It wouldn't be right with ye and Davie under the same roof. Jessie across the way is on her own and doesn't keep too good. She has a bed for ye, but ye'll need to do for her. She'll not keep ye for nothing. Davie can take ye over at the end of the day. Now get this table set. There's seven of us including yourself.'

Isa decided to hold her tongue. Her body ached and craved more sleep but she would not let the woman think she was lazy. She lifted the plates with a damp, shaking hand. Without warning, the dishes slipped from her grasp, crashing to pieces on the flag-stone floor.

Tyna spun around just as the door burst open and the small room became diminished by the solid bulk of male bodies. A melee of voices hushed.

'My plates!' Tyna shrieked. 'They're all I have. Get her out of here.'

'I'm sorry,' cried Isa, glancing round, searching for Davie. The room grew small and airless and before she could stop them, the words rushed from her mouth. 'It's yer own fault! Ye and yer nasty tongue.' With a cry, she squeezed past the men folk, running to the other room and flinging herself onto the bed. As she buried her face in the pillow she sensed rather than heard someone enter.

'Do ye want to tell me what's going on?' said a soft female voice, and the bed dipped as someone sat down.

Isa lifted her face long enough to see a young woman with kind grey eyes and a gentle smile. 'I'm Mary-Jane, Jamsie's girl.'

'She said . . . the bairn wasn't Davie's,' hiccupped Isa.

Mary-Jane stared at the bed-covers for a minute. 'Tyna has a sharp tongue. Just get back into bed. A day's rest'll do ye no harm.'

'Tyna says I can't stay here.'

'Ye'll stay here tonight. I'll have no argument about that. I changed ye last night.'

'Thank goodness it was ye,' said Isa. She wanted her own mother, she wanted her dad and most of all she wanted Annie.

'I'll get Davie,' whispered Mary-Jane.

Within minutes Davie was by her side and the look in his eyes made everything all right. He grasped her hand and pressed it to his lips.

'I'm sorry about the plates,' she whispered.

'Ach, Mam's not as hard up as she makes out. But she'll not

78

put up with cheek. Ye're lucky ye didn't get a clout.' Amusement tinkled in his voice.

'It's not funny! She said . . . she said . . .'

'I know fine what she said, but ye're not to worry. She takes a bit of getting used to.'

Isa leaned her head against his arm. His muscles rippled beneath his shirt.

The door opened and Jack came half way into the room. With a sneer, he looked at Davie and then at Isa.

'Chrissie's no longer spoken for, then?'

Davie's arm tensed. 'Chrissie never was spoken for!' he snapped.

'Who's Chrissie?' Images of Davie and the woman in the field bounced into her mind.

'Just a neighbour. She was here when ye arrived. Don't ye remember?'

'Aye, just a neighbour, eh, Davie?' said Jack. The words sounded bland enough but they carried serious implications just below the surface.

'No, I can't remember. I was too sick to remember anything.' Without ever having met this Chrissie, Isa already hated her.

Chapter 16

'Ye'll have to take treacle on yer porridge for the cows have gone off the milking.' Tyna said the next morning.

Isa helped herself from the pot. 'Anything I can do?'

'Ye can collect the eggs then fill the peat bucket.' Tyna sniffed, and turning away, wiped her nose on the back of her hand. 'As if this house wasn't crowded enough, Davie has to bring *you* here. I don't know what yer own parents are thinking, bringing up a girl to act like that.' Her voice carried on but Isa tried not to hear. She had to get away from this house.

For the remainder of the day it seemed to Isa the workload placed upon her was more of a punishment than a necessity. She did as she was bid, and ignored Tyna's constant complaining. By night time, all she wanted to do was curl up and sleep forever.

Tyna showed a different face to her family. The minute any one of them entered the house her mood lifted, her voice changed and became warm. She laughed so much at their stories her big breasts wobbled. She even cracked a few jokes of her own.

'It's fine to see ye in better form,' said Dan. He dragged off his boots then lit his pipe. 'The lassie seems right enough.'

His wife cleared her throat.

Isa pushed stray curls away from her forehead and lowered her aching limbs onto a hard-backed chair.

'Don't *you* get comfortable. The minute dinner's over ye're off to Jessie's,' snapped Tyna.

It'll not be a minute too soon, Isa thought. From then on she said nothing and sat hugging herself, watching every movement and taking in every word spoken in this close-knit family.

'Isa'll not go till the reading's done,' said Dan when the women had finished putting the dishes away. He lifted a large heavy bible from a shelf. After adjusting his glasses, he began to leaf through the pages. Tyna took her seat at the table and Davie indicated for Isa to do the same.

'One, Corinthians, thirteen, thirteen.' He read the text ending with the words, 'Faith, hope, and charity – and the greatest of these is charity.'

He closed the book, raised his eyes and studied his wife.

'I think that's directed at ye Mam.' Jamsie patted his mother's shoulder.

'Ye'll not find many as charitable as me,' Tyna snorted. 'To them as deserves it.'

'I'm sorry ye have to go lass. We need the chance to get to know ye better.' Dan reached over to squeeze Isa's hand. 'Tyna's right about one thing, ye can't be staying under the same roof as Davie.'

Isa knew one thing. She could not be staying under the same roof as Davie's mother if she wanted to retain her sanity. This Jessie had to be a nicer person, because no one could be worse, she thought.

'She'll never like me,' Isa complained as Davie led her along the shore path.

'Ach, give her time.'

'I could have lost the bairn with all I went through but she doesn't care. It's probably what she wants.'

'She'll dote on the bairn once it's here – ye'll see.'

'Well that's not what I'm thinking.'

Davie stopped and turned to her in fading light. She pushed a strand of hair behind her ear and met his eyes. Being this close to him was a blissful agony.

His fingers brushed her cheek and he gave a half laugh. 'Come on. We've done the hard bit.' Putting his hand beneath her chin, he gazed into her eyes before kissing her gently.

She clung to him, hungry to stay in the warm comfort of his arms. With a low groan he eased her away.

'Don't Isa, I've got to get back.'

'Why? Is it your mam or Chrissie?'

'Who?'

'Chrissie. The one who's no longer spoken for.'

He laughed, a loud, strained sound that hung in the air. Grabbing her by both shoulders he bent down until their faces were level. A lock of hair fell across his forehead. He pushed it away with the heel of his hand and his eyes crinkled. 'It's jealous ye are!'

'No . . .yer mam hates me, and ye didn't stick up for me.'

'She doesn't like scandal. She really has a heart of gold. Just give her a chance.'

Isa pursed her lips and took a sharp breath in through her nose. Was this how life was going to be – him always making excuses for his mother?

The smile slipped from his face. 'Don't be like that. It's not easy for me either. I'll see ye the morn.'

'Maybe ye will and maybe ye won't.' she snapped, turning from him and marching towards the long low thatched cottage. Jessie MacKenzie waited in the doorway, silhouetted by the lamplight.

Isa walked forward and stopped, shocked. This grossly overweight person wore an apron stained beyond repair. Her hair, dull grey, formed a sausage shape around her neck and pillows of fat reduced her eyes to rheumy slits. Placing a meaty fist on either hip, she looked Isa up and down then indicated with her head for the girl to follow her.

'Come away in, Lassie. Ye'll not get a warm welcome from Tyna, things being what they are.' She swayed from side to side as she walked, a waft of sour body odour, stale whisky and pipe tobacco floating behind her. 'It's not much but I've made up a bed for ye.'

If Jessie herself had been a shock, it was nothing to the interior of her house. The walls were smoke-blackened and the arm chairs were the colour of old lard. Ash spilled from the fireplace and spread across the hearth. Damp clothes hung on ropes secured from the rafters of the thatched roof, where no extra timber had been added to create a ceiling. An overlying smell of cat pee, boiled tea and fish permeated the air.

'Ye'll take a drink before bed.' Jessie wheezed and took a fit of coughing. Her face turned red and water filled her eyes. She hawked, brought a blob of phlegm from her throat and aimed it into the fire where it fizzled and spat.

Isa was sure she'd be sick if she ever drank or ate anything in this house. She put a hand on the wall to steady herself and snatched it back. Then studied her palm for signs of grime.

'Can I see my room?' she asked. If it was as bad as this she would leave and sleep in an open field.

'I've put ye in the ben end. I keep it bonny for when my son comes home from London. And I've put a piggy in the bed to air it out.'

Isa shuddered. She hoped the word piggy meant the same in Raumsey as it did in Orkney. Nothing more would shock her in this house.

To her surprise the ben room was clean, tidy and well lit by a large oil lamp. The box-bed had a roof and for that she was thankful. The whole place smelled of damp and the back wall was streaked green with mould. However, it would do – at least for tonight.

'It's the thatch. Leaks in the rain,' said Jessie following Isa's gaze. 'Needs redoing, but I've no man and I've not got the money to pay a' body. I'd have lit a fire but I can't spare the peats.'

Isa could not understand why Davie hadn't warned her or why he let her come here in the first place. Maybe men did not notice these things. At least that's what her mother said. She used to say her father could live in a pig sty. A wave of homesickness enveloped her with a force that brought tears to her eyes.

'Ach, crying is it? Come on Lassie, nothing's so bad it'll not seem better in the morning,' Jessie laid a gentle hand on her shoulder. For the fleetest moment Isa longed to throw herself into the fat arms, to sob her heart out against the great bosom. Instead, she dried her eyes, assured Jessie that she was all right, and bade her good-night.

Pulling back the blankets, she was thankful to find them clean and the piggy, after all, was a stone hot water bottle.

What were her parents doing now? she wondered. Did they miss her as much as she missed them? Her mother's words floated in the air. 'Mind, when ye make yer bed ye lie in it.' Well she would be lying in it tonight right enough.

Yet in her heart of hearts she knew, if by some miracle she could turn back the clock, she would still have chosen to come to Raumsey. She would put up with all this and more just to be with the boy she loved. Then the realisation struck her that this was a ploy by Davie's mother to send her scurrying back to Kirkwall. With the understanding came the conviction that she would never give in to that woman.

Tyna Reid had better learn not to underestimate her. Tomorrow she would turn this hovel into a home. And as she held on to that thought, sheer exhaustion pulled her down into the deep, healing well of oblivion.

Chapter 17

The Reverent Donald Charleston closed the manse door and looked around him. The day was fresh and clear and the tang of the sea filled the air. He was the recently appointed minister on the island of Raumsey, and was still feeling his way with his parishioners and the geography of the place. He would make a couple of calls, he thought, before washing his breakfast crockery and facing the chores he'd set himself.

It was not that he hadn't had offers of help from the female members of his congregation. As a young bachelor of average good looks, every kirk-going mother with an unmarried daughter saw him as a prospective son-in-law. Being wary of their expectations, he believed it prudent to do as much as he could for himself. His own mother had been ailing most of her life and with his father out at work, and his only sister a lot younger than himself and his brothers, he was not a novice in the kitchen. His father hired a lazy lump of a woman who was supposed to come in and 'do' for them. Nevertheless, the reverent and his brothers learned at an early age that if they wanted to eat something that tasted half decent, then they would have to prepare it themselves.

He turned up the collar of his coat and, thrusting his hands into his pockets, headed through the churchyard to the gate at the end of a long drive.

The road was rough and stony with dips here and there that had filled with rain water in the night. A number of people, mostly women, worked the fields Eager to know his congregation better, he made a point of stopping and sharing a few words with each one of them. He made his way past the shop that belonged to Lottie Carter, and along the north road to where Jessie Mackenzie's croft-house backed onto a rocky beach. Jessie was not a church goer but he had been to see her before and the woman intrigued him in spite, or maybe because of, the way she lived. As he approached the cottage he was surprised to see a young girl pegging curtains on the line where they hung like wayward sails.

For a while he watched in silence, enthralled by the picture she made. Her hair fell in black ringlets with auburn glints where they caught the sun. Her blouse sleeves, pushed up past the elbows, showed long slim arms. Her mouth pursed giving a look of concentration to a very pretty face. She bent to pick up another garment and, catching sight of him, jumped.

'I'm sorry,' he said, as if he had been caught spying.

In a fluid movement she raised one arm, lifting the hair away from her face. 'Are ye looking for Jessie? '

'I thought I might call by. I'm Donald Charleston, the minister.' Not yet having come to full understanding of the island dialect, he had to listen carefully. Moreover, her accent was slightly different. More sing-song.

He stepped forward. Her expression became wary. She did not attempt to take the offered hand.

'Isa Muirison.'

'Good-morning Isa Muirison. I don't believe I've seen *you* in the kirk.'

'No, and ye're not likely to either.'

'Why is that?' he asked, surprised.

Ignoring his question, she pointed to the house. 'Jessie's inside.'

'Are you a relation?' He cleared his throat.

'No. I came here to marry Davie Reid.'

'Ah.' He had heard Davie Reid brought a girl back from Orkney. A girl who had broken Chrissie's heart and driven Tyna Reid as mad as a cow at the bulling. Remembering the terminology and the subsequent embarrassment when the good ladies of the parish realised they had been overheard, especially by the minister, he coughed into his hand to hide his smile.

Before he could stop himself, his eyes flicked over her, but with the shawl hanging loosely from her shoulders it was impossible to tell the truth of the rumours

86

'Are ye really a minister?' She turned to stare at him. She pronounced it 'meenister.'

'I am,' he confessed. 'This is my first parish.'

'Ye're still a minister.'

'What have you got against meenisters?' he said light-heartedly.

When she did not reply, he tried again. 'Are you staying with Jessie?'

'Davie's mam thinks it's not right for us to stay under the same roof before the wedding.'

'I see.' He understood that Tyna had sent her here rather than to a more suitable household as a punishment for trapping her son.

'Are ye not going in?'

'Of course.' Reverent Charlton removed his hat and approached the cottage without looking at her again. After rapping his knuckles on the open door, he ducked his head to enter then stopped in surprise. The difference in the room was astounding. As before, a large pot hung from a hook in the chimney, a dresser stood against the far wall, a box bed in the other, a table and chairs sat in front of the window and a battered arm-chair sat at either side of the fireplace – but it was clean!

The room smelt of bread that baked in a tin on top of the smouldering peat, of the peat itself, and slightly less pleasant, the tobacco from the clay pipe that Jessie smoked. Even the woman herself appeared to have had a change of clothing. She sat in her usual position by the fire, her body spread out over the chair, her swollen ankles bulging over woven rope slippers and a ginger cat draped across her lap.

'Ach, it's yersel', meenister.' Jessie pushed the cat to the floor and struggled to sit upright. 'Ye've seen Isa then? She's a grand worker that lassie.'

Isa entered and her eyes met his. A small smile played about her mouth as she poured water from the kettle into the tea-pot.

'You'll want to see me about the wedding,' he said quickly to cover his sudden and surprising unease.

'Aye, but,' she hesitated. 'Do . . . do we have to be married in the kirk?'

'There's a Baptist chapel at the other side of the island if that's your persuasion.'

'I'm not a Baptist nor a catholic either, before ye ask.'

'Then why not?'

'I don't want to go over a kirk door.'

The reverent fingered the brim of his hat while he thought. If she didn't want a kirk wedding, it would solve at least one problem. His superiors, older and more steeped in tradition, would frown on him marrying a pregnant girl in the house of the Lord. He himself had no such reservations but this position was important to him, and the church congress already had doubts about his suitability for the ministry. He was not solemn enough, too tolerant of other's shortcomings, too young and rebellious, were some of the comments he had heard said of him.

He said, 'It's quite usual for a wedding to be conducted from the bride's home.'

Relief spread over Isa's face. 'Then I can be married from here? '

The reverent hesitated. 'Maybe Tyna's – she'll want that,' He did not want to say how unsuitable Jessie's was.

'No,' declared Isa. 'Here's just fine. I'll do it really bonnie – I will.'

'If you're sure. 'His voice trailed off. He knew Tyna well enough to foresee her reaction to this. He also heard the determination behind the girl's words and had no wish to involve himself in their domestic squabbles. In time, he thought he would find out what Isa had against the kirk.

After Reverent Donald Charleston left Jessie smacked her beefy thigh and laughed her hoarse smoker's laugh. 'My, Lassie, ye'd talk a gull into flying backwards! And,' her voice dropped to a whisper. She poked Isa with her elbow. 'Is he not a bonny man?'

'Oh, Jessie – he's a *minister*!' Isa wrinkled her nose.

'Ah, but he's a man for all that.' Jessie laughed so heartily that Isa had to join in.

'And . . .Tyna'll . . . be. . . like a chicken on a hot stove about . . . .about . . . *her* wee boy getting married in my but and ben.' The old woman held her stomach as she shook with hilarity.

Taking a deep breath, Isa placed one hand on her hip and cocked her head. 'Tyna,' she said, 'can go jump in the Pentland Firth for all I care.'

Jessie lifted her hands in the air and let out another howl of mirth and their laughter echoed round the tiny kitchen.

Once the amusement subsided, Isa thought again of Donald Charleston. He did not look like any minister she had ever seen. He was much too young for one thing, tall with a straight back and wide shoulders. His eyes were dark brown, not glittery brown like Jack's, but kind and soulful and his hair – as black as a raven's wing. Jessie had been right he was a bonnie man.

Chapter 18

Isa waited by the shore when the *Silver Dawn* docked.

'I've something to tell ye,' she whispered as Davie secured the ropes. He glanced over his shoulder and followed her up the slope towards Jessie's cottage. The minute they passed behind the barn he grabbed her, but she pushed him away.

'I spoke to the minister today. He's getting back to me with a date for the wedding. He can marry us in Jessie's.' The words came out in a rush as if she had to say them all before she ran out of courage. From Davie, there had been no mention of marriage since her arrival.

He stepped back. 'I can't believe ye've done that yerself! My mam'll want to . . . '

'Yer mam!' Isa snapped. 'It's *my* wedding day Davie.'

'It's not how we do things here. Ye'll have to learn that. And it's *our* wedding day.'

'So that's it.' She settled both fists on her hips. 'Tell the truth. Ye never wanted to marry me did ye? I forced ye to take me from Kirkwall. Ye've never even asked for my hand. Well, that's fine. I'll be on the next boat home.' She turned from him and ran towards the house, tears filling her eyes.

He caught her among the stacks of hay. Seizing her by both shoulders, he spun her round and pushed her against a straw stack. The sharp stubbly ends prickled her back through the thin cotton of her blouse. Heat and a sea-fresh scent radiated from his body. In spite of her heart beating like a rabbit's, she twisted her head away, determined to punish him. 'I should go to Canada,' she feigned a sob. 'It's as well I found out how ye really feel in time.'

'Shut up,' he said. He grabbed both her hands and dropped on one knee on the ground. 'Isa Muirison,' he began, 'will you do me the honour of becoming my wife?'

She laughed, sniffed, laughed again. 'Well, ye know, I don't think I will.' With one quick movement she slipped away and ran around the stack. Taken by surprise he toppled backwards, sprung to his feet and chased after her. Giggling, she dodged this way and that until he caught her and they tumbled together onto the ground.

'Well what's it to be?' he demanded, trapping her arms above her, his body against hers.

'Not if yer mother makes the arrangements,' she shouted, twisting her head away.

His face became serious and their eyes locked. 'Ye don't know how much I've wanted to do this ever since I saw ye again,' he murmured, his hand sliding down, fingers fumbling in the folds of her skirt.

She pushed him away. 'What's it to be?'

'I'll tell my mam ye're going to do it yerself.'

She nuzzled his neck. 'Promise?'

'I promise,' he groaned.

She relaxed, pulling him to her, no longer caring.

Jessie poked the fire and allowed the ash to settle before adding more peat. That done, she swept the hearth. Best to keep the place tidy now the lass had done so much work. The door opened and Isa came in, almost shyly. Jessie glanced at her flushed cheeks, dishevelled hair and the bits of hay on her clothes.

'Ye found Davie then?' she said and Isa's face grew even redder. Jessie turned away smiling. She'd grown very fond of the girl. Nevertheless, seeing her like this brought back a wealth of regret that her own days of being chased among the hay-stacks were so long behind her.

Every day Isa watched and listened as Jessie taught her the crafts of the island people.

'Come on, lassie,' the old woman chastised when Isa's mind began to wander. 'Ye want to be a good wife to Davie do ye not?'

'Yes and I will.' Isa fingered the wooden needle with which she was learning the art of knitting a net. 'But I miss my dad and mam and Annie so much. It hurts, like a real pain – here.' She laid her hand on her chest.

'I know the pain lassie, for haven't there been times in my life when I have known it too? Do ye wish ye'd never come?'

Isa thought for a minute and her eyes leaked. 'No, for I'll only ever love Davie,' she whispered. Her pulse quickened with anticipation of the next time they would sneak behind the haystacks, knowing once she was in his arms there would be no more regrets.

Jessie patted her hand. 'Then go with yer heart. Don't ever accept anything less.'

Chapter 19

Raising the lid from the first small barrel known as a firkin, Isa swilled the salted fish around in the brine to remove any slime. She lifted them out and laid them on a wooden pallet, covering them with canvas and heavy stones to press out excess water. The floating shops were returning.

'Here they come,' someone shouted from the shoreline. Isa lifted her head. The sails were silhouetted against the horizon.

'Take the fish down to the pier. I'll get the eggs.' Jessie sniffed, rubbing her nose on the back of her hand as she came through the door, her great body swaying from side to side.

'I'll do it. I'll do it both.' Isa grabbed the basket. It would be grand to see the boys again, get news of Kirkwall and the girls from the warehouse. More importantly, there might be a message from her parents.

By the time the first shop reached its anchorage, she was on the beach with the others who brought produce with which to trade.

Even the schoolchildren took leave from their lessons, shouted and ran around, often receiving a hefty slap from a parent when they came too near the pails of eggs. The islanders waved to each other, smiled and nodded at Isa, but she was too excited to pay them much attention.

She joined the queue of customers who were waiting to be ferried to the shop when she overheard the conversation.

'Is she still here then?'

'Ach, Chrissie, I don't know what to say. Ye're like one of my own.' Tyna's voice, the kind voice, the one reserved for those for whom she cared, was loud enough for Isa to make out every word.

Isa turned to look at the young woman behind her. So this was

Chrissie. Pretty enough, Isa thought grudgingly, but there was a fullness about her – she would run to fat in later years.

As if sensing Isa's stare, the other girl lifted her head and their eyes locked. Mutual dislike of competitive females sparked through the space between them. Isa straightened her shoulders and arched her back, placing a hand on her stomach so that her condition became obvious. Tyna had told her to slouch, let her shawl hang loose, do anything to hide her pregnancy from prying eyes. Isa, however, wanted Chrissie to see this sign that said Davie is mine – I have something you don't. I have his seed in my belly. She Stared at Chrissie and the look of devastation on the other girl's face confirmed her suspicions. There had been something going on between her and Davie. Isa's mouth tugged upwards in a small, triumphant smile.

Then all other thoughts vanished from her head. Hot blood rushed through her body and her mouth grew dry. An extra man sat in the prow of a returning yole. She gave a scream of delight. Dad.

Picking her way over the shingle, Isa ran across the soft damp sand as the yole beached and her father waded towards her through the shallows. For a moment they stood face to face. He reached out to her, his eyes glistening and damp. Isa hesitated then ran forward to clasp his hands in hers.

'And how are ye, peedie wifie?' A childhood term of endearment. She stared at the well-loved face and breathed in the familiar scent of him.

'I came to see if ye'd changed yer mind,' he said.

She thought of Jessie's hovel, of Tyna's rejection, of the nights she had cried herself to sleep for the want of what she left behind, of the anger she felt a minute ago when confronted with Chrissie.

Her eyes slid to where Davie pushed the *Silver Dawn* from the shore. His hair, highlighted where it caught the sun was tousled by the wind. His shirt, taut over muscles made firm by years of physical labour, was open to the third button and showed a vee of tanned skin. As he caught sight of her, a smile stretched his lips.

Her eyes still on him, she said, 'no, dad. I've not changed my mind.' She turned back to look at her father. 'How's Mam?'

'Ach, she gets no better. It's like the life's gone from her.'

'Maybe if ye stayed . . .'

He shook his head. 'It's all arranged. And yer mam, she'll be better in Canada. There's too many bad memories in Kirkwall.'

'And I'm part of that.' She pursed her lips for a moment. 'When are ye away?'

'This Friday – but I couldna' leave without seeing ye again. I brought Annie's sewing machine and her kist of clothes. I know she would want ye to have them. Now, am I going to meet Davie's folk?'

Isa watched in amazement as Tyna lowered her sack and clasped Sandy's hand in both of hers, her smile as warm as melted butter.

'My but it's grand to meet ye,' she said. 'Ye'll come away up to the house and have a bite to eat before ye go.'

Isa seethed as she listened. To hear Tyna ye would think she was the finest woman on God's earth! Sandy wasn't to worry about his daughter, apparently, for she would be well looked after. How she longed to shout out the truth, to expose the woman as a hypocrite, but she knew that would accomplish nothing.

Chapter 20

Chrissie stood in line, waiting to be ferried to the shop, a basket of eggs on her arm. She held her back straight and kept her eyes focused on the horizon, forbidding tears to spill. Any hopes of Davie's infatuation with the Orkney lass being short lived splintering to pieces.

'If ye hadn't changed yer mind about letting me sail yer boat, ye would be out by now,' said a voice behind her.

She started, placed a hand on her throat and coughed slightly. 'Stay away from me, Jack.' She continued to stare ahead, afraid in case he noticed the raw pain on her face, afraid he would guess the reason.

'I maybe got a bit out of hand that night,' he said gruffly.

'Ye mean forcing yerself on a lassie? I'm not interested in ye Jack.'

'I'll not come near ye again. But ye know damn well ye need my help.'

'I'm in no mood to speak to ye,' she said.

He stepped in front of her, his eyes bore into hers and he took a couple of slow, deep breaths. 'Look, ye need a man to sail yer yole, and I need a boat. I could launch the *Christina* and have ye at the shops in a minute.'

Chrissie rubbed her hands together finding them cold in spite of the warmth of the day. All she wanted was to get her shopping and hide in the sanctuary of her own home. Hide from the smirking face of the brazen hussy Davie brought back from Orkney, and from the pitying glances of her friends and neighbours.

Looking into Jack's eyes she found them impossible to read, yet he spoke the truth. She needed help and she did not have many options.

'I'll let ye sail my boat in return for some labour on the land,' she said, keeping her voice steady. 'But if ye ever try to touch me again, I'll kill ye.'

Anger flashed in his eyes and a muscle twitched along his jaw. She refused to let her gaze waver.

'Well, what's it to be?' she asked.

Jack reddened and gave an exaggerated bow. 'I'll get the boat now then, *madam* – if that's all right with you.'

A heat rose in her and a pulse beat in her neck making her feel sick. She nodded, hoping she'd done the right thing.

Although learning her grandmother's trade as the island 'howdie', delivering babies and supplying herbal remedies, the families she attended, more often than not, had no money to pay her. Now that her grandmother was growing frailer by the day, she had less and less time to work the croft.

Licking her lips with a dry tongue, she gathered up her skirts and followed Jack to where he ran the *Christina* into the surf.

As the sun began to slip westward, Isa walked her father to the shore. He grasped her hand. 'It's a fine family ye're in among; I'll not be too worried.'

How she longed to blurt out the truth, but a lump had risen in her throat and she lost the ability to speak. Sandy fumbled in his pocket and brought out a small bible. 'Yer Mam sent you this. And I put something in as well. All I can spare. If things go wrong, it'll take ye to Canada – and if things go fine, it'll help ye come and see us. Promise me though; ye'll no use this money for anything else.'

She nodded.

'Say it.'

'I promise.'

'Nothing else ever, mind. I can't bear the thought of never seeing ye again.'

As he hugged her, she suffered the pain of regret for all the hurt she caused her parents. She wanted to cry out, to beg him to stay. To stay where it was possible to come, visit, and make her peace. Yet in her heart she knew she had left childhood behind and there was no turning back for any of them.

'I'll come one day – I promise,' she swore. 'And tell Mam . . . tell her I'm sorry.' Suddenly words were beyond her.

'I will. See ye do come lassie.' With that, Sandy Muirison ran through the shallows, leaping over the side of the waiting yole. 'Till I see you again,' he shouted.

She watched the small craft rise on the swell and plunge into the troughs, until the figures aboard became indistinct. She watched the floating shop pick up its passenger and unfurl its sails. She watched until they disappeared into the mists.

Pressing the bible to her chest, she thought of her mam. They had not separated on good terms and Martha Muirison could be a cold and unforgiving woman, yet she hadn't always been like that. Once she laughed, sung and hugged her children often, then she had a bairn who died. For a long time she barely clung to life herself. Was that when she changed? Tears spilled down Isa's cheeks and she cried for the mother she never fully understood.

Only then did she open the bible and count the pound notes lying between the pages. Ten of them. A fortune – more money than she had ever seen. 'Oh Dad,' she whispered through her tears and knew no matter what, she would never break the promise she had just made.

Chapter 21

Isa ran her hand over the top of Annie's kist. She could not open it. She did not know if she ever could for it would be like opening the floodgates to the pain of her loss once more. It was hard enough to look at the sewing machine and imagine Annie pumping the treadle, her hands moving the delicate cloth beneath the needle as she created dresses more fit for a London fashion house than a back street draper's in Kirkwall.

She touched the lock then snatched her hand away. Maybe someday, but not yet – not yet.

'Come on,' she said aloud, jumping to her feet and wiping her eyes. 'There's still a lot of work to do in this house.' Work had become her solace. She lost herself in it and sunk into bed each night too tired to think.

Meanwhile, in Scartongarth, Jamsie Reid waved a letter in the air. 'They've finally agreed,' he shouted. 'We're getting the new pier.' He smacked the page with the back of his other hand. 'We hope to be able to confirm a starting date within the next few weeks. That's what it says.'

'Ye've fought hard for it,' declared Dan, packing a wad of tobacco into the bowl of his pipe with a yellowed thumb.

'Not just me – all of us in the pier committee and the Northern Lighthouse Board. No more rising through the night to haul the boats.'

'It's a proper harbour we need, not just a pier. The jetty at the south side hasn't been a great success.' Dan leaned back in his chair, his lips making a smacking sound as he drew on his pipe, clouds of smoke filling the air around him.

Jamsie rested his knuckles on the table. 'Mind the grand opening. With boat-loads of folk coming from all the islands. Aye even Kirkwall, Wick and Thurso, aye, and a band and all.'

Dan snorted. 'Over two hundred and fifty came that time and they couldna' hold the whisky. At least three fell in the firth.'

'It was a great day, right enough,' said Jamsie and they laughed together.

The door burst open and Tyna came through like a torrent, her eyes bright with fury. 'Have ye heard the latest? Our Davie's getting married in Jessie's ben end.' Particles of spit flew from her thin lips.

'What's wrong with that? It's no unusual for a lassie to be married from home.' Jamsie's spirits were high. He was not about to let anyone put a damper on them this day.

'She should be married in the kirk or from here since she's got nobody of her own. What'll folk think?' Tyna banged her basket on the table.

'They'll maybe think ye're against the wedding,' said Dan with a wink at his oldest son.

'I am that – but I'll no have her making a laughing stock of me – that I will not!' Her chest heaved.

Jamsie walked round the table and took her hand in his own. 'Sit yersel down Mam,' he said. 'Why don't we make it a double wedding? She can be married in Mary-Jane's, same day as us. Saves a lot of work.'

Tyna stiffened and opened her mouth as if to protest but her husband stopped her with a raised hand. He removed the pipe from between his lips and scratched his chin, his nails making a rasping sound against the stubble. He said, 'I think that's a fine idea for she's not likely to come here after the way ye've been to her Tyna.'

Tyna's eyes darted from one face to the other. 'She'll have her own way as usual. No one's going to pay a blind bit of notice to me and that's a fact.'

Jamsie could see his idea taking hold. It offered Tyna a way out without losing her pride. He hoped Mary-Jane would be pleased. Davie wouldn't care one way or the other. He could only pray that the girl herself would agree.

Chapter 22

Isa dragged the tin bath out of the barn and filled it with hot water and carbolic. Finally, she had parted Jessie from her bedding and it needed some amount of washing. It was a grand day with clouds scudding across the sky. The bedding would be dry before night. She removed her shoes, hitched up her skirts and stepped into the bath. She tramped the blanket and hand-sewn quilt until the water turned sludgy grey.

'Ye've got a job there.' Jamsie was striding towards her

Startled, she dropped her skirt and the hem fell into the suds. He took her hand and helped her out.

'What can I do for ye?' she asked, rubbing her palms on her apron. His hand had been firm and dry and the strength of his grip embarrassed her slightly. Looking up at his face, she waited. She liked the look of him, for this would be Davie in ten years' time. Jamsie was broader and more muscular, his hair still blond, his smile quick, his skin weather-beaten tan. He had a steadiness about him and a quiet reliable maturity that his youngest brother lacked.

'I hear ye're getting married from Jessie's.'

'Aye, I am that.'

'Mary-Jane and I . . . we thought maybe you and Davie would be married the same time as us . . . a double wedding, like.'

'I'll not go in a kirk.'

He hesitated, raised his eyebrows but did not ask any questions. 'No, it'll be in Mary-Jane's house. We'll have tables groaning with food if I know her mam and a dance in the barn after.'

'That would be lovely,' Isa cried, tempted a moment to fling her arms around him. Then hesitated, her enthusiasm draining away as quickly as it came. 'Mary-Jane, she'll be wearing a proper wedding dress?'

'I can't say. She's keeping that a secret, for it's not the man's place to know.'

'I'll talk to Davie. We'll tell ye later.'

'And tell him we got the go ahead for the pier. There'll be a real wage for us all for a while.'

'That'll be fine.' Isa's spirits plummeted. The wage would not come soon enough. She would have nothing in her kist that would compare to Mary-Jane's dress. A proper wedding, something she dreamed about had been offered to her and snatched away in the same instance.

'Will ye be moving back to Scartongarth once ye're wed?' Jamsie's voice cut through her thoughts.

'That's what Davie wants. It's just till we get a place of our own.'

'Do you really want to stay with my Mam?'

'No. For she doesn't like me. For myself I'd not come but Jessie's house is not fit to bring a child up in. And what's more Jessie needs the room for when her son comes home.'

Jamsie gave a snort. 'I doubt that'll ever happen.'

'She thinks it will, and I owe it to Davie and our bairn to give Scartongarth a try.'

Jamsie walked away considering the options. Jessie's son had never returned home in thirty years. He did not even send her a card at Christmas. She made a bit by renting out her barn and fields but for most things, she relied on the kind hearts of her neighbours. Having Isa and Davie stay with her would be the best for everyone. He would gladly mend the damaged roof, but if the idea came from him they might realise he did not want them in Scartongarth. Furthermore, there was no guarantee Jessie would agree. It might be advisable, he thought, to keep quiet for now.

'I don't know,' he said to Mary-Jane later. 'At first she seemed delighted, but by the time I left she didn't seem too keen on the idea. Did I say something wrong?' For the life of him, he thought, he would never understand the mind of the female species.

'If she asked about the dress,' said Mary-Jane, 'I think I know what might be the matter.'

Isa sat on the dyke, her face buried in her hands. Life was so unfair! She wanted this wedding more than anything. Arguments chased each other round her brain like dried leaves in the wind. In her pouch lay ten pounds she had sworn never to touch. She could borrow a little – surely her dad would not begrudge her a nice wedding day. She had seen bonny bolts of cloth on the floating shops. But if she bought some, she would have to explain to Davie why she had not told him about the money in the first place. Even if he forgave her for being deceitful, as sure as eggs were eggs he would want to use the rest for other things. Also, it might damage his pride to know his wife had more money than he did. Men could be funny like that, she had heard. Furthermore, if she used it she would be breaking a promise to her father.

'Oh Annie,' she said aloud, 'what would you tell me to do?' She listened as if Annie's voice might come to her on the wind, but she only heard the breeze sighing through the ears of the young corn. A flock of sea birds, crying like lost souls, rose over the hummocky rise making her jump. Mary-Jane walked up the field.

'Can I sit beside you?' Without waiting for an answer, the older girl climbed onto the dyke. 'Jamsie says you're not sure about the wedding.'

'It's just that Davie and I want our own day,' Isa lied.

'I understand. But maybe ye'll help *me* chose something to wear.'

'Ye mean ye don't have a proper dress?' Isa's voice rose and her eyes opened wide. Immediately she cursed herself for being so transparent, for the expression that crossed Mary-Jane's face told her she had guessed the true reason.

'My mam's got a kist in the attic. She's been saving things for my wedding day. Will you have a look in it with me? There might be a dress to fit ye as well.'

'Thank you, but no, I'll get my own dress.'

Mary-Jane reached out and grasped the younger girl's hand. 'We *do* want to share this day with ye both.'

Isa understood that Mary-Jane had intended no offence. She lowered her head and studied the fingers clasping her own. She said, 'maybe I'll find something in my sister's kist.'

'Ye haven't opened it yet?'

She shook her head.

'Would you like me to come with ye?'

'No, It's something I've got to do myself, and I need to do it now.' She stood up and smoothed her skirts.

'I hope ye do find a dress.' Mary-Jane grabbed Isa's hands again. 'Honestly – it will be a grand day.'

'I hope so too,' said Isa, then slipped her hands away and trailed down the hill towards Jessie's.

'Well, here I go,' Isa said to no one, and with churning stomach, she walked up to the chest.

For a long moment she stood and stared at the dark wooden box. She had said she was all right, but was she? She lifted the lid, hesitating when the faint aroma of the lavender and rose water her sister wore wafted into the air.

Her hand shook. She held the lid where it was. The skin on the back of her neck tingled and unnatural warmth seemed to envelope her in a cocoon of love and protection. So strong was the sensation that she knew if she lifted her eyes, Annie would be standing there, fit and well.

'Go on, look through my things.' The words appeared inside her head as vividly as if spoken. Isa lifted the lid all the way up; afraid to lift her eyes in case, after all, her imagination was playing cruel tricks and she would find the room empty.

Gently she removed the patchwork quilt Annie had taken years of snatched moments to complete. One by one she lifted the folded clothes lying beneath, each piece bringing back a sharp bitter-sweet memory. At the bottom, wrapped in plain brown paper, she found an unfinished dress she could not remember having seen before – a simple style, made of white satin. It wouldn't take long to finish, just sew the darts and turn a hem. She would steep in tea of course, to change the colour, as it would be scandalous for a pregnant bride to wear white. With a few adjustments the dress should fit her perfectly.

The realization that Annie might have been fashioning it for her own wedding day brought another rush of emotion so strong her breath caught in her throat. She pressed the material to her cheek as the warmth receded from the room. Annie had gone.

Chapter 23

One of Mary-Jane's sisters met her at the door. The girl was barely a teenager and as thin as a knife, with springy red hair and milky skin.

'Herself's up the stairs. I'll get her.' She ushered Isa through the house.

Children were everywhere, jumping on the box bed and wrestling each other on the floor. The noise deafened Isa, yet Mary-Jane's mother stood placidly, hands deep in a large enamel bowl, flour to the elbows. Sweat trickled down her full rosy cheeks.

'Come away in lassie,' she called. 'I'm glad to meet ye. Are ye going to make this a double then?'

Isa nodded and looked around. Larger than the normal but and ben, the house had a proper staircase and an extension built on the back. In the kitchen area a fire burned so fiercely that the top of the stove glowed red. A low stone sink and a water pump sat next to the back door, beneath a window. The air was full of the aromas of baking bread and stewing mutton. One day, she thought, I'll have a home like this.

'Jeannie, get Isa a cup of tea will ye, and there's scones in the box. Or would ye rather some stew? Don't ye mind the noise. Ye'll have to get used to it soon enough when ye've a family of yer own.' Mary-Jane's mother had a happy smile, making Isa wish she could stay here for ever.

From that moment on, time passed in a haze of anticipation from which Isa never wanted to emerge. The wedding grew closer and women filled Mary-Jane's home, plucking and cleaning chickens, mixing cakes, drinking tea and gossiping. Friends swept and scrubbed the barn. Planks set across oil drums and covered with borrowed sheets, became make-shift tables. A wedding was a communal affair.

A dragging pain started low in Isa's back but she was enjoying herself too much to complain. She did not want anything to spoil this day that promised to be much better than she had envisaged. She missed her own family however. Often, in the still of the night, she would sit on the stone bench outside Jessie's cottage and talk to them with her heart.

On the day, Isa rose early, because a wedding did not stand in the way of work. All the while, she was in a state of unrest, thoughts and fears tumbling over in her mind. For the first time doubts began to plague her. Did she love him enough? Would he ever get her out of this trap of poverty? Was he marring her just because of the bairn? Would she be better off in Canada?

The wedding hour grew nearer and she washed and dressed slowly, imagining a kirk wedding; her own dad walking her down the aisle, her sister Annie as her bridesmaid, her mam crying as mams did. Silent tears welled in her own eyes.

Jessie entered the room, the strong smell of mothballs wafting around her. She wore a bottle green velvet dress with a white lace trim around the neck and cuffs. It might have been beautiful on a slimmer body. On Jessie the waist settled somewhere between her stomach and her breasts, dragging the hemline upward and showing her bulging ankles and rough laced boots to fine advantage. On her head she wore a large brimmed felt hat with a curling orange feather. Her hair rolled around her neck in a sausage shape. She handed a picture, no bigger than a postcard, to Isa. 'It's all I've got to give ye, lass,' she said. 'I've kept it this many years.' Isa took the picture. It was a painting of a dove flying over blue water with an olive branch in his mouth.

'It's real bonny,' she breathed.

'My dad painted it when he was at sea,' said Jessie. 'The dove means peace and happiness. He said if I followed the dove, I would never be sad.' She gave a sharp laugh. 'I think I followed the sea-maws instead.'

'I'll hang it in my room. Thank ye Jessie.'

Jessie twined her fingers together, her lip trembling. 'Ye're right bonny, lass,' she whispered. 'And why so surprised that I can dress with the best of them? I wasn't always so poor. I'm just glad I can still get into it.'

'Ye look lovely,' said Isa, not sure whether to laugh or cry. Events of which she no longer had any control, caught her up and hurled her forward. Whether or not she had made the wrong decision, there was little she could do now.

'Our carriage is here,' said Jessie, grinning and holding the door open. Willie Firth the undertaker, hardly recognisable in his black coat and top hat had come to collect them. His trap, designed to carry coffins, was decked with fresh-cut flowers.

'Now ye didn't think I would let ye down, lass?' Jessie said in answer to Isa's open-mouthed stare. 'Get yersel' here Willie Firth and help an old wifie up on yon cart.'

Davie and Jamsie, waited in Mary-Jane's ben-end. Her father, a quiet, kind-eyed man with scant, faded blond hair, gave both girls away, a bride on each arm. As Davie turned to gaze at her, his eyes full of love and admiration, all doubts vanished and her heart swelled in the knowledge that this was the only man she would ever love.

Presents were few; for the gifts of food and labour were all most friends and family had to give. But what a lovely day. What a lovely week. Isa never wanted it to end.

She had looked forward to the dancing after the ceremony, to socialising with all these people who had become her friends, but the pain in her back was growing worse. Finally, she pulled Davie to one side. He'd already had a mug or two of whisky and his cheeks were flushed, his eyes bright, a soppy smile on his lips.

'What is it, Mrs Reid?' he leaned over to kiss her cheek and staggered slightly against her.

'Let's go Davie.' She did not say home because she did not know whether she would ever be able to call Scartongarth home.

He lifted his eyebrows, turned his head sideways a little, and a slow smile spread across his face. 'I feel the same but we'll need to stay a wee while to be decent.' He slipped an arm around her and nuzzled her neck.

'No – not that.' She pushed him away as a new pain, greater than the last gripped her body.

He took her face between his hands. 'Isa – what is it– what's wrong? Ye're as white as a sheet.'

She pushed past him and outside. She leant against the wall drinking in the air of the late afternoon. A few people stood around talking and laughing in the yard, where a hunk of mutton roasted over a peat fire.

'Will I get the horse yoked up?' Davie waved away a bunch of well-wishers. Someone made a comment followed by a burst of laughter.

'No, I can walk. Just get me back.'

'It's not the bairn is it?'

'It can't be. It's no due for another month.'

He pulled her against him and together they made their way to Scartongarth.

He led her upstairs to his bedroom, 'It'll not be for long. Just till we get a place of our own,' he said apologetically.

'I thought we'd get the good room, or the one at the end,' she said.

'Jamsie and Mary-Jane are to have the one at the end for a while, and Mam will never give up her best room. Ach,' he yelled as he tried the knob, 'they've covered it in treacle.'

Isa knew it was the custom to play tricks on newlyweds, but tonight this brought hot tears to her eyes. She almost lost control when she saw the bed full of peats, and a single bed at that.

Like a dull sword ripping her body in two, the pain returned, doubling her over. She screamed and the scream tore at her throat and hung in the air.

'Isa, what . . .what is it?'

'The . . . bairn,' she gasped as the spasm passed.

Davie raised his hands, his mouth opened and shut like a landed cod. 'I . . . .I'll get my mam.'

Isa for once, did not complain – but she was not staying in this room. 'Help me down the stairs and hurry.'

Tyna returned alone and the minute she entered, she assumed command. 'I've sent Davie for Lizzie, the howdie,' she said. 'Yer not to worry. A seven month bairn can survive.' While Isa paced the kitchen floor, her mother-in-law prepared her best room. She stripped the bed and covered it with a layer of fresh straw, on top of which she spread a white sheet.

'Lie down,' she ordered. That was the last thing Isa wanted to do. Crossing to the window she grabbed at the sill, looked out and looked again, wondering if the pain had muddled her mind.

'The men are coming,' she cried, 'but Davie's pushing someone in a wheelbarrow.'

'He got Lizzie then.' Tyna brought a chair that she placed by the bed. 'Ye'd best get yer clothes off. It's not lucky for a lass to deliver in a wedding dress.'

Dan and Davie entered supporting an old woman between them. Dressed in black, the woman had sunken eyes in a dried prune of a face and a pale pink scalp showed through cobweb-fine hair. Stick legs protruded beneath a sack-like skirt and booted feet scraped along the ground. The men positioned her on the chair beside the bed. Tyna reappeared with a basin in which the howdie washed her long bony hands.

'Now for the goose fat,' Lizzie the howdie said, grinning, showing a solitary blackened tooth. From her pocket she took a small jar.

As the woman massaged the fat into her gnarled knuckles, Isa turned her eyes to Davie in a silent appeal. Surely this person was not going to deliver her bairn. Already Tyna was shooing the men from the room. The minute they were out of sight, the howdie, Lizzie Adams took control, the strength of her voice surprising Isa.

'Have you boiled the rags?' she shouted to Tyna.

'I'm at them now.'

'How long between the pains?' Without waiting for an answer, Lizzie laid the side of her head against Isa's belly. 'Strong heartbeat,' she shouted after a minute. It seemed she only talked with a shout. She straightened up and placed her palms on Isa's abdomen as another contraction forced the breath from the girl's body.

'It's as well it's early for yer a peedie lass.' She nodded at Tyna. 'It maybe wouldn't be a bad idea to put a sheet over the peat stack'

'What's wrong...what sheet?' asked Isa.

'We place a white sheet over a peat stack on the other side of the island, and when the doctor from the mainland sees it, he'll know that a boat is coming for him afore long.'

The light outside was fast becoming a dull grey. 'But. . . it's getting . . . dark.'

'If it's too dark they'll set a bonfire. But that's the men's job.'

'What... if the doctor... disna' get here in time?'

'We don't need him really, but Davie needs something to do. Ye're not to worry. I've delivered over a hundred bairns and I've never lost a one.' Now lie still. It's going to be a long night.'

The sun shone full in the sky the following day before Isa's first born son took his first breath and hands held the infant to where she could see him. He was tiny and blue, covered in blood and what looked like lard. For a second he opened his eyes and stared unblinkingly into hers. The anger at her own body for having rejected him, tempered the sudden surge of love. Tears filled her up and overflowed from her eyes.

'Hurry, bring him here,' someone said and the child was lifted away.

'It's the lass I'm worried about. She's lost a lot of blood,' the old woman shouted.

'Ye go home and rest. We'll take care of her.' That voice again. Isa struggled to recall where she had heard it before but everything dissolved as she drifted into a deep sleep born of sheer exhaustion.

She awoke to a heavy weight on her leg and pushed her hand against the softness of hair. The weight moved and lifted and she realised it had been Davie's head. He had fallen asleep lying half over the bed. Straightening up he gazed at her, his hair rumpled, marks of the quilt in the skin of his cheek.

The room was too quiet. The only sounds were the ticking clock, the gentle whoosh of a settling fire and the faint creak of a rocking chair. She struggled to sit up, her eyes darting around. Where was the infant?

A woman sat by the fireside, gazing down at a small bundle in her arms with an expression of rapture on her face. Slowly she lowered her head and pressed her lips against the fuzz of dark hair showing above the dull white of the shawl

Recognition and anger flooded through Isa.

Chrissie!

Isa moaned. 'Give me me bairn!'

Chrissie lifted her head. She rose and walked towards the bed.

'How dare ye touch me bairn!'

'Quiet Isa,' Davie held her arms pinning her down. 'Ye've lost a lot of blood. Ye have to lie still.'

'It's all right Davie, I'll go now.' Chrissie lowered the child onto the bed. 'I've rubbed him with olive oil and wrapped him in sheep's wool. Keep him warm. And feed him a little every hour. If ye've any worries come for me.'

Davie released Isa's arms, grabbed Chrissie's hand and looked up into her face. 'Thank ye – for everything,' he said.

'Take care of your wife Davie.' Chrissie glanced at Isa, a small tight smile on her lips as she left the room.

'What was *she* doing here?' Isa cried.

'She helped with the bairn. Ye were exhausted and my mam's not fit.'

'*You* sent for her!'

'No, Chrissie often helps her granny. The lad wouldn't have survived without her.'

As he spoke Isa loosened the tightly wrapped blanket around the child.

'Isa, what are ye doing?'

'I want to see him.'

Free of their strapping, the tiny fists flailed in the air. The baby opened his mouth and gave a thin wavering cry. Suddenly, the responsibility for this tiny scrap of humanity overwhelmed Isa. Fresh tears gathered in her eyes. 'Oh, Davie, he's so wee. I'm scared. I want me own mam.'

'We'll be fine. Let Chrissie help. She's worked with early bairns before.'

The words cut like a knife through her heart. He had not seen the way Chrissie had looked at the baby and the way she had looked at him. 'She wants you. And she wants me bairn!'

'We needed her. We went for the doctor and he wasn't at home.'

The door opened and Isa clutched the child as tightly as she dared, relaxing her hold when Mary-Jane walked into the room. 'Ye have to feed the wee laddy now.'

She started to cry again. 'I don't know what to do.'

'Hush now. Why would ye know about babies? Ye're not much more than one yerself. Move over, Davie. I'll help Isa.'

When they finished, Tyna brought her a cup of warm milk, and milk had never tasted so good, yet there was something else in it, some bitter after taste. The old woman picked up the child. 'Ye sleep now. I'll see to wee Daniel.'

'Daniel? Who said he is to be called Daniel?' As she spoke, Isa felt her words slur.

'The first boy is always called after his father's father,' said Tyna.

'He's to be called Alexander, for my own dad.' Isa tried to shout but her voice was fading. Her strength ebbed, the room spun and she drifted away.

When she next woke, daylight seeped around the curtains. Her body was heavy and sore. The door opened and Dan came in carrying a wooden cot with rockers. 'Ah, yer awake,' he said. 'I've brought down the boys' cot and cleaned it up for the bairn.'

'Where is he?' She had been barely aware of the child being brought to her and laid at her breast several times during the night. Now she longed to hold him.

'With Mary-Jane. Tyna's off to her bed, she's been with him all the time, keeping him warm and bringing him to ye for feeds.'

'Then surely we can stay in this room – for the bairn's sake. Ye can't squash us all up the stairs.'

Dan took a long draw at his pipe. 'That room is not as wee as the one we lived in when we first wed, and we raised three of a family and all.'

'It's not like ye haven't got the space. Ye could tell her. She might listen to ye.'

'Tyna listen to me?' He gave a short laugh not unlike the bark of a seal. 'Ye have to understand why she's the way she is. She was brought up in a family of fifteen, and in a smaller house than this.

She always wanted a good room, a parlour she called it, for she worked in service for a while. She came home to take care of her mother. We married late, after her folks died and her oldest brother claimed the house and croft. The time's not been long since my own mother passed away, and at last Tyna has a room to call her parlour. No grand mind ye, but I'll not go against her wishes. It's little enough I've had to give her.'

'But the state of Davie's room! Full of peats, and from what I could see, not even a sheet on the bed.'

'Ach, the lads always get up to devilment. It's well cleaned up. And as for the sheets, we only have the one and it was kept for the birthing. Ye'll maybe have been used to better things in Kirkwall.'

Isa lowered her eyes. 'Nothing was grand about the house in Kirkwall.' She felt chastised without understanding why. 'And another thing, about the bairn's name. I want to call him after my own dad.'

'That's for the second son,' said Dan, 'not that I care what ye call him, for it's the bairn that's important, not the name. Tyna now, she's a great one for tradition.' As he patted her hand, she laid her head against his arm and he smelt like her own father, of sea and the outdoors and tobacco.

Sniffing back another surge of tears, she smiled into his kindly

114

eyes. 'Maybe Daniel's not such a bad name.'

Dan nodded as he rose. 'It'll keep the peace, lass.'

'David Alexander Daniel Reid,' she added. 'But we'll call him Danny.'

Dan stopped at the door, turned to her and said, 'If that lad's got your spirit, he'll no go far wrong in this world.'

Chapter 24

Pleased with the morning's catch, Davie stared into the water as the last creel sunk, landed on a rock-shelf and slid away to settle on a bed of green-brown weed. He tossed the buoy over the side and the connecting line uncoiled in the clear water. They had left the house at three o'clock that morning to catch the flood tide that carried the boat towards Dunnet Head. Now the current had changed direction and he was ready for home and a quick nap before helping the women in the fields. 'All done,' his voice sounded hollow in the lee of great towering cliffs.

Jamsie extinguished his pipe, pushed it into his pocket and grabbed the oars. 'A steamer's coming,' he said. 'If we hurry we'll catch it.'

In the distance, the blurred form of a large ship sailed through the channel between the islands and the mainland. Hands clumsy with haste, Davie unfurled the sail.

Once near enough Jamsie used the oars to steady the yole and Davie stood upright, legs apart, holding his balance as the boat heaved and rocked beneath him. He raised his arms above his head, a lobster in each hand. The ship drew alongside, he dropped the lobsters, caught the rope thrown to him and threaded it through the iron ring on the prow of *Silver Dawn*.

'We want to trade,' he called. 'We need cigarettes, twine and paraffin.' After months at sea with only salted meat, the crew of the steamer was more than willing to barter. Once the goods exchanged hands, the skipper leaned across the rail. 'I've an injured crewman. I'm in need of a good man to take his place as far as Hull.'

Davie looked at the large vessel, heard the creak of the timbers, and the call of adventure filled his veins like a fire. 'Just as far as Hull?' he asked.

'Maybe further for a good man.'

'I'll have a look round.'

'What d'ye think yer doing, man?' Jamsie grabbed his arm. 'Ye've got responsibilities now.'

Davie hesitated. 'We need the money. Isa'll understand.'

'I hope ye're sure of that.'

The image of Isa with his son in her arms sprung to his mind. From the first moment he laid eyes on the child, such a rush of emotion filled him up he had been unable to stem the tears. And what a little fighter the lad turned out to be. Now at three months he was thriving as well as any. Jamsie was right. No way should he leave. Yet with the arguments between Isa and his mother worsening daily, he often wished himself a hundred miles away. A surge of water rose beneath the vessels, throwing them together and squashing the cork buffers between them. Davie stumbled and fell backwards into the yole.

'Well, what's it to be?' shouted the skipper.

Davie regained his balance. The answer had to be instantaneous for the tide had begun to drag them towards the treacherous waters known as 'The Merry Men of Mey.' He shook his head. 'I'd better not, man.'

The skipper shrugged his shoulders. 'How about you?' He raised his eyebrows at Jamsie who instantly turned him down.

'I've too much to lose at home,' he said, with an accusing look at his brother. 'How could ye even consider going?' Jamsie asked as the yole rolled in the backwash and the distance between the vessels widened.

'I only wanted a look,' Davie mumbled. 'I wouldn't have gone.' His cheeks flamed. He adjusted the sail and checked the sun's position. They would make it home before noon. With a heart full of longing, he watched the retreating ship until it slipped over the horizon.

Back on the island, Isa twisted a length of straw around a sheaf of corn and tied a knot. 'I tell you Jessie, I'll no put up with this for much longer,' she said. 'Tyna dotes on Danny but she'll never accept me.'

'Ach, she likes you well enough.' Jessie took the sheaf from her and leaned it against the others to form a stook. 'But ye know she'll not admit it. Maybe if ye'd go to the kirk once in a while. Appearances mean a lot to Tyna.' She used the back of her hand to wipe the sweat that trickled down her face.

Isa gathered another armful of corn stalks and began binding them together. 'Her own man doesn't go to the kirk. And the boys only go now and then to stop her harping.'

'Ach, men. They get off wi' it. And ye'll get no peace till the bairn's christened.'

'If Davie wants him christened he can take him.' Isa crossed to where her fractious baby lay wrapped in blanket at the edge of the corn field. She picked him up, marvelling at the strength in the little limbs.

'Tyna was great at first but now that the Danny's fine, she's never done complaining. I'm getting no sleep. It's stifling at nights in the attic. Let us stay with ye, just till we get a place of our own.'

Isa and Davie shared a small attic bedroom with a narrow skylight. The only furniture was a chest of drawers and a table holding a paraffin lamp. The single bed was hard and lumpy with not enough room for two.

Jessie's face flushed and her breathing came fast. 'Just a minute lass.' With difficulty she lowered herself to the ground where her bulk spread around her. The unaccustomed field work tired her out. 'It was good of Jamsie to fix the roof, but I'll need the room for when Matt comes home.'

Isa tossed her head and bit back sharp words. Sick of hearing of this wonderful son, Matt, who had done so well in London but didn't have the time to send his mother one letter, she said; 'If he does, we'll leave right away.'

'I wouldn't want to fall out with Tyna.'

'Ye'll not fall out with Tyna, for she'll be glad to see the back of me.' Isa's eyes strayed towards the bay where the men ran *The*

Silver Dawn onto the beach. Her face broke into a wide smile. 'Davie's home. Ye'll no mind watching wee Danny for a while?'

'Look lassie, Tyna'll no want her granbairn brought up in my house . . .'

Isa was already running across the field.

Later that afternoon, Davie followed Isa down the stairs of Scartongarth. 'Don't be daft,' he pleaded. 'Mam, tell her ye want her here.'

'What I want means nothing,' snapped Tyna.

Isa glared at her mother-in-law. 'I'm fed up with being squashed in a wee attic room. And I'm fed up with her constant harping.'

'A good wife would not go against her man's wishes.' Tyna's eyes narrowed to slits and her bottom lip quivered as she spoke.

'So I'm not a good wife am I?'

'Think about the bairn,' pleaded Davie. 'And I couldna' live in Jessie's.'

'But I could? Ye didn't think about me when ye sent me there.' Isa turned to face him, hands on her hips, breath coming in short angry gasps.

Davie wrinkled his brow and blew out some air. 'It was for the best at the time.' His eyes flew to his mother in a silent appeal. The look that passed between mother and son angered Isa more than ever. She drew breath into angry lungs, ready to launch into a new tirade when Dan interrupted.

'The lass is right, Davie,' he said. 'This house is too small for these two women.' He spoke to his wife. 'And ye are too hard on the lassie.'

'Take her side against me, would ye? Ye know she's far too wilful.'

'Och Tyna. My own mam said the same about ye a long time ago.'

'Aye, and she was a wilful old besom an all.'

Dan clapped his son on the shoulder. 'What we suffer for our choice in women.' His eyes twinkled. 'The trouble is,' he turned to Isa. 'Ye and Tyna – ye're too much alike. Go on to Jessie's if she'll have you. I'll sort things here.'

'Oh, she'll have us. I'm welcome there. Get our kist Davie, and the cot.' She shot a look of ice at her mother-in-law, tossed her hair over her shoulder and strode through the doorway.

Chapter 25

Chrissie finished the milking and drove the cow through the open door. As she picked up the bucket a shadow fell across the floor. She dropped the pail with a clatter and spun round, grabbing the pitchfork as she did so. Jack stood in the doorway his hands held up as if in defence.

She jabbed the spines towards him. 'Take one more step and I'll run ye through with this graip,' she warned.

His fingers curled into slow fists. His voice became low and angry. 'I've no intention of touching ye. I only came to ask if ye needed anything before I went away.'

She lowered the fork but continued to hold the handle. 'I'm fine.'

'Ye can't have him, ye know – not now with a wife and bairn.' He spun on his heel and marched away.

Chrissie dropped the graip. Tears were not far off, but then they seldom were these days. When she had held Davie's baby she had experienced new and disturbing feelings. He should have been hers. Maybe if she had a child herself it would ease some of the ache inside.

She watched Jack's retreating figure, her eyes following the contours of his body. Tall and broad, the shirt stretched tight across muscles that rippled as he moved. He had not bothered her since that night, yet something about him plagued her still, like a dangerous undertow that lurked beneath a deceptively calm ocean. Jack excited her in a way Davie never had. With a deep sigh dragged up from the hollow place where her heart used to be, she finished her work in the barn and plodded back to the house.

Up above, sea birds circled, their cries not unlike that of a new-born baby. In the distance she heard a dog bark, the plaintive bleat of a ewe and the cheeky answer from its lamb. A large merchant steamer ploughed through the firth, and smaller boats returning from the fishing, dotted the bay. The breeze was gentle and the wild cotton on the marsh barely nodded their heads. She looked up at the thin clouds stretched across the washed out blue of the sky. The weather signs were good. At least that was something for which to be thankful.

The cottage stood before her, door closed, no trickle of smoke escaping from the chimney. That was unusual. A clammy ringer reached up her spine and she quickened her steps.

'Granny,' she cried as she opened the door. 'Ye've let the fire out again.' Her grandmother's chin had dropped on her chest; her wispy hair fell around her face like errant cobwebs, her hands lay in her lap, palms upward, fingers curled. A dullness lay about the body as if the inner glow had faded to nothing.

'Please God no!' Chrissie breathed as realisation hit her and she ran to wrap her arms around her grandmother's still, cold form.

Chapter 26

Davie walked along the beach, gathering drift wood and coal lost from passing steamers. He set everything he found above the high tide mark, thus proclaiming ownership. Jamsie had helped him to weave heather stalks into baskets, which they filled with long flat stones. That done, they attached them round the edges of the net covering of Jessie's newly mended roof. This would hold it securely through the winter storms. The room he and Isa shared, known as the ben-end, still smelled of damp however, and to dry it out, it needed all the fuel he could find.

Now he had settled, Davie did not know why he'd been against the move. It might not be their own house, but it was the next best thing. Jessie was hard of hearing and usually snoring long before bedtime. Freed from the fear that his parents in the room below would hear every sound, Isa had become a much more enthusiastic lover. Whistling a tune, he threw another chunk of wood on the pile. He batted away the midges that hung around him in swarms, hungry for any exposed flesh.

Lowering himself onto a rock, he allowed the stillness to envelop him. The wind was almost non-existent, the sea rattled gently across the shingle and from somewhere over the hill, the sound of accordion music drifted on the air.

Now the pier was definite he would be earning a wage, and the thought of extra money filled him with hope. Once he had enough, he would buy shares in a boat, he thought. Not a wee one like the *Silver Dawn*, but one large enough to chase the herring. He would not stop at Kirkwall or Wick; he planned to sail across the horizon, as far north as Shetland and south to Aberdeen or even Yarmouth. He would bring back coffers full of money. Then he would build Isa a house, bigger and better than any on the island. And all with her blessing, not by sneaking away on a passing steamer. He did not think he could have actually done it but he was glad Jamsie had been by his side that day.

In the half light of the gloaming, he walked back to the cottage. Isa sat on the flagstone seat in the soft night, hugging her knees and staring at the darkening sky. With shadows in her eyes, she turned her head and waited until he joined her before she spoke. 'Ye've been a while.'

Davie gazed upwards. A single seagull flew silently across the moon. 'I got a lot of driftwood. Is Danny sleeping?'

'Aye. Jessie's rocking the cot. Where's the music coming from?'

'Maybe the loft at the mains farm. The lads and lassies often get together for a dance on a Saturday night.'

'Do ye wish ye were with them?'

'No, I want to be nowhere else than right here.' He slipped his arm around her.

'Are ye still mad at me for making ye leave yer mam's?'

He gave a short laugh. 'I don't blame ye.'

'Davie,' she whispered and waited until he looked into her face. 'I've never danced.'

'Never?'

She shook her head.

'Then how about now.' He sprung to his feet, pulling her upright.

'I don't know how.'

He put one arm around her waist and clasped her free hand in his. 'Now watch my feet and do as I do.' He swirled her round and led her over the green. A wave of sound flowed through her until it was part of her and her first awkward steps became fluid and easy. And as their baby slept, Davie and Isa danced among the stooks of corn, under the light of a harvest moon.

For Isa, the following weeks were some of the happiest she had ever known. She made friends her own age, and the laughter and gossip as they gathered the crops reminded her of her days in the warehouse. She either left Danny with Jessie or, when the old woman had had a dram too much, carried him tied to her back in a shawl. The outdoor life gave her an appetite and her thin body began to fill out. A healthy tan glowed on her skin and she drew admiring glances wherever she went.

She liked labouring in the fields and once the new pier was complete, and Davie had enough money put by, she imagined they would go to Canada and work side by side on their own piece of ground. At night they snuggled together in the comfort of a mattress newly filled with chaff and dreamed their different dreams.

Once the harvesting ended, the farm workers swept and prepared the loft of the mains farm for the thanks-giving celebrations. Isa had already discovered how much she loved to dance and refused leave the floor. Her mother-in-law happily cradled the sleeping Danny. Now they lived apart and the gossip regarding the early arrival of the child had died down, an uneasy peace had developed between the two women.

Life was good for Isa in the summer of 1900.

For Chrissie however, this became the loneliest year she had known. She forced a smile on her lips and pretended to the world that she was still the strong confident girl she had always been. In reality, she was continually tired and plagued by a sensation of dread.

Persuaded to go to the harvest dance by friends, she wished she had followed her own instincts and stayed at home. Most women her age were already part of a couple, many with bairns in their arms and the sight of them made her more aware of her own loneliness.

Her eyes met Jack's across the hall and she turned away quickly from his penetrating gaze. Her heart, bruised and broken, was not ready for any relationship and certainly not with a man whose very eyes upon her made her nervous. Yet he made her feel something else too – a flicker of desire, brief, but dangerous and strong.

She left early. What reason had she to look forward? A woman alone, almost twenty, few attractive, eligible men on the island and her body crying out for the love she had once experienced with Davie.

As she tossed and turned in her lonely bed in the heat of late August, her fantasies transported her back to the time Jack had tried to force his attentions on her. No matter how much she told herself she hated him, the memory of his body and lips remained in her mind.

He had danced most of the night with Deanie Green, and the silly young girl had never once taken her eyes off him. He would be in her arms now and she was glad. For she wanted none of a rough bugger like him, she told herself.

Still, as the weeks passed and the fine nights turned cold and dark she found her thoughts turning more and more towards the broad young shoulders and firm buttocks of Jack Reid.

Chapter 27

By late September the weather had taken a downward turn. Reverend Donald Charleston stepped outside under a lowering sky. He loved the sense of freedom of these endless frontiers, so different from the city where he grew up. Here there were no high buildings, no mountains to obscure the landscape, no trees against the skyline – only acres of rolling farmland ending in the broad plateau of the Pentland Firth, the entire scene topped and influenced by an ever changing dome of sky. Today, the water was slate grey and oil-smooth. Shrouded in mist, the neighbouring islands rose above the surface like slumbering hump-backed creatures.

He straightened the collar of his greatcoat against the fine drizzle filling the air and, turning his steps northward, walked along the narrow stony road. As he neared Scartongarth, he recognised a lone figure making her way from the beach, a straw basket slung over her shoulder.

'What brings ye out in a miserable day like this minister?' she asked. Bareheaded with her shawl lying round her shoulders, a silvery film of moisture outlined her hair and upper body. He did not say there were times he liked the inclement weather – less likelihood of curious parishioners waylaying him. He did not tell her that for some reason he failed to understand, she was the one person he had been hoping to meet. 'I wanted to speak to you about Danny.' At least this was partially true.

'You want me to have him christened?'

'It's usual, yes.'

'Did Tyna put you up to this?'

'You two would get on better if you weren't so against the kirk.'

Isa's eyes narrowed. 'I don't believe in God. Is that not enough?'

The reverent started, both at the tone of her voice and the hardening of her face. 'Can't you at least tell me why?'

'He let my sister die. She was a good person – much better than me.'

'I'm so sorry. I didn't know. It's hard to understand why the young are taken.'

Isa looked into his eyes, her face solemn. 'Can ye help me understand?'

He faltered, willing his god to place the right words in his mouth. When it did not happen, he answered honestly. 'I don't know.'

'That's what I thought.' She turned away.

Anxious to keep her talking he hurried alongside. 'I wish I could. If there's anything I can do . . .'

'There's nothing.'

They walked in silence for a few minutes.

'Do you miss Kirkwall?' he asked.

'In a way.' After a pause she spoke again. 'Where are ye from?'

'Glasgow.'

'Ye speak posh.'

He gave a laugh. 'My father's a banker. Both my brothers followed him into the business. We were educated in England.'

'Why aren't ye a banker?'

He took a hesitant breath. This was a question he found hard to answer. Lacking in the drive and ambition of his brothers, he had dreaded entering a profession for which he had neither interest nor expertise. His one talent was having a good speaking voice and the church offered him a means of escape whilst maintaining the respectability he craved. Having made the commitment, he meant to do the Lord's work to the best of his ability. 'It didn't suit me,' he replied at last.

'And there's not a woman in yer life?'

'No. The girl with whom I had expected to share my life had higher ambitions than being a minister's wife.' Uncomfortable, he changed the direction of the conversation. 'About the christening.'

'Can ye do it in the house?'

'Of course.'

'Make the arrangement then. I've got to go. The postman's coming.' She twisted around and ran down the cart track. He watched her go, surprised at how easily she had agreed to dedicate her child to the Lord. She was a strange contradiction of mind-sets, this girl-woman with the thick dark ringlets and fire in her eyes.

Isa caught up with Sanny the postman and he grinned at her, his funny eyes looking in opposite directions at the same time. Still grinning, he pulled something from his bag. 'Got a Canadian stamp.'

Every Thursday she met him, despairing when there was no letter. She jumped the ditch, her feet slipping on the wet grass, snatched the envelope and tucked it under her shawl.

'How're they doing'?' asked Sanny, eager for news.

'Fine.' Ignoring his disappointment that there would be nothing more forthcoming, she ran to the house and into her own room, impatient to read every word written in her father's sprawling hand.

When the *Silver Dawn* beached that night, Isa, waiting by the shore, waved the letter above her head and ran towards Davie. Grabbing his arm, she pulled him a little way from the others.

'Dad wants us to come and join them in Canada.' She held her breath, waiting for his reaction.

'Do they live near the sea?'

'No. It's a place called the North West territories. Dad says they've got miles and miles of grasslands called prairies stretching as far as the eye can see. Ye can ride a horse all day and never come to the edge. 'And,' she added after a moment's hesitation, 'They're giving land away for free.'

Davie studied her face and wiped his brow. 'I hope ye've not got a mind to go.'

'Why not? Ye're always restless. I know we can't afford it yet but once work on the pier starts . . .'

'Work on the pier!' he snorted. 'That's something else. They've wasted so much time talking about it that it's too late in the season to start. We'll no be getting the work till next year. That's if they don't find ways to drag it out even further. Jamsie's getting the pier committee together tonight.'

'About Canada . . .?'

'I don't like farming Isa. I can't be away from the sea.' He turned and nodded to the vastness of the Pentland Firth and the Atlantic Ocean beyond. 'There's *my* prairie. And that there's my horse.' He pointed to the *Silver Dawn*. 'At least for now.'

A tremor of unease ran through her. For the first time she had to face the fact that Davie's ambitions might be different from hers.

Chapter 28

The first storms of winter came on the back of an unsettled autumn, sooner than expected. Fierce gales carried hail and sleet from Arctic shores, dragging spindrift in long ribbons across the firth and over the land. Like an angry beast, the wind moaned round the houses, pushing chilly tendrils around windows, beneath doors and along floors, making the edges of the rugs and curtains tremble and flames flare up the chimney.

The latest storm lasted for two weeks. Boats remained tied up, sheep huddled behind walls, cattle were brought into the byres, men took themselves to the sail-sheds or the store to mend nets, make lead sinkers, play cards and smoke. The women spun wool, knitted, made rag rugs and baked what they could with the last of the supplies.

Isa hated the days she had to spend confined indoors. Keeping the baby away from Jessie's constant bronchial coughing, dodging washing hanging on lines tied to the rafters and trying in vain to dry clothes in a house where water still found a way to drip through the roof. Once the straw in the new thatch had soaked and swollen it would be watertight, Jessie had told her. Nevertheless, as night melted into monotonous night, she doubted the wisdom of moving from the solidly built Scartongarth.

The lamb sales had been good that year and the earth had yielded well. The island's prosperity was at its peak. Davie however, not owning any livestock or land, had only his share of fishing and whisky. Although the diet was limited, Scartongarth had enough food for them all until spring, but they needed money for other things. Salt for preserving the meat and fish, oil for the lamps, fuel for the fires, twine for the nets, lead for the sinkers, new boots for the winter. And Isa had ten pounds hidden in her bible. It chewed at her conscience as she darned Davie's socks that were more darning than sock, when she lined his boots with another wad of paper, when she cut up her last warm skirt to make something for her baby to wear, and when she finished her sewing by the light of the fire because the lamp had run out of oil.

She had to be rid of the money before the pressure to use it became too much to bear. There was only one person she could ask for help. The first chance she had she set out, booted, a scarf tied round her waist and her bible hidden beneath her shawl. The wind was nearly strong enough to sweep her off her feet and as sharp as gutting as knives. Yet there was something exhilarating about the wildness of the elements and the crazy dance of water in the firth.

Once in the shelter of the kirk she leaned against the wall, welcoming the sudden calm. She stood until her heart slowed from its rapid beating, arranged her shawl around her shoulders and smoothed her hair, tucking strands behind her ears

The day she told the minister she did not believe in God, a sense of terror hit her. She had experienced that terror once before when she made a similar declaration back in Kirkwall after Annie died. Nothing terrible happened either time but her outspoken statements still left the dread in her heart.

First, she had to put that right. She knocked at the manse door.

Reverent Donald Charleston, surprised but pleased to see her, stood back to allow her to enter.

'What can I do for you, Isa?' He cleared his throat and adjusted the cuffs of his jacket. Motherhood had made Isa, if anything, more beautiful, for now she had a confidence about her and a fullness of figure that had changed her, physically and emotionally, from a girl into a woman.

Her lips pressed together, her nostrils flared slightly with each rapid breath, her eyes darted round the room, lingering when they fell on his well-stocked bookcase. She breathed deeply and turned to face him.

'When . . . I said I didn't believe in God before – I didn't mean it.'

'I'm glad to hear that. Come on, take a chair.' He placed his hand on her elbow and led her towards the fire.

'It's just that he broke our bargain. He let my sister die.'

'It is not for us to make bargains with the Lord. It was your sister's time.'

'Maybe,' she said, bringing out her bible.

'Is there a passage you want to discuss?' he asked hopefully.

She shook her head, 'It's a present from my mother. But it's really what my dad gave me I want to talk to ye about.' Opening the book, she took out the pound notes.

As she explained, Reverent Charlton's perplexity grew. He walked to the window and stared at the shredded clouds and slate grey firth. Nothing in his training had prepared him for a situation like this. Nothing in his life had prepared him for a girl like Isa. He ran his hand over his head, trying to think up a suitable answer. Surely it was wrong for a wife to keep a secret from her husband, yet equally wrong to break a solemn promise given to one's father.

Being a minister in this parish had sounded simple. Hold a service on Sunday, visit the sick, arrange funerals, weddings and christenings. To have peace and quiet to follow his own pursuits – his nature study, his reading, his sketching.

Now this girl who refused to go to kirk, who had little respect for the cloth and who had aroused feelings in him he'd never expected, had come to him with a problem and he wasn't sure why. Whatever his personal beliefs there was only one answer he could give her. 'You have to tell Davie.'

'It's too late. If I tell him now it'll put a rift between us.'

He paused for a moment. 'Then you did not come to me for advice?'

'In a way. I need someone to bank the money for me.'

'Ah.' He let out a long sigh. So this was it. If he turned her away now, he might lose her forever. 'It should be your husband.'

She shook her head.

'Then you, yourself.'

'I'd have to go to town and I've no reason. Please. I trust ye and there's no one else I can ask.' She looked up at him, her eyes large and beseeching beneath thick dark lashes, her lips pursed together, her cheeks wind-stung pink. One work-roughened hand clasped the money, the other pressed the bible to her bosom.

'Put the money away Isa. If I helped you and the kirk session heard of it, I would not last long in the ministry.' He spoke sharply, wishing her gone so he would not have to look into those eyes again.

'I'm sorry – I didn't think . . . no . . . ye mustn't get into trouble for me.' Replacing the money, she turned to go. Her dejected expression reminded him of her youth and naiveté. Now she was leaving he was eager to make amends.

'Do you like reading?' he asked, remembering how her face had lit at the sight of his books.

She stopped but did not look up. 'I do.'

'Would you like to borrow something?'

'Aye, I would.' Her smile was wavering but grateful. She set the bible on the table and moved along the shelves. Now and again she would stop to remove a book and run her finger almost reverently over the cover. 'So many,' she whispered, 'Annie would have loved this.' Finally, she gave a cry of delight and held up a copy of Wuthering Heights. 'This one? I'll keep it good.'

'I'm sure you will. And you'll come back and talk to me?'

'About the book?'

'About anything you want.'

'Maybe. And I'm sorry . . . I shouldn't have asked ye to help.'

He steepled his fingers together and pressed them to his lips as he came to a decision. For reasons he did not understand, he knew he was going to put his whole career in jeopardy. Surely, he told himself, the end would justify the means if he could draw this soul back into the fold.

'I'll bank the money for you Isa. I'll get you the papers next time I'm in town and bring them for you to sign.'

Her whole countenance became animated. 'Ye don't know what this means.'

He studied her for a moment, then said, 'Just don't tell a soul.'

'I won't. I promise.'

He watched her walk away clutching the book as if it was the most precious thing anyone had ever given her. He watched her lean forward into a wind that pulled at her clothes and tossed her wild curls. And he knew, despite any resolution he might make, he was helpless to deny her anything in his power to give.

When he returned indoors he saw that her bible still sat on the table

Chapter 29

During the long hard months of winter, the community became closer, as if the cold drew the islanders together in a warm huddle of humanity. Every so often, when the monotony of daily grind grew too much to bear, someone arranged a spree in their ben-end. Friends would meet to sing, play music, sample the latest batch of whisky, drink tea and gossip. On one of those occasions, Isa and Chrissie came face to face again.

Chrissie did not intend to allow the animosity to continue. 'How's wee Danny?' she asked, steeling herself for the possible rebuff.

'He's fine.' Isa's eyes darted around as if searching for a means of escape.

'Sometimes early bairns come on the best.' Heartened, Chrissie forced a smile to her dry lips. She would never know how Isa might have responded, however, for at that moment, a hand fell on her shoulder. She turned round and looked directly into Jack's face.

'So ye two are friends now.' He gave a low amused laugh.

'Excuse me. I have to go.' Isa glared at him before pushing her way past and across to the furthest side of the room.

'Leave it be Jack,' said Chrissie, annoyed the chance had been lost. 'It's best to put things to rest. I'm not going to be able to avoid her forever.'

'Ye don't fool me. It's only to get closer to *him*!' He turned, grabbing a jug of whisky from the dresser and taking it with him.

Davie stood nearby. He turned to Chrissie.

'Ye heard then,' she snapped.

'Couldn't help it. Is something going on between ye and Jack?'

'No. Not that it's any business of yours.'

He smiled. 'I know I've no right . . . but my own brother . . . ye wouldn't.'

Chrissie stared at him, for the first time noticing the weakness in the line of his jaw and the hint of arrogance in his eyes. 'I'll do what I want,' she said too loudly, 'and if that means taking up with Jack, so be it.'

Her face flamed. She had to get out of there, away from the roomful of eyes suddenly turned in her direction. Away from the silence that followed her outburst.

Outside, the wind tore at her skirts and battered her body like a determined fiend. She adjusted the shawl about her head feeling strangely liberated. For the first time since a schoolgirl, being close to Davie Reid had not made her tremble.

A faint glow seeped through the half-open barn door. Curious, she crossed the yard and peered in. Jack leaned against the wall under the light of a storm lantern, tipping the jug of whisky to his lips. She studied his strong features and determined chin, and found herself wondering if a more sensitive nature lurked beneath the façade. If this was so, perhaps there could be some kind of future for them. She edged the door open and on soft feet walked up to him and, placing a hand on either side of the jug, she pulled it away.

He looked at her, startled. 'What the hell do you want?' he snapped.

'I think we should talk.'

'What is there to talk about? Ye made yer feelings clear.'

'I don't think they're clear at all.'

While the wind lifted loose wisps of hay, scattering them across the floor and wrapping them around their feet, they studied each other.

She was close enough to smell the whisky on his breath, to see the furrowed line between his brows and the stubble along his jaw. His eyes, dark pools in the faint light, slid over her face and down the length of her body. Without warning, he reached out and pulled her roughly towards him. His arm was like a band of steel across her back, the muscles of his chest hard as he moulded himself against her. A gasp escaped her lips. She let her head fall back. Her hair, already windblown, tumbled free from the roughly tied bun. He covered her lips with his own.

She slipped her arms round his neck, returning his kiss with an urgency that surprised her. She wanted him now and she wanted him to know it. For a long moment they stood locked in an embrace. Then with one swift movement he drew away, grabbed her upper arms, gave a derogatory laugh and flung her from him. 'Did he turn ye down? Well ye needn't come here, for I'll not be second best.' Still smirking, he reached for the jug. Before he could raise it to his lips, Chrissie grabbed the vessel from him and threw the liquor in his face.

'I do not want Davie. I am no longer a young silly girl. Whatever made me think you would be man enough to accept that is beyond me.' She stared at him, her body shaking with rage and shame.

His eyes registered shock and then anger.

Chrissie ran from the barn. She ran through the wind and rain towards her own cottage and threw open the door. A flame flared up the chimney in the unexpected draught and a sudden shower of hail rattled the loosely fitted windowpanes as if protesting at her anguish. She leaned back on the door closing it against the gale, hot tears coursing down her face. Never had she missed her grandmother as much as at that moment.

Chapter 30

On the first day of April, Isa climbed to the highest point of the island and gazed down into the quarry where primroses spread in a yellow carpet. In spite of the warmth, snow still huddled in shadowy corners. From here she could see the entire coastline of Raumsey, the blue mounds of surrounding islands and the misty shores of mainland Scotland.

She lifted her face, allowing the southern winds to run through her hair like fairy fingers. The birds were returning, filling the air with their voices, and the sweet smell of damp earth and young grass drifted around her. The cycle of life was beginning again. With it, Isa too experienced a quickening of spirit bubbling up inside her, making her want to laugh aloud. She spread her arms and spun in a circle. A crofter working in a nearby field stopped to watch her. He grinned and waved.

She waved back, picked up her basket, skipped down the slope and away. The grinding poverty of the past winter had failed to erode Isa's bouts of youthful optimism.

Lottie Carter's wee shop sat at the crossroads, in the centre of the island. To the right stood the school and to the left the church and manse. Huddled around were six cottages known as 'the village.'

The shop itself was the hub of the community. Although it sold a little bit of almost anything, the main purpose for visiting was the social aspect. Here the women met to exchange gossip – who went out with who, who was having a bairn and who might be, and who had the best vegetable garden this year.

There were always a few old men there too, and apart from tobacco, it seemed they bought very little. They would cluster around a long table in the corner, play cards, smoke, discuss fishing, farming, past shipwrecks, and who was set to win the cup for the model yacht racing next season.

As Isa entered, the bell jangled above her head. Inside was over-warm, smelt pleasantly of oatmeal, earthy potatoes, and paraffin oil. Old Morag Sinclair, a woman Isa barely knew, was the only customer.

'How are ye this fine morning?' Lottie remarked from her usual stance leaning against the counter. Her ample breasts lay on top of folded arms and her frizzled grey and red hair sprung out of an untidy bun. She pronounced each word with a slight hiss, most of her teeth having long gone.

'Fine. And we've two new lambs at Scartongarth already.' Isa set the basket down and produced a written list.

Morag leaned over, nudged Isa and dropped her voice to a whisper. 'Is it true Mary-Jane's expecting?'

'Aye, but don't say I told ye.' It was common for the island women to keep a pregnancy secret for as long as possible although Isa had never seen the sense in it.

'I knew by the look of her!' said Lottie, straightening up triumphantly.

'An me,' said Morag. 'Was I not just saying that very thing before the lass came in?'

'Aye, ye always had a nose for things like that.' Lottie pushed her glasses onto the top of her head, picked up Isa's list and peered at it. 'How did Jamsie and the pier committee get on with the cooncil?'

'Good. They marched into the council offices in the middle of a meeting and demanded a hearing. They've finally been given a start date for the pier. The first day of next month.'

'Jamsie Reid's a man to get things done,' giggled Jeannie. 'Can ye no just see these fat cooncillors on the mainland quaking at the sight of a bunch of Raumsey fishermen bursting into their grand offices.'

They all laughed together.

Isa handed the note to Lottie. 'Can I leave Tyna's linie with ye? I have to get a book back to the minister.'

'Aye, away ye go.' Lottie looked at her friend and settled her glasses back on her nose. 'I'll swear, I've never known a lassie to read as much. It can't be good for the eyes.'

Leaving them to discuss the state of her vision, Isa walked the short distance to the manse. Although glad things had gone well for the pier committee, she had something else to worry about — Davie's exuberance at the sight of the herring fleet in Wick harbour. The sheer volume of boats, the herring, the number of gutters and coopers working on the quayside, so impressed him that he could talk of nothing else for days. She had always known about the restlessness in him, but could not contemplate the thought of him leaving her, even for a short time. And what was the point? From what she gathered, the men who followed the silver darlings came back poorer than they left. Thankfully, building the new pier would bring employment, which would give him something to focus on for a while.

She hoped Reverent Charlton was at home. A completely different world existed out there that only he could talk about. The more he told her, the more she wanted to know. He had a sister, Elizabeth, who joined the suffragette movement. Every other week a letter arrived from her. Encouraged by Isa's interest the reverent often read them aloud, each word an unfolding episode in the exciting life of a woman she had never met but already admired. If she had been born further south, she knew she would be marching too. Not that women getting the vote would make any difference to the islanders, she thought.

She pushed the heavy manse door and it swung back with a low creak.

Reverent Charlton sat at the kitchen table, pen in hand and a stack of papers before him. The kettle sang on the stove. A pile of dirty dishes lay in the enamel basin beside the pump. As he looked up she saw to her surprise his eyes were puffed and red, as if he had been crying. He smiled a greeting, a hard, forced smile that did not travel beyond his lips.

She set the book beside him. 'I'll not be needing another till the dark nights come back.'

'I'll miss our chats,' he said, his voice flat.

Isa tensed. There was something very wrong. 'Any news of Elizabeth?'

He appeared to be struggling to compose himself.

'Surely she's not been arrested?' asked Isa.

The reverent cleared his throat. He stood up and crossed to the window. 'She *was* arrested and refused to eat. She was force fed.' He leaned forward resting his knuckles on the sill. 'God knows what she had to endure.'

'Is she . . . is she all right?' Isa asked.

'No.' He spun round, his face ablaze with uncharacteristic rage. 'She caught pneumonia in prison. She's dead Isa. I had the telegram from my father today.'

One quick stride took him to the stove. He spooned tealeaves into the pot.

Isa ran to him and laid an impulsive hand on his arm. 'I'm so sorry.'

'I'll be gone for a week or two. I have things to sort out,' he said without looking at her.

'But . . . ye will come back?'

He nodded. 'Of course.' Then added so quietly that later she was not sure whether she'd imagined it, 'there's nowhere else for me to go.'

She took the cup of tea he offered but did not drink. To do so would have choked her. She wanted to tell him she knew exactly how he felt, but in spite of all their discussions, their talk had never become personal. She hoped he would come back, for if he did not, there would be yet another void in her life.

Spring dissolved into a blistering summer, and still the Reverend Charleston did not return. Young missionaries, who stayed for a few weeks and then replaced, performed the services. Work was hard and the long hours gave Isa little time to think, yet at some point during every day, she wondered what had become of him.

Danny, who had started to walk, toddled after his mother as she worked the fields. His pale skin took on a new glow. When the men went to sea he held up his hands, wanting to go with his dad.

Davie laughed and tousled the boy's hair, dark and curly like his mother's. 'A real fisherman's son,' he said. 'Give it a year or two and he'll be able to come with me.' He picked the toddler up and tossed him in the air until his screams turned to laughter.

'Ye'll have that bairn black and blue,' scolded Isa, but her heart swelled as she watched the two of them together.

She placed her hand on her stomach. It was as well Davie proved such a devoted dad, for she knew that before the end of this year there would be another mouth to feed.

Chapter 31

As promised, on the first day of May, to the accompaniment of a piper and a delegation from the mainland, a fine lady from Caithness laid the foundation stone for the new pier. Tables covered with food prepared by the women had been set up on the green, and there was music and dancing afterwards. When the boatloads departed, most of the men were fairly inebriated.

'We'll have an even better day once the pier is completed,' shouted Jamsie after them. Clapping and jeering echoed across the water.

After the first few days of breaking rock, Davie often lifted his head and gazed at the sea. He imagined the salt winds in his face and no man to tell him what to do. He cursed as he swung the pickaxe at increasingly stubborn slabs of stone, every sinew of his body burning with the effort.

It happened on a Saturday. The crinkled blue of the firth beckoned to Davie. He watched the crashing breakers; the white spumes of spray reach into the sky, splatter over the rocks and run in rivulets back to the sea. He pulled a packet of cigarettes from his pocket and prising the top open, shook one into his hand. The white cylinder rolled to the centre of his palm, so light he barely felt its presence and he allowed it to travel downwards, catching it between his finger and thumb. Cigarettes were a new novelty and the young men of the island had just begun to enjoy them. He placed the tobacco-filled tube in his mouth, felt the paper stick to his lips and pulled a matchbox from his pocket. The small wooden stick ignited and flared as he struck it against the sandpaper and for a second the smell of phosphorus filled his nostrils. Cupping his hand to protect the flame from the wind, he applied the flickering light to the end of the cigarette and sucked deeply. The smoke filled his lungs with a warm, pleasing sensation. Shaking the match to extinguish it, he threw it into the air, watching it lift in the wind then tumble towards the gravel by his feet.

'Hey, you! You're not getting paid to stand around daydreaming.' The unpleasant voice of Alex Barton, the foreman, cut through the air. Davie stifled a sharp retort.

'The rock won't move,' he answered.

'I thought you fishermen were a tough lot,' the man sneered.

Davie ground his teeth. He pinched the end of the cigarette between his finger and thumb and tossed it onto the ground. He swung his pick with renewed force. A shower of sparks flew into the air.

'It'll not budge. We're going to have to use the dyna . . .' A searing wind lifted him off his feet. A hail of fire and stone threw him backwards. Sand and debris fell around him. Something heavy pinned him to the ground. The scream shot from his throat. The body of Alec Barton, the foreman, lay across his chest. Half his head had gone.

All at once, the great rushing subsided, replaced by a ringing silence. The smoke around him cleared. Men staggered about; their mouths open in soundless screams. Bodies lay scattered. People came from every direction. Then a roar of sound flooded over him, the rush of the water, the moans and cries of the wounded and the screams of the women.

Davie struggled to his feet, freeing himself of the mangled piece of humanity lying on top of him. He did not see the rocks that crashed into his head from the cliffs above.

When he next opened his eyes, it was to darkness. Two upright boulders had trapped him, but undoubtedly saved his life. A searing pain filled his head. The warm stickiness of blood trickled down his face. Stone and rubble had imprisoned him in a cold tomb and the tide was rising. He felt around the walls. There was barely enough room to sit upright.

Icy water seeped to his waist freezing out the will to live. In the distance he fancied he could hear Isa calling his name. Then he was not cold anymore and drifted in a quiet place, the desire to sleep heavy upon him.

When Isa heard the explosion, she handed the baby to Jessie and raced to the shore. Her shoes filled with sand and she stumbled on her skirt hem as she ran across the beach. Above the high tide mark, rescuers were already tending to the injured. Isa hurried from one to the other calling Davie's name until her throat was hoarse. Her heart hammered so hard she feared she might die.

'We think he's under here,' someone called to her. She ran to the base of the collapsed cliff. She tore at the fallen rocks with her bare hands.

Before the sky darkened they found three bodies – the foreman and two local boys. Working more slowly as their energy depleted, the rescuers continued to remove the stones and boulders by the flickering lights of lanterns. The tide had receded, making the work easier.

'He's here.' Finally, the muffled shout for which they had all been hoping spread into the night.

'Is he alive?' Isa sobbed.

Jack laid a shaking hand against his brother's neck. 'He's alive.' He straightened up. 'Get him home. I'll find the doctor.'

They carried him on a makeshift stretcher into the kitchen of Jessie's cottage.

'What's happened?' Jessie cried and talked at the same time. 'I couldna' leave the bairn. I wanted to come down, I did – I did.'

'Just help me Jessie.' Isa laid a folded towel under Davie's head. The blood had congealed and the wound was swollen and ugly. He moaned. His eyes flickered. Fear filled her as she chafed his frozen limbs, for she knew of men dying once the cold got through them. Together they tore off his sodden clothes. Isa lay down holding him tight against her, trying to warm him with her own body. Jessie dragged the quilt from her bed and wrapped it around the couple.

'He needs heat. I'll get the bath.' Beads of sweat ran down Jessie's fat cheeks. Her wheeze worsened. 'Is he any warmer?' she asked, once the pots of water were on the fire.

Crying too hard to answer, Isa shook her head.

Jessie lowered her great body onto the floor and enveloped the young couple in her big arms, but Davie remained cold and unresponsive.

'Have ye any whisky?' Isa remembered how the heat of the liquid had revived her on her first night in Scartongarth.

'Aye, thank the good Lord I didn't finish it all.' Jessie rose to her knees and lifted the tin from which she had been drinking earlier. 'There's a fair droppy left.'

At that moment the door opened.

Expecting the doctor, Isa jumped to her feet. But Chrissie entered, her skirts billowing behind her in the swirling draught.

'Where is he?' She barged in almost knocking Isa over. Jessie had raised Davie's head and held the whisky cup to his lips.

'No!' Chrissie ran forward, slapped Jessie's hand and the cup fell and rattled across the floor.

'What are ye doing?' shrieked Isa.

'No whisky.' Chrissie stared at the steaming pots and the tin bath. 'And no hot water unless ye're going to make him drink it.' She knelt beside Davie, put her fingers on his pulse and laid her cheek close to his mouth. From her pocket she brought out a small green bottle, which she pressed to his lips. '*This* will warm him inside.' He coughed and spluttered, but she continued to force the liquid down his throat until the vessel was empty. Then she wrapped her arms around him, holding him against her bosom.

'Get away from my man. You have no place here,' shouted Isa. She started forward, teeth clenched, fingers curled into fists.

Jessie struggled to her feet and grabbed Isa's arms. 'Chrissie knows about such things. Leave her be,' she hissed.

All at once Isa's bravado gave way and she covered her face, her body shaking with suppressed sobs. 'Get her away from him,' she cried.

'Don't be so foolish.' Chrissie snapped. 'He'll need all the help he can get. Jessie, get hot bricks and a stone bottle if ye have one.'

Without another word Isa swallowed her tears.

'Let's get him on the bed,' said Chrissie.

Isa nodded.

Chrissie placed hand around his back, grasping his arm with the other. She indicated for Isa to do the same at the other side. 'Now when I say so, lift.'

Together they hoisted him into a sitting position.

He moaned, his eyes flickered open and his head lolled backwards. 'Dad and Jamsie?' he muttered.

'Dan's got a broken leg, Jamsie's cracked his shoulder and has some pretty bad cuts and bruises but they'll be fine,' said Chrissie. 'Now we're going to get you into the bed. Can you help yourself?'

'I think so,' he replied through chattering teeth. His whole body started to shake. It took a bit of heaving and pushing but eventually they got him onto the bed. He slumped back gasping in pain as his head hit the pillow.

Chrissie studied the swelling. 'Don't let him sleep. If he does and you can't wake him, come for me at once. I'll have to go now for there's others that need me.' She stood up and locked eyes with Isa.

'Will he be okay?' Isa whispered, her hands bunching the cloth of her apron.

'He's shivering and that's a good sign. Get in beside him. Your body will help warm him.' At the door Chrissie stopped, looked at Isa and said, 'he loves *you*.' Then she turned and was gone, swallowed up by the soft darkness, until the bobbing pinprick of light from her lantern was all that remained.

When Jack returned with the doctor, the worst was past. Jessie had gone to bed in the other room beside the baby.

'It's been a hellish night.' Jack's eyes glittered in a face as white as bone.

'The heat's back in Davie. Ye helped to save his life,' said Isa.

Jack gave a snort, 'Aye, well, don't tell him that.'

'How are the others?'

'Five dead – the foreman, Davie Dixon and Sanny McCormack, and Beeg Nellie's two lads.' He named a few others who were badly hurt.

All young men she danced with at the harvest thanksgiving. 'Did you hear how it happened?' she asked.

'Anything could have set it off – a spark – anything. The explosives should never have been stored so near where the men were working.' Isa could sense the tension in his body and heard the way his voice splintered as he fought for control.

They turned at the sudden moan from the bed. 'It was me – my fault,'

'It's the bloody council trying to save money,' Jack shouted, bringing his fist hard against the doorjamb, 'The stuff should have been kept in a building! By God, it's as well that foreman had his head staved in for had he lived, I'd have killed him with these bare hands.' He held trembling hands up, fingers hooked into claws and clenched his teeth.

'Easy now.' The doctor closed his bag and stood up. 'Anger helps no one. Davie is doing well but he needs quiet. Who next?'

'Will there be any kind of compensation for the families?' Isa asked, following Jack and the doctor to the door.

'Don't make me laugh,' hissed Jack. 'We're only ignorant fishermen. Who the hell cares what happens to the likes of us?'

'But yer alive, and I give thanks for that,' said Isa.

'Many will think the wrong ones died,' Jack replied.

Towards the northeast a bright band of hazy sunlight slashed the horizon. 'It's going to be a bonnie day,' he said grimly.

'Will you be all right?' The doctor patted Isa's shoulder and she nodded, turning to look into the sad, kind eyes, noticing the heavy bags beneath them and the grey stubble on his chin. The small horse waiting between the shafts of the trap snorted and shook his head as though in relief that this night was nearly over.

She watched until they had driven well along the road before sinking onto the stone seat. She wrapped her arms around herself and began rocking slowly.

The weeks passed. Work on the pier resumed and the island gradually returned to a type of normality. The young men whose cuts and bruises had healed, once again lifted their picks and began to clear the area.

Although physically recovered, Davie sunk, night after night, into the dark recesses of his nightmares. Each time he closed his eyes he was back in the small cave with a mutilated corpse lying across him. Again he felt the cold water creeping up his body – the breath of death. And he would wake screaming. Isa calmed him, grabbing his flailing hands, holding him close. Once awake, he clutched at her like a dying man as the realisation of what had happened hit him over and over again.

Daytime was little better. He had thrown away the cigarette end that might not have been properly out. Sparks shot from his pick. Whatever the cause he blamed himself and believed only he knew the truth. Guilt lay on him so heavily he could not face the other islanders – not yet. Comfort came from the whisky that Jessie had hidden behind a false wall at the back of her barn.

Chapter 32

It was almost midnight. The wind blew strong and the sky above filled with bulging clouds of a summer storm. Chrissie set the pail of water at her feet and opened the door as a splattering of rain hit her face. Inside the fire smouldered under a pot of soup. A good plate of broth was all she had to look forward to these days. A few weeks after the tragedy, a depression still hung over the island, and with it her sense of melancholy deepened.

In the distance the carbide light of a passing ship dipped and rose in the swell, and Chrissie heaved a sigh of relief when it turned northwards away from the treacherous currents of the Swelkie. She cupped her hand over the top of the lantern, the glass warm against her cold skin, and blew out the flame.

'Chrissie.'

She jerked round. A guttering glow swayed towards her.

The figure stopped and held up the lantern so she could see the face.

'What do ye want Jack,' she said.

'Ye've to come. Mary-Jane's started labour.'

Fear, nothing to do with the man before her, crawled up her back like a snake. 'Go light a fire on the beach and pray to God the Doctor takes notice.'

'What's wrong?'

'Mary-Jane is carrying twins. The bairns are big and they're lying the wrong way. I told her she should be in hospital.'

'She never said.' He hesitated, his face misshapen in the flickering light.

'Just go!'

Without another word he hurried away, bare feet making whispering sounds on the soft turf. Boots were kept for the coldest days of winter.

She rifled in her cupboard knocking bottles over in her haste. Just like Mary-Jane, she thought. As with so many other island women, she would rather put herself in danger than spend much needed money on a hospital bed.

How dare she risk her babies' lives! Chrissie railed mentally, packing all the items she might need in a bag, her hand shaking. She should have told Jamsie. Surely her man would have talked some sense into her. This was the first problem birth she would have to deal with alone. Oh granny, she thought, why couldn't ye be here?

Several hours later Chrissie wiped away the perspiration trickling into her eyes. The smell of burning peat, paraffin lamps, sweat and blood filled the room. Mary-Jane's screams had become exhausted moans. *Where was Jack with that doctor?*

'How is she?' whispered Tyna clutching the bedpost, her hands white and veined. Her eyes were round, the lines across her forehead intensified. Her lip quivered. Chrissie needed more help than this old woman could give however willingly, and she needed it now. The nearest house was a short walk away.

She said the only thing she could. 'Get Isa.'

Isa came at once. 'What do ye want me to do?'

Chrissie handed her a thick length of pleated cotton. 'Hold her steady and give her this to bite on, for it'll not be easy.'

Mary-Jane opened glassy, fear-bright eyes and her lips moved as if to form words. Instead she screamed as her body arched. Isa held her, muttering words of encouragement, tears streaming down her own cheeks.

Chrissie located the feet of the first baby and pulled them gently downward.

Mary-Jane cried out, grabbed Isa's arms and bit down hard on the wad of cotton. Chrissie set one hand on her patient's stomach and felt the strength of the contraction. The baby did not move.

Unwinding a cotton bandage, Chrissie wrapped it round the tiny feet. 'Now, Isa,' she commanded and pulled, ignoring everything but the need to get these babies into the world. Mary-Jane had no more strength in her. At last the inert form of a little boy, his face faintly blue, slipped from his mother's body.

She cleared his mouth with deft fingers and lifting him by the ankles tried to slap the breath into him. Finally, a thin wavering cry announced that James Daniel Reid had claimed his right to life.

'Mary, Mary, ye've got to stay awake,' Isa shouted. Mary-Jane's face was ashen, her eyes closed, her head lolled to the side.

Chrissie wrapped the baby in a towel, laid him in a drawer that served as a makeshift cot and leaned over to check Mary's pulse. It was fluttering and weak.

She looked at Isa and the moment their eyes met a strong bond of solidarity formed.

'We've got to get the other bairn,' Chrissie whispered.

As the grey fingers of dawn snaked around and below the curtains the second child, a healthy, angry little girl lay in Isa's arms.

'Clear out her mouth,' Chrissie told her, 'I've to tend to Mary.' She lifted a needle and thread from a pan of boiled water by her side.

A sudden flurry outside drew her attention and the doctor burst into the room. 'I'm sorry I took so long, I was called to a young lad who'd been kicked by a horse.' He knelt by the bed and pressed his fingers against Mary-Jane's neck.

The examination was prolonged and thorough. When he removed the stethoscope from his ears, he glanced at the babies. 'They're fine?'

Chrissie nodded.

'Then it seems you did a good job without me.'

'Will Mary – Jane live?' Isa asked in a low whisper, her fingers twisted together.

The doctor did not reply immediately but packed his instruments with care. At last he spoke. 'She's in God's hands. I'll speak to her husband, for if she should survive there must be no more children.'

No one relaxed until Mary-Jane's eyes flickered open and she was able to take some tea brewed with fennel seeds and thistle and laced with whisky.

Chrissie studied Isa. Saw the flushed damp face and untidy hair, the way the long slender fingers twisted in the material of her skirt, the way she turned her head too late to hide the tears, felt the pain that matched her own. 'She'll be fine now,' Chrissie said.

Isa gave an uneasy laugh, 'I was terrified.' She sniffed and pushed the hair away from her face. 'Ye were so calm – ye saved her – ye saved them all.'

'I wasn't all that calm,' said Chrissie.

Isa put her hands over her mouth and gave a barking laugh – or was it a sob. Her eyes filled with tears that spilled over her fingers. Chrissie's own throat filled. She walked over and rubbed Isa's shoulder. 'I *really* couldn't have saved them without ye,' she said quietly.

Chapter 33

With nothing left to do Chrissie allowed Jack to walk her home. She had not spoken to him since the night he had spurned her in the barn. Now the incident seemed petty and unimportant.

'She'll . . . she'll be all right?' he asked.

'We can only pray.'

He did not answer.

'When did ye last eat?'

'Yesterday, sometime, I forget.'

'I've a pan of soup I can warm up once I get the fire going. I think I'm past being tired.'

'I'll not stay long. I'll need to go back to the pier.' He gave a bitter laugh. 'I'll not have it said I don't do my share of the work.'

'Ye've a good excuse.'

'I make no excuses.'

His face reminded her of chiselled granite in the half light.

'What's wrong, Jack?' she asked. 'Why are ye always so angry?'

He turned to scowl at her. 'Angry? This bloody life would make anyone angry.'

'Ye can tell me what's on yer mind if ye want.' She kept her eyes on him.

'If ye saw what's in my mind ye'd never sleep again.'

She gave a laugh. 'I'd take the chance.' She glanced away suddenly shy before the intensity of his gaze.

'We'd best get the fire going.' With one quick motion Jack turned from her and bent down to poke the embers. A green flame shot from the smouldering timber, spat and settled as the wood split into its ash-drawn squares. He threw some small dry peat on top and waited until they caught fire before adding more.

As he worked she studied the stoop of his back and the tired lines of his face and sensed a pain within him that had nothing to do with the events of this night. She ran an impulsive hand over his shoulders and hesitated when he flinched. He turned to look at her. There seemed no anger in him now – just a deep weariness.

For a long time their eyes met and held and without knowing what prompted her, she moved towards him and pressed her lips against his. He did not instantly respond nor did he draw away. They sat like that, bodies apart, only touching where their lips met and her hand rested on his shoulder. When they finally separated she dropped her head.

Silence stretched between them for what seemed an eternity.

'Say something.' she snapped, unable to bear it any longer. He grinned, reached for her and jerked her against him. His lips claimed hers; his tongue filled her mouth. She clung to him. Months of pent up emotion rushed to the surface, blotting her mind to anything but the needs of her own body. His fingers fumbled with the buttons on her bodice until, impatiently, he tore at them and pushed her backwards. The pain of her shoulder striking the blunt edge of the fender brought her back to her senses.

'No – not like this.' She pressed her hands against his chest.

He trapped her in his grip, his body tense and hard. The cold stone of the flagstone hurt her back and the draught from beneath the door chilled her skin. She had the impression that she'd awakened a sleeping beast and now lay at his mercy. Simultaneously, fear and excitement raced through her.

'Don't ye dare play with me like this,' he said.

'I'm not playing with ye,' she gasped, going limp beneath him. 'Take me if ye want but it'll no be willingly.' She had been jolted back to reality just in time. She had given herself too freely once before and lost the man.

He released her, the old anger once more showing on the lines of his face. For a moment she waited, trembling, afraid he might strike her. Instead he sprung to his feet. 'I'm not that hard up.'

Controlling her breathing she met his eyes. 'I do want ye but not before I'm wed.'

Astonishment replaced the anger in his eyes. 'Me?'

'If it's what ye want. Otherwise we'll no speak of this again.'

He stared down at her for a long time. Long enough for her heart to thunder and her stomach to churn. Long enough for her to see the distrust darken his eyes.

'By, ye're some girl right enough.' He let out a loud laugh. 'Now why would ye want to marry me?'

'Can ye not guess?'

'Ye can't have the man ye want and ye could do a lot worse.'

'If that's what ye think then forget it.' She struggled to her feet and pulled her torn bodice around her. Her face burned and her hair fell over her shoulders, her large breasts rising and falling.

Jack stared at her, thinking how magnificent she looked. Never had he wanted her as much as at that moment. He always suspected a strong passion lurked within the bold exterior and now she had proved it. She proved something else as well. That she was a lady – the kind that would save herself for the marriage bed. If he could really believe her words, a light would shine in the darkness of his soul.

'I want a proper wife, not one who hankers after another man,' he muttered, dropping his gaze.

'I'm over Davie. Why can't ye believe me?'

Reaching behind her, he grabbed a handful of hair and pulled her head backwards, firmly but gently. 'Swear it,' he hissed, his face inches from hers. He had to see the truth of it in her eyes, force it out of her if need be.

With her face flushed, her eyes half shut and her pupils dark, she answered, 'I swear.' Her mouth remained slightly open the tip of her tongue showing between the white ridges of teeth. A soft growth of hair, almost invisible, lay above her lip. A pulse beat in the hollow at the base of her neck.

The heat of desire rose from her in waves. She had to be telling the truth. And if she wasn't – he closed his eyes against the possibility. 'I wouldn't have any other kind of lassie,' he told her. He released her then and laughed. A laugh harsh enough to cover an uncharacteristic rush of emotion. He left before the temptation to take her right there and then grew too strong.

Chapter 34

On the 10th of June, the day of Jack and Chrissie's wedding, Davie moved along the rows of embryotic turnips. He hoed several young plants away, leaving enough space so the others could flourish. Midges seemed intent on eating him alive but they bothered him less than the music drifting from Chrissie's house on the ridge of the hill.

With so many men injured after the explosion, and the women nursing them, the farm work had been neglected. It gave Davie the excuse not to go back to the pier. He used the same excuse not to go to the wedding. Not because he still cared for Chrissie, he told himself – at least not in that way, but because he could no longer tolerate noise and crowds. God, he hoped his family understood.

Davie believed Isa despised him for his weakness as much as he despised himself. He'd watched the dark circles grow more pronounced round her eyes, her once smooth hands grow rough and red, the spark that had drawn him to her wither and die. His guilt over what he had done to her deepened every day he lived.

For the sake of peace, he promised Isa he would follow her later but even as he said the words he did not intend to honour them. He stared at the shoreline knowing that for all their sakes, he had to conquer the demons inside him.

A sudden explosion as they blasted away even more rock froze his body. He dropped the hoe and pressed his fists to his head. *He would not cry again – he would not. Crying was for bairns and women! What was wrong with him?* Lowering his hands, he looked at them in horror. They were shaking.

He reached into his back pocket and drew out a flask which he tipped to his lips, emptying it in one go. The drink would steady him; help him make it through the day.

Drawing in a deep breath, he forced himself to walk to the bay, fear closing his throat like a thick wad of paste. His insides felt high in his chest and they worsened with every step. At the top of the brae he looked down at the men working and listened to metal clanging against rock.

The horror in his head began to replay. As he cried out a flock of sea birds rose from the hummocky shore-line, the noise of their screeches and beating wings filling the air and the inside of his skull. Turning he stumbled towards Jessie's and into the barn where he scrabbled behind the stalls for the hidden whisky. After a few mouthfuls the shaking eased. Another long swallow and the world began to look a lot better.

There were voices approaching. The wedding was over. 'Here's to the happy couple,' he sneered, raising the tin can once more to his lips.

Outside, Isa took a sleeping Danny from Jamsie's good arm.

'I could throttle Davie for not coming,' he said.

Isa adjusted the weight of the child on her shoulder and he gave a grumbling cry, slipped his arms around her neck and relaxed again, his breath hot against her cheek.

'Davie's changed,' she said.

'We've all noticed it.' Jamsie laid his hand on her arm and the warmth released something inside her, bringing the pressure of tears up behind her eyes.

His voice dropped. 'Ye're a strong lass. I'm sure he'll get well with ye at his side.'

Nodding, she swallowed to rid herself of the lump in her throat. 'I'd better go in. I don't know where he'll be.' She did not add, or in what state.

She found him in the barn, sleeping on a pile of hay the smell of whisky hanging in the air. Picking up the pail she filled it from the rain barrel and threw the water in his face. He groaned and sat up, blinking stupidly, water streaming onto his shirt and the swollen bodies of drowned flies sticking to his skin and hair.

'I'm sick of this Davie,' she shouted. 'If you don't stop drinking and bring in some money, so help me, I'll take Danny and go to Canada myself.'

He stared at her for a second before he spoke. 'Ye'd be better off for I'm no good to ye. I don't know what's gotten in here.' He hit his forehead with the heel of his hand. Then he began to cry in earnest, uncontrollable sobs that shook his body. Her anger melted. She ran to him, pulling him into her arms where she rocked him like a baby.

'I wish I'd died with the others,' he hiccupped, clinging to her. 'I'll get you money from somewhere, I will . . . I will'

Chapter 35

It was Chrissie's wedding night and the guests had gone home. She looked at her new husband. In the flickering candle-light. He took her hand and they stood like that, neither one moving. Then he touched her shoulder, a gentle fairy touch, traced his finger along her neckline, and very slowly, he unbuttoned her bodice. It fell open and his hand brushed her nipple sending a bolt of lightning through her body. Grabbing her head in his hands he brought her face towards his and kissed her long and hard. She melted into him as the snows of winter melted in the heat of the sun. Her whole being quivered yearning for more, her skin so sensitive that her hair tumbling over her shoulders and down her back, touched her like an added caress. Never had she felt this alive. Something wild and dangerous about Jack heightened her desire beyond the point of reason. Taking his hands and ignoring the slightly surprised expression on his face, she led him towards the bed.

She awoke in the dawn and stretched as memories of the night before flooded over her in a warm sweet wave. Her body was languid, content. For the first time in her life she felt complete. With a little moan of pleasure she reached out to touch her man. She started, fully awake when her hand fell on an empty pillow. She raised herself on one elbow and looked around the room.

'Jack,' she called but there was no answer. Pushing the blankets aside, she swung her feet out of bed jumping when they hit the cold solidity of the flagstone floor.

She found him outside sitting on the front step, crouched forward, his shoulders covered with his work jacket.

'Good morning.' Shivering in the thin September sunshine, she grasped his upper arms and pressed her breasts against his back.

He sprang to his feet, knocking her sideways.

'What's wrong?' she cried, her head throbbing where it hit the door jamb.

'I wasn't the first was I?'

'What do ye mean?' She staggered to her feet.

'Ye had me for a right fool. Ye wouldn't let me touch ye till we were wed. How many more have touched ye though?'

'No one. I swear. There's only been you.'

He hesitated. Doubt flitted across his face and she seized the advantage.

'There's not always blood,' she said hurriedly, and lowered her head unable to meet his eyes. He had to believe her – she was a midwife after all – she knew about these things. If only she had held back, acted coy, he would have been more easily convinced, but with the long denied fires raging through her she had given him her very soul.

He grabbed her chin between his thumb and forefinger, tilting her face up, forcing her to look at him. 'Swear it.'

Lying did not come naturally to her. How could she do it convincingly now, under the scrutiny of his gaze?

She saw his eyes harden to brown granite and knew what her hesitation had cost her.

'Davie!' He spat the name out.

'No, please,' she pleaded.

'I would have never wed ye had I known the truth. I'll sleep in the hay loft from now on.' He threw her aside and strode away, fists clenched.

Chrissie ran after him, oblivious to the stones on the path under her bare feet. 'Jack please. I swear it, I swear it,' she cried, grabbing his arm but he shook her off. Suddenly devoid of strength, she fell to the ground. Crying aloud she curled herself into a tight ball, her head buried on her knees.

Chapter 36

Davie carried sacks of barley, sugar, yeast and malt down the steep brae, across a patch of shingle and into the cave where the men brewed the whisky. The cave was one of many branching from a larger hollow or gloup, which joined the sea by a long narrow tunnel. The position provided excellent cover, hidden from prying eyes on either land or sea.

The Reid's still sat idle, surrounded with several kegs of the amber liquid, neglected since both Dan and Jamsie had been laid up. They had not asked Davie to do this, probably assuming it was beyond him. He was determined to prove everyone wrong, and, after counting the small kegs, he arranged them against the far wall. There was not enough whisky to warrant a run to Orkney this year but if he put his mind to it, he could distil a fair amount by spring.

Using drift wood and dry grass, he built a fire between two large flat stones. From a burn that cascaded down the cave walls, he collected water. With all the ingredients in the pot that made up the base of the still, he positioned it over the flames. Once the mixture began to steam, he doused the fire, put the lid on the pot sealing it tightly and left the mash to ferment.

Pleased with his efforts he picked up a full keg to take home. One of his father's strictest rules was that there would be no drinking in the caves. A drunken man could slip on the loose shale and fall to certain death in the still green waters that lay below. Although the island men lived half their lives on the sea very few ever learned to swim.

The men were still clearing the site at the pier and another explosion rent the distant air. Davie flattened himself against the rock face and covered his ears with his hands. Behind him, damp slime caused by years of water trickling down the cliff face, smeared his clothes. The shaking began again, bringing a weakness that made his legs crumple beneath him. The sweat poured down his cheeks and he struggled to catch his breath, clutching at his stomach as his gorge rose. Air slammed into his lungs, his fingers scrabbled along the rock beside him until they made contact with the little barrel he had dropped. He needed a drink. He needed one badly.

Picking up the keg, he pulled out the cork and breathed in the odour.

Just a wee drop, he thought, his father's dire warnings still ringing in his head. For he would never find the strength to climb the slope otherwise. Tipping the cask to his lips he took several long swallows and the fiery liquid burned its way down his throat, instantly relaxing him.

The roar of the blasting faded into silence and the only sounds around him were the cry of the sea birds, the gentle thunder of a somnolent ocean, the worried bleat of a lone ewe and the thudding of his own heart. He would give himself some time before going back to the fields. Time to get himself together, time for the nausea to settle, time for the shaking to cease. He took another drink, and then another.

Chapter 37

'Let me do that.' At the sound of Jamsie's voice, Isa stopped beating the rugs she had slung over the clothes line. She wiped her brow on the back of her hand.

'Yer arm's still bad,' she protested.

'And ye are doing too much for a lass in your condition.' Jamsie indicated her swollen belly. He threaded the staff through his fingers. 'The secret is in turning the stick while ye swing it upwards. Once ye get into the timing it's just like threshing – easy.'

Her face grew hot. It was not a man's place to refer to a lady's 'condition.' An amused smile played along his lips and his blue eyes crinkled.

'Have you seen Davie?' she asked huffily.

'Is he not seeing to the animals?'

Isa shook her head. Davie had been gone since early morning and in unusually high spirits. He had something planned, of that she was sure. Her eyes met Jamsie's and silently they communicated a common concern.

'I think ye'd better get Charlie or Angus to look for him. Then get in the house and have a cup of tea with Mary-Jane. Ye look done in,' he said.

Charlie and Angus were Mary-Jane's brothers, hired to help on the farm. They were twins, a few inches separating them in height and breadth but otherwise they shared the same carrot red hair, freckled faces, pale blue eyes and gap-toothed grins.

She found them mucking out the byre and as usual they were laughing about one thing or another.

'Ach, why worry about Davie when there's a bonnie lad like me around.' Charlie, the taller of the two, puffed out his chest. Isa laughed at his cheek. Although they were only marginally younger than she was, she felt years older. They were like boisterous children, miles apart from their mild-mannered sister, Mary-Jane.

'Aye, well, if I'd met ye first,' she teased. 'But I've got a man and I'd thank ye to go looking for him.' She turned away knowing the boys would have better knowledge than she of where a young man might go for a secret drink or a crack with his mates.

A sudden wave of nausea swept over her. Jamsie was right. She was done in. With a well advanced pregnancy, Davie still prone to nightmares and Danny wakening early, she got little sleep. Nevertheless she could not rest. Mary-Jane had never regained her strength and Tyna's rheumatics were all but crippling her. There was so much to do before winter.

She gazed at the hesitant blue of the sky and the dark clouds drifting across from the east. More and more often, memories of the minister, Donald Charleston flashed into her mind. Where was he? Why had he not returned? A letter would not have been too much trouble – or did their friendship mean so little to him? Shivering, she hurried towards the house and the welcoming warmth in the kitchen of Scartongarth.

Chapter 38

Meanwhile, outside her but and ben, Chrissie removed her washing from the line. She folded her pillow-slips and towels in the basket and started back towards the house when she heard her name called softly but urgently. In the gathering gloom she could barely recognise the figure behind the barn holding onto the wall as if for support.

'Davie, what are you doing here?' She walked towards him, stepping back as she caught the stink of whisky from his breath. Weed and mud stains covered his jacket. Dirt smeared his cheeks and hands.

'I can't go home like this,' he whispered, 'I need to wash – sober up.'

'Well, ye can't do it here.'

'Please Chrissie.'

She looked at him for a long time and saw the slackness of his mouth, the desperation in his bloodshot eyes, the way his clothes hung on him as if no flesh lay underneath. How had the fun-loving, bonny lad she had once been in love with come to this? She still cared for him, but her feelings were now more like those of a sister for a wayward younger brother.

'What happened to ye?'

'I was in the caves when the blasting started. I . . .' His voice broke and he placed a hand against his forehead.

He'd come to her for help and she could no more turn him away than stick a knife in her own heart. 'If ye strip to the waist ye can wash in the barrel there, for ye can't come to the house. I'll get ye a towel and wipe down yer clothes. But hurry.' She glanced at the bay, thankful that there was still no sign of the *Christina*.

Davie struggled out of his jacket and shirt, his teeth chattering as he dipped his hands in the rain water and splashed his face.

Goose pimples covered his upper arms and his skin stretched over a visible rib cage. Just the sight of him made Chrissie shiver in spite of the mildness of the evening. With a worried glance out to sea she came to a decision. 'Come inside, but hurry.'

From where he beached the *Christina*, Jack could see his house standing on the high ridge, silhouetted against the final rays of a suffused sun. A glow lit the window and he imagined Chrissie setting the lamp on the table. In his mind he saw her walking to the fire, then pulling the pot of soup over the flames.

No matter what she had done he still ached for her touch. Perhaps he could forgive her if she showed enough remorse, for it was growing cold in the barn at nights and a man had his needs.

He would never let her forget however. She owed him and she would pay by the barb of his tongue.

Already looking forward to the night ahead, he hitched the rope to the winch and strained against the handle until the yole was dragged clear of the water. With the boat secured he turned his eyes back towards the cottage and stopped. Two figures stood in the light from the door. Though impossible to tell who it was from this distance he guessed, by the shape of him, the man had to be Davie. The figure walked away, past the hay-screws and vanished in the lengthening shadows. All the while the heat rose in Jack's body, filling him with a greater anger than he had ever experienced before.

Davie. It had always been Davie. First his mother and now his wife.

All the way home his tortured mind spun with questions. How would he handle this? Should he accuse her right out? Should he go to Jessie's now, wait for Davie and have it out with him? Let Isa know what was going on? By God, to think he had saved this brother's life.

By the time he reached the house the heat of his temper had changed into a cold fury. He would wait and see what she had to say for herself. If she was guilty he would see it in her eyes, know it by her silence and then, by the devil, he would kill them both with these bare hands.

Chrissie stirred the contents of the pot, jumping as Jack came through the door. She licked her lips and fought to breathe normally as she turned to watch his face. He had arrived sooner than she expected and it was possible that he had seen Davie leaving.

Since their wedding night he had kept his distance only talking to her when absolutely necessary and only coming into the house for food, which she continued to serve to the best of her ability. Knowing she had done wrong she strove to always look her best, to greet him with a smile and pray within her heart that he would eventually forgive her. Tonight she could not afford to act differently.

However, patience was not a virtue that Chrissie had in abundance and she already felt her resolve beginning to crack. Innocent though Davie's visit was she had no desire to give Jack any more reason for jealousy.

'I made tatty-soup,' she said as her mind searched for a plausible explanation. 'Tam dropped by a wee while ago, ye just missed him.' She used the first name that sprung to mind. Davie's friend, poor, gormless Tam. If she asked him she knew he would lie for her. Tam had never like Jack.

'Tam?' he asked, his voice both surprised and suspicious.

'Yes. He wondered if we had any jobs.' Funny how a lie once started could grow so easily. Tam, a feckless joker, well liked but without a piece of land of his own, worked where he was needed and then only to earn enough to eat.

'I hope ye told him where to go.'

'I did no such thing.'

His next words shattered her tentative security. 'I could have sworn I saw Davie coming out the house.'

As blood rushed to her face she clenched her hands and turned on him, her fear sparking to anger. 'I am sick of yer constant suspicions,' she yelled. 'Davie means nothing to me now.'

He banged his spoon on the table. 'Ye lied to me once. How can I be sure ye're not lying again?'

Weeks of pent up emotion rose in her like a sea.

'Ye did well marrying me – now ye've got a croft and boat. And what have I got in return? No even a body to share my bed.' She took a deep breath ready to renew her onslaught. 'Maybe ye can't. Is that it? Maybe once is all ye're good for. I wish I'd known in time that ye were such a poor excuse for a man.'

He shot to his feet knocking the chair over. 'A poor excuse for a man, am I?' Grasping her hand he jerked her against him, his free hand groping her body, his unshaven chin scouring the skin of her throat and face. 'Well if this is all ye want ye can have it.'

'No – stop,' she cried.

His body, a solid mass of tense and trembling muscle pressed against her and in spite of her rage, her own excitement rose until the hands that fought him off clasped him to her. Then they were on the bed locked together, the fire of their passion all consuming. He took her roughly, urgently, without any tenderness and afterwards he rose immediately leaving her needy and empty.

'Is that my dues paid?' he growled without looking at her.

Still trembling in the aftermath of passion, she followed him to the door and watched as he disappeared into the barn. How dare he, she thought. How unfair that he could treat her this way yet lay claim to everything that was her birth right. Her fury turning into frustration, she rearranged her clothes and pressed her head against the window pane welcoming the cool of the glass against her brow.

Maybe he was right. Maybe she was a whore. For she did know that she enjoyed the physical act of love. She enjoyed it so much that it filled her mind for a great deal of her waking hours and the lack of it tortured her in the still of the night. Her parents brought up to believe that nice girls merely tolerated it as part of their duty. Yet here she was, her body already tingling, her mind still alive with images of what had just happened.

'If a whore is what I am then so be it,' she said to no one. She pulled off her apron and hurled it from her. She shook her head allowing her thick mane of hair to fall around her face and opened her bodice so that the greatest part of her breasts bulged out. Nipping her cheeks until they glowed pink she then marched across the farm yard and climbed the ladder to the loft. Jack lay on his straw mattress staring at the rafters through the dim light of a storm lantern.

He turned his head as she entered. 'What do you want?' he snapped.

'Ye asked me a question.' She spoke slowly her mouth dry, her heart beating faster with every breath. 'And the answer is no. Yer dues are not paid. Not at all.' She walked towards him and knelt beside the bed pulling her bodice open so that her breasts burst free.

However much he tried to fight it he wanted her again. She could see it in his eyes, hear it in the sharp intake of his breath, see the bulge inside his trousers. With growing confidence, she ran her tongue over her lips and lowered her voice.

'What's it to be then? Do I get a husband in every sense of the word?'

'Ye've had all a whore deserves.' His voice dashed like cold water. 'And if I ever find out ye've lied to me again it will be a bitter day for both of ye. Now get out of here.'

She shot to her feet and pulled her bodice across her breasts. 'Then am I to tell everyone in the island that I married a man who cannot perform his marital duties?'

'I'd kill ye first.'

'Then kill me now for I will. I won't live like this for the rest of my life.' She stood upright, her chin jutting out, defying him to do his worst.

For a moment he looked at her in astonishment then his face crinkled and he started to laugh. A wild, high pitched laugh that for an instant made her want to turn and run.

'By god, if it's marital duties ye want I'll show ye marital duties.'

He leapt to his feet, seized the front of her dress, tore it apart and grabbed her breasts so roughly that she cried out. Positioning one leg behind hers, he pushed her so that she fell backwards onto the straw. His body landed heavily on top of hers knocking the breath from her. He eased himself up on his arms so that he could look into her eyes. 'Ye are the worst slut I've ever bedded,' he hissed.

She felt her breath quicken and all doubts disappeared in her need of him. Grabbing the front of his shirt, she ripped it open and pulled him against her. 'But the best,' she said, her body arching against his. Her teeth sank into the skin of his shoulder so that he yelped and drove into her with a sudden exquisite force.

Several hours later she awoke, her body sore and tender. Reaching for her dress she pulled it over her chilled skin and snuggled up against the sleeping Jack. The lantern still glowed, hanging motionless from the rafter above, its light shimmering in a spider's web which stretched from beam to beam. Outside a cockerel crowed and an unhappy cow bellowed. Chrissie flexed her muscles. She felt both fulfilled and apprehensive, yet stronger and more alive than she had ever done. From now on, she told herself with conviction, *she* would be the one in control of her own destiny. Little did she know how difficult that would prove to be.

Chapter 39

Isa's pregnancy gave her little bother and she had little need of Chrissie's expertise, which was just as well. For since her marriage to Jack, Chrissie was seldom seen in public.

It was late in August and the men had already taken the lambs to the agricultural sales on the mainland when the mild contractions Isa suffered since early morning became crushing pains. Within hours her second baby, a small slippery, black haired girl, made her entrance into the world.

'Ye did a good job of that,' laughed Jessie as she sat beside the bed nursing the infant. 'Chrissie barely had time to get through the door.'

'What will ye call her?' asked Chrissie as she closed her bag.

'Annie,' Isa answered without a moment's hesitation. The infant pursed her mouth and made sucking motions with her lips. The feathery eyelashes fluttered. One tiny fist waved in the air. She was perfect. Davie was in for a grand surprise when he returned. His mood had been a lot lighter lately and he promised he would bring every penny home tonight. Stroking her new born daughter's cheek, Isa decided to trust him. She wanted no negative feelings to sully this moment.

'Wait till your daddy sees ye,' she whispered pressing her lips against the downy forehead and breathing in the milky scent before drifting off to sleep.

The job of loading lambs onto the large flat bottomed boat, sailing to Wick and herding them to the mart left Davie with little time to think. The prices were good, and in high spirits the men took themselves to the public house at the foot of the black-stairs near the harbour.

Davie hesitated outside the smoke-filled bar room, inhaled

the warm beery aroma and ran his tongue around his mouth, taste buds already alert. Inside, the loud male laughter and clinking glasses beckoned him. Yet, as the others entered, calling out to old friends and finding seats at the long wooden table or a space against the bar, he hung back. He knew that if he started to drink they would have to carry him home with empty pockets. Reluctantly he turned away, putting as much distance between himself and temptation as possible. Anyway, he thought, he did not need to indulge here. He was making all the whisky he needed back on Raumsey.

He pushed his share of the money deep within his pocket, enjoying the feel of the notes against his fingers. That done, he headed into the bustling street, across the cobbles, past the salt cellars and towards the harbour.

The sounds and smells of industry were all around him. The rattling of wheels over cobblestones, warning shouts, the bark of a dog, screams of gulls hungry for fish guts, the clomp of horses hooves, the singing of gutters and packers in the endless yards and the ring of hammers from the cooperages where they made the barrels.

The atmosphere flooded through him giving him a new spring in his step. He was well aware of the admiring glances the fisher lassies threw his way, their hands working so quickly he could hardly see what the knife did. One girl in particular caught his attention. Small with dark hair and a quick smile, she reminded him of Isa – the way she used to be. As he passed her he met her eye and gave her a cheeky wink.

His head higher, his shoulders straighter, no longer Davie Reid; failure, drunk, killer of his friends, he became once again a carefree young lad dreaming of adventure.

His main purpose in coming to the harbour was the boats, especially the steam drifters. They were the latest thing and at least ten of them bobbed within the harbour walls, six more than the last time he was here. He crossed to the nearest, *The Girl Georgina,* studied her lines and listened to the creak of her timbers.

'She's a beauty isn't she? Just brought her up the other week.' The voice came from behind him.

'She's yours?' Davie asked surprised. The lad was not much older than he was.

'Six of us have a share. A steamer is three times the price of a sail ship. But I'm the skipper.' He grinned. 'Would you like a look?'

'Definitely.'

'I'm Don Swanson.' He held out his hand.

Davie introduced himself and both leapt aboard.

'Raumsey, aye? I've heard it said Raumsey men are the best seamen around.'

'They are that. I'd give anything for a berth in a boat like this.' Davie ran his hand over the wood of the capstan. 'I'd love to see how she handles in the sea.'

'I'll give ye a try any time.'

'Ye mean that?'

'Aye, but ye'd have to come now. We're on our way to Yarmouth this very night.'

This had always been his dream, and now it was within his grasp. He clenched his fists until the nails dug into his palms. He needed time to talk to Isa – make her understand.

'Well, how about it?'

He screwed up his face and drew in a slow breath. Possibilities raced through his mind. Money – freedom from poverty – the creak of those great timbers beneath his feet. Then the doubts. Isa, ready to have another bairn, waiting back home. If he explained to his brother – maybe . . .

'Hi, lad, we're off.' Jamsie's voice hailed him from the shore.

One glance at his brother's curious and disapproving face told him all he needed to know. There would be no support from this quarter. He turned to the young skipper and shook his head. 'I'm sorry man, too short notice.'

'Ye know where to find me,' Don called after him as Davie followed the others up the quay.

It was almost dark when the lads pulled the boats high over the shingle beach. The old men, hungry for news of the day, met them. The stories flew, growing in magnitude with every telling. Davie laughed too, envious of their inebriation, longing to put the situation to rights. He turned his eyes towards Jessie's small thatched cottage with its thin wisp of smoke spiralling from the chimney into the still air. The lamp, already lit, emitted a yellow glow in the fading light.

'Is there not a drop of whisky for a dry lad like me?' he shouted. Dan came hobbling down the slope and pointed at Davie with his pipe. 'Something's going on at your house lad,' he said. 'Chrissie came out a wee while ago, a bag in her hand and all.'

'What?' He threw down the coiled rope he held and turned so quickly he tripped and stumbled against the sea wall.

'Aye and he never had a drink,' someone laughed.

He scrambled to his feet, cursed good naturedly at the cheering men and ran home.

Isa sat up in bed, her face flushed, her eyes bright. She looked as bonny as she had ever done. She stretched out her hand and touched the small bundle in the cradle.

'It's a girl,' she whispered as Davie fell to his knees by her side.

'And she's every bit as beautiful as her mam,' he breathed staring at the small face in wonder. At this moment he thanked God he had come home sober and with money to get the essentials for the winter. Then there was the whisky. By spring he would have enough to bring in a fine penny. Maybe even enough to put down a deposit on a boat of his own. He grasped Isa's hand. Her fingers felt small and fragile. In the silence, the wood in the fireplace crackled and spat.

'What is it then?' Davie, not having heard the door open, started at the voice. Jamsie and Tam followed by the other lads poured into the room.

'A girl,' said Davie. He stood up a smile stretching from ear to ear.

'And a bonny wee thing she is too.' Jamsie leaned over the cot.

'Will we be wetting her head then? ' laughed Tam, waving a keg of whisky in the air.

'Na,' stated Davie with resolution. 'This night I've to care for my wife, for she'll be fair worn out.'

'Glad to hear ye say that Davie.' Jamsie clapped him on the shoulder. 'Put the keg away Tam, for this here's a sensible man.'

As laughter filled the room Isa drifted to sleep, her face relaxed with contentment. Everything was going to be all right.

Chapter 40

The winter was hard. Davie's demons still plagued him and Isa often lost patience with his mood swings and his binges. Finally spring spread across the land and life began anew.

At the mouth of the cave, Davie pulled the stopper out of the last keg, sniffed the contents and congratulated himself. This had to be the best batch yet. He poured a little in his tin can and drank, closing his eyes and tilting his head back as the nectar trickled down his throat. A smile tugged at the corners of his mouth and the sun warmed his skin. Soon, he thought, everything would fall into place. He planned to ask Tam to help him get this lot out of the caves and down to the pier.

Isa deserved better than the way he had treated her since the tragedy. Now spring was here and the whisky run had started, it was time to make amends. Once he came back, money in his pocket, everything would be fine. He took another drink – then another. The echoes of his father's warnings grew fainter with every sip.

The tunnel leading to the sea from the gloup glinted in the sunlight. The rock formation was impressive in browns, greens, oranges and purples. A colony of seals lazing on a ledge just above the water line picked up their heads. Moving as one, they dived into the green depths hind flippers flashing through the foam, and disappeared below the surface leaving only a settling ripple. The splashing of a boat heading into the tunnel had disturbed them.

Davie rose to his feet and his legs gave way beneath him. He grabbed the boulder, pulling himself upright. A pah of relief escaped his lips when he recognised *The Christina*.

Jack manoeuvred the yole through the channel and ran her onto a patch of shingle. His face darkened. 'What in the name of

Hell are you doing?' he shouted, leaping ashore. 'I could have been the excise man.'

'Na, na, they'd never make it here. They don't know the tides.' Davie tried to articulate his words but suddenly the whole thing seemed hilarious and he started to laugh, wrapping his arms around an upright rock.

'Ye know the rules – no drinking in the gloups,' Jack shouted.

Davie steadied himself and waved a keg towards his brother. 'There's no harm in it. I've been drinking for the past six months and I've brewed . . . ' His words stopped as the blow caught him square on the side of the face and the barrel spun from his hands to burst open on the rocks below. Humiliation and shock rose in his throat like bile as he staggered backwards, sobering.

Jack stood over him, his breath coming in short snorts, lank black hair falling across his lowered brows, his eyes icy. 'Get out of here,' he hissed. 'You're not fit to be let near the whisky.'

'What . . .?' Davie rubbed his jaw. 'But I . . .' His mind flew to a time when they were children and jack often used his boot or fist to subdue the younger boy. He never told, simply avoided being alone with his tormentor. He was not a child now and he would not be treated this way. Not anymore.

'It's not the whisky that's bothering ye . . . it's Chrissie is it not? What's wrong man? Ye've got her.'

'I'll never have her. Not when you've had her first.'

Davie stared at him before realisation seeped through his brain, filling him with the cold desire to strike back, to hurt as he had been hurt. 'Aye, I had her. And I could have her still.'

'Then it *is* true.' Jack turned away pushing his fingers through his hair. His shoulders heaved and he spun round, pointing a shaking finger at his brother. 'Get up that damn hill,' he shouted taking a threatening step forward, 'or so help me . . .'

Davie stumbled and fell against the sharp rise. He knew he should not have said that about Chrissie. To his horror his eyes pooled. He bit on his lip, his chin trembled and he blinked rapidly. His hands found the cliff face behind him and he welcomed the solidity as he fought for control. Jack's back was already turned, his shoulders and neck bulging as he strained at the boulder which normally covered the mouth of the cave where they hid the still.

Davie struggled up the steep incline and fell on his face at the top, the rough heather scratching his skin. He rolled onto his back, lay for a long time staring up at the indistinct blue of the sky and finally gave way to tears.

'Ye've been at the drink again,' accused Isa when he returned home. With the baby balanced on one hip and Danny clinging to her leg, she kicked a basket of peat across the floor. Tiredness showed in her eyes. Her hair fell free and untidy. Threadbare clothes hung on her body.

Still smarting after his run in with Jack, both her appearance and her accusation irritated Davie. 'Can't ye just leave me be.' He banged his fist on the table.

'Oh, I'll leave ye be. And if ye want something to fill yer belly ye can cook it yerself but first ye'll need to find it.' With a final kick at the basket she stormed from the house, a screaming Danny scurrying after her.

In an effort to release the well of emotion that stretched his nerves to breaking point, Davie rammed his fist into the wall repeatedly, welcoming the pain. Eventually he sank onto the floor, finding comfort in the rocking motion of his body.

He could not tell how long he sat in that position but when he lifted his head the room was dark and had grown cold. His mouth was dry and pain stabbed inside his skull. He wanted another drink but Jessie had hidden her stash somewhere else. He knew because he had searched for it before. She would be away for hours and come home far merrier than she had left. Aware of the ache in his hand he lifted it, finding it swollen and painful, his knuckles skinned.

Pushing himself to his feet he fell against the wall. He stood for a minute sensing the chill air on his face. Isa had left the door open.

Isa had gone.

He looked round the room; at the walls they had white-washed together, at the beginnings of mould in the far corner, at the empty grate and the basket of peat on the shiny flag. He breathed in the scent of the geraniums Isa had cultivated, and looked at the curtains so carefully sewn. She had turned a hovel into a home. Once the whisky money was in his pocket he would make it all up to her. By God he would! If only she gave him the chance.

'Are ye there Davie?' The voice and slow dragging steps of his father were instantly recognisable. Davie straightened up, flattened his hair, adjusted his jacket, ran his tongue over his teeth and swallowed the sour taste.

Dan Reid hobbled in, leaning on his crutch. He had a fierceness about him Davie had seldom seen.

'Ye were drinking in the gloup.'

'So Jack couldn't wait to tell ye.'

'If ye were any younger I'd flay you alive this night. We'll sell the whisky but it'll not be ye that's going, I'll tell ye that.'

Davie grabbed the back of a chair and leaned forward. 'Ye can't stop me going with the whisky. We sorely need the money and I did all the work.'

'Work? What work is in setting up a still? If ye wanted work ye should have gone back to the building of the pier like a man.'

Davie closed his eyes. How could he explain how terrified he was of going anywhere near that pier, when he did not understand it himself. Instead he said, 'it's not fair.'

'No son of mine will lie around drinking whisky then make money running it.'

'But it's for me and Isa. It's our future. Ye can't stop me. I won't drink any more. Ye've got to give me another chance.'

'Another chance ye say? And what of yer wife and family while ye lie wallowing in self-pity? She's down at the beach gathering limpets and whelks for ye've no other food in the house. Get the tatties from the pit and at least have that ready by the time she gets back.' He turned and hobbled out, hawking spit from the back of his throat.

'And the whisky run?' Davie shouted after him.

'No. And that's the end of it.' There was no arguing with Dan when he had his mind made up.

Davie hit his forehead with the heel of his hand. He had tried to make amends. He had worked like a horse all winter. Most of the money from the whisky run was his by rights. The thought of it was the only thing keeping him sane.

If it were not for him, there would be no whisky. What thanks did he get? Well to Hell with them – the lot of them. How could he ever make it up to Isa now? She did not deserve this. And Danny and the bairn had cried – frightened of their own father.

They would all be better off without him. He remembered how good he had felt walking along Wick harbour and his thoughts turned to the fine lines of the steam drifters and Don Swanson's offer.

With the heel of her boot Isa kicked another limpet free from the rock and threw it into the pail. Her hand against the small of her back gave the muscle little relief. The wind whistled around clusters of upright rocks producing a hollow, eerie, undulating melody that made the air seem twice as cold. It was almost May but the warmer southern winds had yet to reach the shores of the northern isles.

With frozen fingers, she tucked the shawl more tightly around her baby and picked up the pail in her free hand. She called to Danny to follow and trailed home. In the house she laid the infant on the bed, washed the limpets and put them on to boil. Davie had prepared the vegetables, an act of contrition she knew, for that was not a man's job. He had tidied himself too. His eyes now followed her as meekly as a chastised hound as she moved about the room.

He was the first to break the silence. 'I thought ye'd gone.'

'Where on earth could I go?' She gave a short unhappy laugh.

'Isa I think it better if I went to work on the mainland for a while.'

Sudden fear leapt into her heart. However justified her anger the thought of actually being without him hit her with the force of a cold winter wave. She shook her head. 'I need ye here. I need ye back the way ye were.'

'I'm not the way I was Isa. I can't go near the pier. Every blast stabs me here.' He laid a hand on his stomach. 'I love ye an the bairns an it tears me apart that I can't provide for ye.'

'We get by.'

'Get by. And what's the most we can expect? To slave all our days and still end up with nothing.'

'Ye have me.'

Davie reached forward and grabbed her hands. 'And I'm grateful. But it's not just the money. It's the way everyone looks at me. They think I'm a coward, a useless drunk. Even my own family.'

'Ye can change. Stop the drinking and there's still the croft and the fishing.'

He ran his fingers through his hair. 'It's not enough.'

She bunched the corners of her shawl in her hands. If she told him about the ten pounds she had in the bank would that keep him?

'If we did have some money . . .' she began.

'The thing is we don't.' He lifted his hands and brought them down, slapping his thighs. 'I want to give ye everything I promised. A man should be able to provide for his wife. Without that he's useless.' He paced to the window and back.

'Ye're not useless Davie. Ye *can* be yerself again. Give it a wee bit more time . . . please.'

She waited, hardly daring to breathe, afraid to tell him about the money her father had given her – afraid not to.

Watching her face Davie saw her colour rise and her eyes blink rapidly. The skin stretched over her cheek bones so that they stood out sharply. She appeared so deceptively fragile. He pulled her against him and hugged her fiercely. Her heart beat against his chest and the clean fragrance of carbolic soap and sea salt rose from her. Yet however strong his feelings, the future was one long black tunnel. Just to keep Scartongarth producing he would need to do the work of three men and still have nothing extra in his pocket. And why should he anyway, after the way his father had treated him? Along with his nerve, his dreams had been shattered and that was hardest of all to take.

'I'll try Isa but I don't know if I can,' he whispered.

Danny tried to wedge himself between his parents. Isa bent and scooped him up and he wound his hands in his father's hair, giggling with glee. Davie screwed up his eyes feigning pain and breathed in the warm milky scent of his son. The baby gave a snuffling cry from where she lay.

This was his family. After everything he'd done they still loved him. A sudden determination seized him like an angry sea filling him with the undeniable desire to put things right at any cost.

Isa's hand gripped him through his shirt, her breath shuddering. 'We can make it,' she whispered, with enough force that he could almost believe her. Burying his face in her hair he knew, for the sake of his wife and children, he would stay and somehow find the strength to fight back.

Chapter 41

By the beginning of May, the seas had calmed enough for the first trip to Orkney. Barrels of whisky filled the hold of *The Silver Dawn*, and Jamsie and Tam pulled the boat away from the shore pointing her towards South Ronaldsay, the nearest island. They sailed for less than twenty minutes when a large pale mass gradually appeared, blotting out the coastline of mainland Orkney – a fog bank stretching west to east, diluted by the feeble light of the sun.

'Maybe we should turn back,' said Tam, not the most experienced of seamen.

Jamsie consulted his compass. 'It's not that thick.' An uneasy sensation stirred in his gut. Although calm enough, it was still early in the year and he would have been happier with a third member of crew.

The fog did not worry him, for now and then it dissipated in the breeze and the blue hills of Flotta again became visible. They had picked their way through worse, but something indefinable niggled at him. Ach, it's the bad feeling between Davie and Dad getting to me, he thought, shaking off the cold finger that traced its way down his spine.

The wind was fair and the *Silver Dawn* cut through waves at a steady pace. Eventually he relaxed enough to allow his mind to wander as it often did since the explosion. His thoughts turned back to his youngest brother. Davie had a brave lass in Isa but the youthful light was already beginning to dim in her eyes. Jamsie did not believe that banning Davie from the whisky run was the best way forward, but Dan had been adamant.

All of a sudden the wind died and the sail collapsed, as if the world had taken a deep breath. Lifting them up on the swell the ocean pitched them sideways and a wall of water broke over the deck.

Jamsie shot upright, realising what had happened. 'By the living God we're too near the Swelkie,' he yelled, as the thundering of the great whirlpool filled his ears. 'Jesus Christ, Tam. How'd ye no see where we were headed?'

Tam howled and scrabbled for the oars. Hanging onto the mast to maintain his balance Jamsie leaned forward and touched the end of the boat hook. Only touching cold iron would remove the curse brought about by taking the Lord's name in vain while at sea.

Why was he saddled with this fool? Tam, who fell easily into a state of panic, was no use in certain situations. And yet the fault lay within himself – he knew what Tam was like. He also knew the problems he had been experiencing in his own lapses of concentration. Only he had been too proud to admit to them.

As if with a mind of its own the boat heaved and bucked in a slow circle as the draw of the whirlpool grew ever stronger, the roar of it blocking out their shouts to each other. In hopeless desperation, Tam threw away his oar and began to toss the kegs of whisky into the swirling water. The old men of the sea believed that feeding the vortex satisfied its hunger, thus persuading it to release the victims.

An ancient resident of Raumsey, Daisy Sinclair, in her ninety-eighth year, gathered driftwood along the shore. She watched the boat appear in the dispersing fog. Shielding her eyes with her fingers, she peering into the distance, shrugged her shoulders and returned to her task. Once she had filled her basket she painfully straightened up and squinted through the drifting mist. The yole had made little headway. It was tossing in the swirling foam dangerously near the Swelkie. Something was wrong. Daisy dropped her basket and turned to run for help, at the same time realising the hopelessness of it. Her running days were long gone and in the few seconds she had turned away, the boat had disappeared.

Jamsie looked up and saw no sky at all. A great wall of water was all around them, bearing down with white frothy claws, impatient to crush the vessel and her crew into oblivion. He saw his whole life as a road leading to this moment. In his mind, Mary-Jane and his babies appeared before him. 'I'm sorry, Mary,' he screamed as he reached his hand towards her. The yole spun in its final circle before disappearing into the depths of the ocean forever.

Back at Scartongarth Mary-Jane burst through the kitchen door, her eyes wild, her hair in disarray around her face. Tyna nursed one twin and rocked the cradle containing the other with her foot.

'My, lassie, what are ye doing out of bed? Take yer rest while ye can. I'll manage fine.'

'It's Jamsie.' The younger woman gasped, one hand steadying herself against the doorpost, the other clutching at the shawl that covered her nightdress. 'Something's happened to him.'

'Ye've had a bad dream. Ye're still not yerself.' In spite of her words ice chips filled Tyna's blood.

'I saw the boat break up. I saw him reach out his hands and heard him call my name.' With a sob, Mary-Jane collapsed on the floor.

Chapter 42

For several days no one was able to let go of the thread of fragile hope that the tragedy had not happened. The desperate desire to believe a terrible mistake had been made, that an old woman, alert though she appeared, could be prone to flights of imagination. Even now, the *Silver Dawn* might emerge from the mists, sailing home with a plausible reason for having stayed away so long. However, try as they may to conjure up the sails on the horizon, the skyline always remained empty. After a fruitless search round the neighbouring islands, the inevitable had to be accepted.

Torn apart by anger and grief Dan, Jack and Davie Reid, helped by several local men, hauled the whisky stills out of the caves. They dragged them to the highest cliff and threw them over. With grim faces, the men watched as the equipment bounced and broke, falling to the sea in helpless tangles of twisted copper and wood. Shaking his fist at the sky, Dan Reid swore an oath that he would never again distil whisky on the island of Raumsey.

The remembrance service was held the following Sunday for there was little hope of either body ever being recovered. Davie adjusted his jacket and dusted his collar. 'Are ye coming?' he asked his wife.

The steady stream of black-clad islanders moved up to the high road where they joined and marched along like a colony of ants. Isa watched them from the doorway of Jessie's home and tightened her shawl around her, knowing she should pay her last respects to a man she esteemed and cared for. Her stomach churned and she wanted to be sick at the very thought of stepping inside a kirk. She met Davie's eyes and shook her head. 'Take the bairns,' she said.

He spun round on his heel and followed the rest of his family who walked along the beach path like ghosts, faces white, eyes unfocused, not knowing or caring whether Isa attended or not.

She started after him but stopped. Her hands were damp with sweat. She rubbed them down the sides of her skirt. 'I'm sorry.' She called to Davie's retreating back. Her voice seemed to come from a long way off.

She waited until the last mourner disappeared into the kirk and the steady peal of bells fell silent. Only then did she leave the house to walk northwards in the opposite direction. The road was deserted, the cottages empty, the wind almost non-existent as if even nature held her breath. Everyone it seemed had turned out for the service.

She came near the lighthouse sitting on an outcrop, gleaming white in the thin sunshine. Someone was working within the compound and the sound of hammer blows rang through the still air. A new keeper. Someone who had not known Jamsie and Tam. Sea birds screaming defiance at an unjust world soared above her or settled on the roofs and chimneys of the light-keeper's homes. The land was flat here, and heather on the ground beneath her feet was soft and springy. When she reached the cliff top she stopped and stared into the churning foam of the Swelkie.

Sea pinks covered the shore line and she gathered a large bunch. She clambered down to the beach and walked on careful feet over the flat, often slippery rock formation until she could go no further. For a moment she stood and then, bringing the flowers up to her lips she kissed them and tossed them into the breeze where they scattered and fell into the dark swelling water. 'For you Jamsie,' she shouted through the air.

The mourners returned to the farmhouse and left in the early evening, filing through the door as quietly as they had entered. Many brought offerings of bannocks, bread, cheese and soup. There had been little talking and no whisky at this wake. Throats were too full and hearts too shocked.

Isa followed the neighbours when they left, thanking them all. The men walked together to the bottom of the rise and in silence lit their pipes or cigarettes. She stood for a time watching her eldest child draw shapes with his finger in the earth. She marvelled at how he seemed to know that this day, above all others, he needed to stay quiet.

Searching for Davie, she walked around the house. She stopped when she saw the lone figure of Jack. His hands were flat on the barn wall, his shoulders shaking. With a bellow like a bull, he suddenly beat his head several times against the brickwork until blood poured down his face.

Isa's heart began to pound so hard she feared it might break free from her chest. As if mesmerised, she watched Jack sink to his knees sobbing like a baby, unaware that anyone witnessed his grief. Without making a sound, she withdrew.

There was still no sign of Davie Maybe she should have gone to the service. Maybe she should have forced her rebellious legs to carry her over the kirk threshold but it was too late for maybes. Hoping he had not found solace in the drink, she picked up her children and returned to Jessie's. Tonight she would leave Scartongarth to mourn in peace.

Back home she alternatively paced the floor and gazed out into the darkness. The wind rose and rain splattered against the pane. She constantly peered through the window, seeing nothing but her own reflection behind the rivulets of raindrops dragged sideways across the glass by the buffeting storm. Finally, unable to keep her eyes open, she lay fully dressed on top of the quilt. As soon as she closed her eyes, sleep fled from her and she lay trapped in wakeful exhaustion.

Davie returned in the early hours and he walked steadily without the scent of whisky. Isa waited until he came to bed, hoping he would turn to her for comfort. Instead he moved as far away as possible, his back to her. In the dawn he rose and left. She remained where she was, staring into the grainy morning, silent tears trickling down her cheeks.

After feeding the children and exchanging a few words with

Jessie, she made her way to Scartongarth. All disagreements between her and Davie would have to wait until another time.

Isa walked slowly, knowing that with the service only a day behind them, the grim reality of life without Jamsie would have to be faced. Dan did not seem to notice her until she was an arm's length away. He stood in the farmyard staring out at the ocean. When he did see her, he turned away immediately.

Noticing his tears, she put her hand on his shoulder. 'It's all right Dan,' she said. 'A man should be able to cry.'

'It's all over,' he said. 'The life I planned – the hopes I had for my family. My first born son is dead. The boat I helped my father to build is smashed to drift wood. The two lads I have left are at each other's throats.'

Isa rubbed his arm. She thought it best to say nothing — to let him talk if he needed to. She moved closer and placed both arms around his shoulders.

'Oh God,' he said, raising his hands to his face. When he spoke again his voice was broken and an octave higher than usual. 'I've listened to the sobbing of the women folk every night and I can't do a thing to help them. Mary-Jane has lost her man and Tyna has lost her bairn.' He straightened his shoulders and took a deep breath. 'How could an able seaman like Jamsie have sailed too close to the Swelkie? If he suffered an ailment, why didn't I see it? If Davie had been with them would it have helped, or would we now be crying for them both?'

'There's no point in torturing yerself, Dan – we all need ye.'

'Aye. I'll be strong. But between ye and me, nothing's going to stop these questions from torturing me for the rest of my life. Go Isa, leave me now. And don't mention this . . . what I said. What I was like.'

'I promise, I won't.' She could say no more. To the other islanders it would appear Dan Reid had coped with the death of his son as he had coped with all tragedies in his life — calmly and without emotion. His outward appearance would show nothing of the turmoil that twisted in his soul.

Indoors she found Tyna hunched over a cold stove. Jamsie's death had diminished his mother, making her appear older, her face more sunken and as grey as the hair that fell round her shoulders in thin wispy strands. Loose skin beneath her eyes lay in dark unflattering folds; sad evidence of the fact that she had not slept for days. The sight of her tugged at Isa's heart, for whatever Tyna was, she had loved her son. Only since having her own children did Isa fully understand that love. She bent down and covered the age-speckled hand with her own. 'We'll get through this,' she whispered. 'Where is Mary-Jane?'

Tyna shook her head. 'She rose to come to the service, but apart from that, she'll not speak nor eat and never rises from her bed.'

'I'll see to her.' Isa kept her voice low. She knocked gently on the bedroom door. 'Mary-Jane, it's me, Isa.' The room remained silent.

Tyna's cracked tones floated from the kitchen. 'God knows I've done my best, but I'm no fit for two young bairns. If she carries on like this she'll soon be joining her man.'

'We'll not let her. First let's get a fire on.' Isa returned and, opening the stove door, began to pull out dead cinders and ash. 'Can I use this paper?' She pulled a journal from a pile beside the fender.

'No, that's Jamsie's.' Tyna stopped then nodded. 'Go ahead.'

'And food. Have ye eaten the day?'

'I've not the inclination.'

'I'll get some eggs,' Isa said. 'Could you peel a few tatties if I bring a basin to ye?'

'I think I could do that, lass. It's the bairns I'm worried about.'

Both children, small and thin for their age, stared at her. Their eyes were large and dark, their faces solemn. Without any conscious thought, the plan appeared in Isa's head. With a child in each arm she carried them into the bedroom where Mary-Jane was lying, her back turned to the door.

'Yer bairns need their mam.'

From the mound on the bed, no movement came at all.

'I'll leave ye to see to them in peace. Tyna's not fit any more.' She set both children beside their mother. 'Mind ye don't knock them off the bed now. I've got work to do.' Walking to the door, she slammed it. Mary-Jane had to believe she had left the room.

The twins looked at their mother then at Isa and began to cry in unison. Christabel crawled to the edge of the bed and stopped, just short of falling. Isa could hardly bear it. When she thought her plan was not going to work, Mary-Jane stirred. Easing herself into a sitting position, she gasped and pulled her daughter back from danger. As she gathered her son in her free arm, tears began to run down her face until she was crying so hard she could barely hold the children. She lifted her eyes and saw Isa. 'Come here,' she called, reaching out a hand.

Isa ran to her side and hugged her. Beneath the nightdress was nothing but bones. 'We'll get over this,' Isa whispered through her own tears.

Chapter 43

Several weeks passed and, as usual, Isa finished her own work and made her way to Scartongarth where she helped with the twins and the farm. Mary-Jane seemed to be coping with her grief, although she was prone to bouts of weeping that came upon her often and without warning. With no boat, Davie caught barely enough fish from the end of the pier to keep them going. Mary-Jane's twin brothers, Angus and Charlie had come to help on the croft.

'How's it the day?' Isa pulled off her shawl. Mary-Jane peeled potatoes in a basin perched on her knee. Never having regained her strength since the birth of the twins she was pitifully thin, her eyes like dark bruises in her face. The sophisticated attractiveness that had once been hers had gone forever.

'He's a good shot, young Charlie,' Tyna said, laying a dead rabbit on the table. Steadying the corpse with one hand, she produced a knife from the pocket of her apron and began to part the animal from its skin.

'I'll get the eggs.' Isa picked up the basket, opened the front door and stepped back in surprise. A tall figure dressed in black strode up the farmyard towards her, the wind raising the tails of his coat, chickens scattering before him. He stopped a few feet away from her and smiled almost awkwardly.

'Jessie told me you were here,' he said, his eyes travelling across her face.

Isa stared at Donald Charleston the minister, not quite deciding if he was real or something her mind had conjured up to confuse her. He looked older, his features sharper, harder somehow.

'Ye . . .ye came back.' Her mouth went dry.

'If only I'd known. I'd have returned sooner.'

She stepped aside. 'Ye'd best come inside, then.'

He removed his hat and ducked under the top of the doorway.

Tyna stopped what she was doing. With a dull thud, the rabbit and his skin joined his entrails in the bucket by the table. Concealing whisky and newspapers from the men of the cloth was commonplace, and it appeared Tyna believed Reverent Donald Charleston would find a naked rabbit equally offensive. She wiped her hands on her apron. Isa recognised a brief hint of amusement on the reverend's face. He placed a hand on the older woman's arm.

'I'm so sorry,' he whispered, his face once more solemn.

Tyna sniffed and gave her fingers another rub with her apron before offering him a chair and some tea. 'Ye've been gone a long time minister.' She wrung out a scouring cloth and wiped the table.

'To my regret.'

'Aye, well if it's God's will there's no room for regrets. Why minister – why was he taken?'

'It's not for us to question. He's in a better place.'

'And what of Mary-Jane and the twins?' snapped Isa unable to help herself. 'Are they in a better place? Why would a loving God let all this happen?'

Tyna gasped. Mary-Jane said nothing but kept her head bowed, the muscles of her throat working as if she had words that would not come out.

Reverent Charlton fed the brim of his hat through his fingers. 'I believe,' he started without looking at Isa, 'our time on earth is not important. Yet our lives are eternal. We are sent here so we may know pain and grow spiritually.'

'Then I'd rather not have come at all,' cried Mary-Jane, her voice shrill in the quiet room.

'You've got the children. Part of him that will go on.'

'To starve?'

'Will you send them to school?'

'Of course,' she said without hesitation.

'Even if they may be unhappy and suffer in the time they are away from you?'

Mary-Jane's closed her eyes. The disciplinarian in charge of the classroom was strict and often cruel. Many a child came home in tears having been caned for very little. 'It's better they learn,' she said slowly.

'Exactly. And does our heavenly father love us any less?'

Except for the ticking of the clock and the settling of the fire a silence descended around them.

'Is there anything I can do for you?' he asked at last, straightening up.

'We'll be fine,' answered Mary-Jane quietly.

He nodded. 'Do you mind if I say a prayer before I go?'

'Well that's what ye're here for but there's no enough prayers in the world that can put things to right in this house,' said Tyna.

Reverent Charlton cleared his throat and his eyes briefly met Isa's again before he folded his hands and bowed his head, his strong voice filling the small room.

'*Our father which art in heaven, bless this house and bring comfort to all who dwell in it.*' he began.'

Isa kept her mouth pursed and stared at the far wall trying not to listen. What good did words ever do?

She followed him to the door. 'Will ye be taking the service this Sunday, minister?' she asked.

He raised his eyebrows. 'You used to call me Donald.'

'Donald,' she repeated.

'I came to say goodbye.'

'What . . . but why?'

'I'm not cut out for the ministry Isa. You must know that.'

She shook her head. 'Ye're good. Everybody likes ye. Ye're different to any minister I've known. Ye're . . .' She wrung her hands unable to put her thoughts into words. She wanted – needed him here. 'Don't ye like the island?'

'I love the islands, but that's not a good enough reason to stay in the ministry.'

'What else can ye do?'

'I can get a job as a clerk. I've been promised a permanent position starting at the end of the month.'

Her breath caught in her throat. 'Donald, ye mustn't give up the ministry. Ye're mistaken when ye say it is not for ye.'

'I came here because I was running away.'

'Maybe ye think ye were. Ye could have been a clerk from the beginning. Ye were brought here for a reason.'

He clutched the rim of his hat and to her relief doubt sprang in his eyes.

'Give us another try please, we need ye.'

Lifting his head he gazed past her, across the firth. 'The kirk session wants me to reconsider but I don't know.'

'The things ye said in there. They made sense. No one's explained it like that before.'

'It's the way *I* see God. I doubt everyone would agree.'

'And . . . also.' She lowered her voice and looked at his feet. '*I* . . . miss ye.'

He turned his wide brimmed hat round in his hands as if it was a ship's wheel. His forehead crinkled.

'I've no one to talk to – about books and things,' Isa continued.

'I would like to stay. But . . . '

'Then don't go.' She laid her hand on his arm.

His eyes lingered on hers. 'I promise you I'll pray about it then we'll see. Thank you Isa.' He turned and walked up the hill towards the church, his head bent against the wind.

Chapter 44

As the day ended, Davie threw the basket of small fish at his feet and glanced towards the sky, heavy and leaden with unshed rain. The day had been long and for little return. He needed a drink to rid himself of the voice of his conscience, to clear his mind of the cries of the wounded, of the faces of his schoolmates now lying in the graveyard and most of all, Jamsie and Tam. For they too would still be alive if it hadn't been for the whisky – his whisky.

He glanced at the gleam of the paraffin lamp in Jessie's window. Isa seldom spoke to him these days yet her silence screamed in his ears. She blamed him for everything. Yet surely she had to take some of the responsibility for the gulf that now widened between them? At least she should have been by his side at the memorial service for his brother.

Deep down he knew he was looking for reasons to transfer the blame. Without the unwavering faith of his parents, it mattered little to him that Isa never went inside a kirk door. He had even admired her for daring to be different.

What had changed? Lifting his face to the sky he closed his eyes. Suffering the first fat drops of rain he knew the answer. He had changed. Not Isa. Hadn't she always been by his side? Oh, he could blame his relapse on the death of his brother and friend, he could blame the fact that his wife did not sit beside him at the remembrance service, he could blame the continuing trauma of the explosion, but deep in his heart he knew where the real blame lay – within his own weakness.

Isa and the bairns would be better off without him. To get any vestige of self-respect back he had to recapture his dream. Never here though, not now.

Back in the house he set the basket of fish on the kitchen floor. Isa lifted her eyes from the wool she spun but remained silent.

Jessie slept in her chair, snoring. The fire settled and spat.

'A few of the lads are going to the mainland tomorrow. I've a mind to go with them.' he said.

'Why,' asked Isa.

'There's word of a crofter selling off his livestock in the mart. We may get another pig for the winter or a stirk even.' A young female calf could be bought cheaply and sold four years later at a profit.

A worried frown flitted across her face.

He knew why. 'I'll no come home drunk,' he said.

Going into the bedroom he opened a drawer in the dresser, found a pad and pen and began to write. He took a long time to commit his deepest feelings to paper. Once the ink had dried, he folded the note and slipped it into his pocket. Tomorrow he would leave this letter for Isa to find.

Returning to the kitchen he studied her small pinched face, the dark half-moons below her eyes, the riot of black curls pinned haphazardly around her head and thought how beautiful she still was. He bent down, cupping a hand to either cheek and kissed her. Her lips felt rough, the skin beneath his fingers firm and warm, the hair that brushed his cheek soft as eiderdown. She smelt faintly of peat and carbolic. 'Ye know I love ye,' he said, lifting his face from hers.

She gazed at him, her eyes widened and darkened, her mouth open slightly and she slipped her arms around his neck and hugged him fiercely to her.

'I've missed ye so much.' She dropped the spindle and rose.

'I'm so sorry Isa.' He crushed her against him, pain and regret welling in his heart – both for what had gone before and for what he planned to do.

Their kiss was long and hungry, leaving them both shaken. Davie cast a sidelong glance at the sleeping Jessie, then indicated towards the door. 'Come on.'

She smiled almost shyly and followed him to the bedroom.

Next day, as Isa slept on, Davie rose and crossed to the window where he stared into the still morning. Lifting his jacket, his fingers fumbled in the pocket for the note he had written last night. He cursed silently when he heard her rise. There was no way now to leave the letter discretely.

Padding over to him, she slipped her arms around his waist. With a low groan he turned and held her close, burying his face in her hair. She was warm and yielding, the scent of their lovemaking still clinging to her. He would miss her more than there were words to tell, but it was impossible to turn back now.

'Ye'd best make ready for they'll be leaving in a minute,' she whispered, tilting her head, eyes still heavy with sleep. He noticed the fine blue veins in her eyelids and the long sweep of her lashes. He grabbed her arms, sinking his fingers into her flesh. 'Believe me Isa, whatever happens, I'll always love ye.'

She tensed, suddenly wide awake. 'Davie what's wrong?'

'Nothing.' He let her go and picked up his clothes. 'Go back to bed; get yer rest while the bairns are sleeping.'

'I'll see ye off.' Her voice was guarded. He could see she was worried.

'I'm fine,' he whispered.

At the top of the rise he turned and looked back at the cottage. She stood at the door clutching her shawl around her, hair lifting in the wind.

'See ye the night,' she called.

His heart lurched. He would hold that image of her in his mind for a long long time.

Half an hour later he stood in the prow of the boat, staring as the misty line of mainland Scotland grew closer. His stomach churning with conflicting emotions, he spoke little to the other men. All too soon they sailed into the shallows and he leapt out, his hands shaking as he helped the others to run the boat up the beach and secure the ropes.

'I'll not be coming to the market with ye.' He spoke at last, finding the words difficult to say.

200

'Then what else will ye be doing?' snapped Alec Cavie, a friend of his father's and a pillar of the church. 'No one ever goes to the pub till the sales are over.'

'I've to see someone,' Davie mumbled and stared at his feet. The other men eyed him with suspicion and he knew what they were thinking. Useless, drunken Davie, who had to have a drink in him before he could do anything. Suddenly he did not care. He lifted his head and straightened his shoulders. 'After we get to Wick I'll be going to the harbour,' he stated. 'Ye don't need me for the sales or the buying.'

A communal grumbling rumbled through the crew. 'And who would do the buying and selling if we all took to the harbour?' someone asked.

'Ach, leave him,' said another voice. 'He'd be no damn use in the mart anyway.'

Davie's face reddened. He was still fuming when they reached the town. The others had largely ignored him on the way.

'Well damn you lot,' he muttered, striding away. Before long, the excitement that the busy harbour scene always instilled in him melted his anger.

'Is Don Swanson's boat in?' he asked a group of men who were walking up the cobbles.

'Aye,' said one, turning to point. 'He's just finishing washing the deck. He'll be in the pub soon enough.'

Davie searched the crowded quay until he found the *Girl Georgina*. Don Swanson was coiling a rope around his arm. He raised his head as Davie called to him.

'Ye'll maybe not remember me but we spoke not six months ago.'

Don eyed him for a moment then grinned. 'Aye, I remember ye fine. The lad from Raumsey. Have ye changed yer mind about that berth?'

'I'm free if ye'll have me.'

'If ye mean that, I'll hire ye this very night.'

'I do. But I've no lodgings. Can I sleep on the boat?'

'Aye, but there'll be little sleeping, for we leave for Shetland within the hour. Come aboard and have a look around.' He bent down and offered Davie his hand.

Davie vaulted aboard and stood on the desk, revelling in the feel of timber beneath his feet, listening to the creak as she swayed in the gentle swell. 'She's a beauty,' he said.

'Davie, what the hell are ye doing?' someone called from the quayside.

Davie jumped and wheeled round. For a moment he thought the voice was Jamsie's. But hands on his hips, his brows screwed down, stood Jack.

'Ye followed me?'

'Someone had to find out what ye're up to.'

Davie shook his head. 'Well, ye'll be pleased to know I'm not coming back.' He leapt from the boat to stand opposite his brother.

'What d'ye mean?'

'I've got a job on a drifter. I'll send Isa money and I'll be back between trips.'

'Ye had this planned?'

'It's the only way.' Davie, his heart crying for understanding, thrust out his hand. Jack stood still for a long moment, then reached out to grasp the hand loosely.

'Take care, man.' With a ragged voice, Davie looked at this brother to whom he had never been close. He experienced a sudden uncharacteristic urge to throw his arms around him. Whatever had gone before, Jack was his only remaining sibling.

'Ye too,' Jack studied him for a long moment then turned and walked back along the cobbles.

'Just a minute.' Davie ran after him pulling out the letter he had written last night. 'Give this to Isa. I meant to leave it, but I didn't have the chance.'

Jack pushed the folded paper into his pocket. There was a gleam in his eye.

My God, he's pleased, thought Davie, and the knowledge was like a fist in the stomach.

'Mind see she gets it,' he said.

'I'll do that.' Jack opened his mouth as if to speak, closed it again. For one brief, mad moment, Davie imagined he was going to say something kind, but instead he pressed his lips together and nodded curtly. 'Good luck, man.' And he walked away.

Chapter 46

'Hi, Don. Want a can of tea?' The lass standing on the quay seemed familiar.

'No I'm done.' Don coiled the last of the rope round his hand and set it on the deck. The girl met Davie's eye and lowered her head. A slight blush crept up her face. Only then did Davie remember the gutter who had smiled at him the year before.

Her friend, a buxom lassie with springing red hair, was first to speak. 'Ye're new.'

'I'm from Raumsey. I've been offered a job by Don here.'

She elbowed the dark girl. 'Hear that Lizzie. He'll be around for a while.'

Lizzie's face turned crimson. Shooting a look as sharp as gutting knives at her friend she scampered away.

'I think my little sister likes ye,' laughed Don. He leaned over and whispered to Davie. 'And the other one likes me. Come on. I'll take ye back to the house for a bite to eat before we sail.'

'Yer mate seems to have embarrassed ye,' said Davie, catching up with Lizzie.

'That Connie. She's aye doing that – thinks it funny.' Two bright pink dots remained on her cheeks. Her eyes met his for the briefest of seconds then fluttered away, but not before he had seen the spark in them and that spark lifted his spirits.

Once in the house he accepted a dram, which he tossed back, welcoming the familiar burning in his throat and stomach. It had been too long since anyone had looked at him with neither condemnation nor anxiety. Laughing along with the others, he relaxed. Then Isa's face sprung into his mind and the image brought with it a crushing stab of guilt. Silently he vowed to make everything up to her once he returned home. Gladly he accepted the second dram pressed into his hand.

Later that same day, they sailed north and through the Pentland Firth. The wind was fresh and the air clear. They passed Raumsey so close Davie would have recognised Isa had she been near the shore and the wrench of leaving her hit him anew.

'Not changed yer mind?' asked Don, coming up behind him. Davie sensed the throb of the engines beneath his feet and licked the salt from his lips. As Raumsey slipped behind them, he swallowed and said, 'Na, I'm all right.'

Davie lifted his head and breathed deeply. 'Ye may think I'm daft, but I can almost smell the herring,' he said.

Don punched the air. 'That's great, man. Ye're certainly not daft. Ye're maybe one of them that's blessed with the gift.'

'The gift?' asked Davie.

'Have ye not heard of it? Some men can tell where the herring are by the smell in the air. I'm lucky to have ye.'

Don slowed the engines and lowered the lead weight on a length of wire, known as a seeker, over the side. Within no time at all the wire jolted and shook as a shoal of herring swam against it.

'Herring.' someone called, and every member of the crew congregated on the deck.

'What did I tell ye? Ye're blessed right enough,' said Don. He went on to explain the workings. 'The youngest lad will be in the locker below deck and he'll feed out the messenger here.' He set his hand on a thick tarry rope. 'Jim will pull out the nets. Yer job is to attach the corks and buoys that will keep them hanging from the surface. I'll send the lot on their way overboard myself. It's all team work here Davie.'

'Let's get to it,' Davie grinned and reached for the first cork. Other thoughts vanished as each man took up his individual task, everyone a different part of a well-oiled machine. Davie had to keep his wits about him more than most, for fishing on a drifter was very different to that of a yole. Nevertheless, he took to it quickly and worked with every ounce of his strength.

Hours later, when all the nets hung like giant cobwebs in the sea, Don clapped him on the shoulder. 'Rest now. The food'll be ready soon.'

Alone on the deck, Davie gazed around him and breathed in air sharp enough to sear his lungs. The sky was a navy dome pierced with stars. The distant lights of carbide lamps attached to the mast heads of other boats, dappled the vast darkness around them. Out here he felt almost invincible and with a flash of insight knew he was capable of doing anything he had a mind to. When the season finished he would return to Isa, free from the drink and be the man she deserved. He pressed his eyes closed, ran his fingers through his hair and offered a silent prayer that he would find the strength.

In the galley men sat round a table, eating, drinking tea, smoking and telling yarns. They moved over to make room for Davie. He ate and drank, laughing with the rest, yet fear of his recent past still lurked behind the dark curtain in his mind.

The narrow bunks, mere slots in the walls where the men slept, reminded Davie of rows of coffins and, tired though he was, he could not imagine lying in such an enclosed space. He spent much of the night on deck leaning against the rail, watching the cold lacy glitter of froth on an ever roughening sea. Eventually he settled himself on a pile of rope in the lee of the cabin where he dozed. As dawn bled into the horizon he was jolted from impending dreams by incessant shouts, and the deck filled with seamen pulling on thick jumpers and oilskin overalls.

'Ye should have taken yer sleep when ye had the chance,' shouted Don his voice sounding hollow above the throbbing engines. He drew on his pipe and peered over the side and a smile spread across his face.

The capstan strained and turned with a great grinding sound and Davie joined his skipper at the rail. His breath caught in his throat as a misty shadow materialized from the gloom, gradually changing into a pulsating silvery shimmer. Herring! And never had Davie seen so many all at once. The buzz that rattled through him was a hundred times better than anything out of a bottle. If only this boat was his.

The capstan's complaining increased in volume as the weight on the messenger intensified.

'Go with the roll,' instructed Don. 'Grab the net when the boat tips and pull with all your might as she rights herself.'

As the boat tipped sideways until the deck touched the surface of the water, Davie joined the others and grabbed onto the net.

'Heave ho,' shouted Don.

Davie, his hands frozen and muscles burning clung on as *Girl Georgina* righted herself and rolled the other way. High on excitement, he slipped into this new rhythm as if he had rehearsed it all his life. With each roll the men dragged the net further from the water until, bursting open, it spewed its silvery, pulsating innards over the deck.

Don handed him a large, flat wooden shovel. 'Scoop them into the hold as fast as ye can.' Ankle deep in twisting, slippery fish, Davie obeyed. The others gathered in nets, buoys and ropes. Every man was part of a larger force.

By the time the night ended Davie had no second thoughts. He was born for this and he felt more alive than he had done for a long, long time.

Chapter 47

'You're lying.' Isa shouted.

Jack shook his head.

Her teeth clamped together. She stamped her foot, tore the shawl from her shoulders and threw it to the ground.

'He'd better not come home. For I'll kill him when he does!'

'Don't take it out on me. It's hardly my fault,' Jack snapped, turning his back and walking away.

All the worst swear words she had heard the men on the quay utter when they did not know there was a women within hearing distance now crowded her mind and she fought the urge to repeat every one of them. She ran into the house where Jessie, with Annie asleep on her lap, lay in her chair

'Davie's gone,' Isa cried. 'We've no one to fish for us now.'

The baby woke with a start and Isa fell on the other chair, sobbing dry frantic sobs. Jessie picked up the child and laid her on the bed beside her sleeping brother. She went to Isa and folded her in her arms.

'No man's worth all this lass,' she said. 'Davie has to find his own salvation like many a-one before him. He'll be back because few men love the way that lad loves ye.'

Nothing anyone could say now would make Isa feel better. Davie had gone. Until he returned she needed to find a way to bring in enough money to feed herself and her children.

For most of the night she paced the floor. Life had been hard enough with Davie here. How would she manage when the meal kist was empty, when the oil for the lamps dried up, when the frost came and they had no shoes for their feet?

Anger and distress prickled through her, chasing away the luxury of sleep. At the first sign of light spreading across the horizon, she left the house. By the time Jessie and the children woke Isa had already completed a morning's work. She sat down, leant her head against the back of the chair and closed her eyes.

'Make the porridge Jessie,' she sighed. 'For I'm done in.'

Half an hour later after breakfast and a cup of Jessie's strong black tea, Isa stood up. 'If I can do this one morning, I can every morning,' she declared. 'But ye'll need to tend the bairns for me Jessie.' With a flurry of skirt and shawl she left the house and headed up the road towards the manse.

Surprised to see her, Donald Charleston invited her in.

She stopped mid floor and spun around. Her eyes flashed. 'Davie's gone.'

He pulled out a chair for her. 'Gone?' he asked, unable to comprehend.

'Aye. Gone.' She declined the offer of the seat and instead paced to the window. Her hair shone red where it caught the shafts of early sunlight. Her narrow shoulders slightly stooped.

'Not even a note – nothing.'

'I'm sure he'll be back.'

'Oh, I'm sure an all. But what am I to do in the meantime?'

'Sit down a minute Isa. Calm yourself.'

'How can I sit down? What time have I to sit down?' Nevertheless, she sank into the chair and began to drum her fingers on the table.

'Anything I can do?'

Her face was paler than usual and the dark circles round her eyes even deeper. 'Ye could give me a job as your housekeeper. Ye said yerself ye'd need to get one sooner or later.'

He shook his head. 'You're doing enough.'

'I need the job. Mary-Jane has her brothers, Charlie and Angus, helping at the farm. And . . .and . . .' Her voice trailed away as she stifled a sob. For a time she stared at the table.

At that moment he would have gladly given her anything she asked. 'If you're sure you can manage,' he said.

'Thank ye.' Her face brightened marginally. 'I'm sorry I don't come to the kirk. Maybe I'll will someday.'

'It's not a condition. Now you'll have tea?'

She shook her head and her curls fell round her face. 'I don't have the time. I'll be back tomorrow and I'll make a start with the cleaning then.'

'If I'm out, I'll leave the door open for you.' He followed her to the outside. She walked with small quick steps along the road.

Jack saw Isa coming towards the cottage and tensed. To his relief she carried on past with no slackening of pace. He turned his attention back to Chrissie. He watched as she led the cow into the lee, ran her hand along the flank, and felt around the tail. He knew she was checking to see whether the birth of the calf was imminent.

The letter Davie had given him hung between his thumb and forefinger. He *had* considered giving it to Isa, until he read it.

Darling Isa,

I know I have no right to ask your forgiveness, for I know I've hurt you badly. I couldn't come back to say good bye because I knew you would plead with me to stay, and I would have to give in, my darling, for I have always given in to you in the end. I know how difficult I've been these last few months and I would never have done this if there was any other way. I had to get away from the island, to get myself back to what I was before, for my own sake and for yours. It's not because I don't love you, but because I do. You and the bairns will be better off without me for a while. I have a job on a drifter and am going after the herring. I promise you I will save every penny and come home a richer man. I'll think of you and the bairns every night.

The skipper is a man called Don Swanson and he is a fine person. He is not much older than me and, Isa, he has a part share in the boat. You should see her, she's one of the finest drifters I've seen. If he can do it, I can and all and I will, some day.

If only you can understand. I couldn't go back to the pier. I shook and felt sick at the thought of it. I realise that maybe you've had enough of me and cannot find it in your heart to forgive me.

Please write to me at Don Swanson's house. I'll put the address at the bottom. His family will make sure I get the letter. If I hear no word,

I will know you can't forgive me and are getting along better without me. I won't blame you. But I will be back whatever happens and I pray I'll find you waiting.
My love forever
Davie.

Jack did not want Davie to return – ever. He saw him as the major obstacle between himself and Chrissie. If only there was a way to make his brother believe Isa wanted no more of him. Then he would surely stay away. Jack carried the page to the grate, hesitated and looked again through the window. Chrissie was returning. There was no time for indecision. He dropped the letter into the fire and watched the corners curl and blacken. Realising that if Davie was to write again, Isa would know what he had done. His mind whirled.

'She'll calf before the night's out,' Chrissie said coming through the doorway. She stopped and took a second look at Jack's face.

'Why are ye looking at me like that?' he snapped.

'Like what?'

'Like ye're accusing me of something.'

'I'm sorry. I didn't mean to. I'll go and get the peats.' Chrissie picked up the scuttle.

Why did the bitch always turn away when he tried to speak to her? Even now, with every chance of a new start, she couldn't act like a normal wife. He grabbed her arm, yanking her back with such force that she stumbled against him dropping the scuttle. The flash of fear in her eyes pleased him.

'Ye heard Davie's gone?' he asked.

'Why should I care,' she said, but her voice trembled.

Tension tightened his muscles. She was lying again. 'A lass never forgets her first Chrissie.'

'Davie's no threat to ye.'

She wasn't going to fool him, he thought. With a snort he said, 'he won't be, not anymore.'

Something flashed across her face; fear, concern, shock. In the same instant as he felt the tightening in the muscle of her arm.

'Ye care right enough. Ye think I've hurt him.' He laughed aloud. 'Well ye can believe what ye want. It's time ye learned who's the man in yer life.' He flung her away from him.

Her eyes narrowed. Her nostrils flared slightly. 'I am no longer in love with Davie. I warn ye I'll not try to convince ye forever.' She looked him in the eye and he saw a new hardness, almost a challenge. 'We could have been good together – but it's ye and yer vile temper that's driving us apart.' Then she banged out of the door.

A sudden fear that he could actually lose her gripped him. He ran after her, grabbed her arm and turned her to face him. 'Ye know I love ye, Chrissie. I don't know what gets into me sometimes. I don't want to hurt ye – but ye make me so angry.'

'I'm sorry, I don't mean to. Ye've got to trust me Jack, ye've got to,' she said.

'I'm so scared I'll lose ye. Ye don't understand. Nobody understands.' He pulled her against him. He held onto her with desperation. He would never, could never let her go.

She pushed against him with her arms. 'I can't breathe,' she said. And when he loosened his grip she slipped her arms around his neck. 'If only ye would stop being so angry,' she whispered, pressing her face against his, 'things could be different. We could be happy.'

Yes, he thought. With Davie gone things would be different. He did not want him to come back, ever. How could he make sure Davie stayed away? He had to think – think. His head roared with problems and solutions.

The idea came to him like divine inspiration. There was a feeble minded lad working in the post office. Daft Larry, they called him. The family who ran the mail boat had taken him from an institution on the mainland and used him to sort the mail, for he could read well enough. Jack had befriended Daft Larry, and had basked in the lad's devotion and total loyalty, finding it amusing. Larry, a social outcast, saw Jack as his one and only friend. It would not take much to persuade him to set aside letters addressed to Isa, and he would reward him with cigarettes and whisky. He would not tell a soul, of that Jack was sure. Just in case, Jack would enforce his silence with the threat of fire and brimstone. Larry was a God-fearing lad, and believed Jack's version of the scriptures. Isa would soon turn elsewhere. Women were like that. They needed a man's strong hand to keep them in their place. Isa was already over-friendly with the minister.

Jack decided he would make sure his brother found out what a deceiving cow his wife really was. Then Davie would never come back. All the pieces were falling into place so neatly that believed the hand of the gods were guiding him and his spirits took an upward turn.

Her body was soft and warm and he felt himself stiffen against her. 'Everything's going to be fine now, ye'll see,' he said, and smoothed the hair back from her face. Their kiss was long and hungry. She clutched him to her, her body trembling, and he knew her need was as great as his.

Chapter 48

Davie had not been gone for three weeks when the sickness started. Isa marked the days off the calendar with growing dread. She could not have another child. She just couldn't! Worn out, she had no time for the two she already had. Furthermore, pregnancy had never been so bad before. Each day she just wanted to curl up in a miserable heap. She suffered nausea too severe to eat and had pains in her head and bones.

When working in the harvest fields she heard talk among the young girls about herbs that brought about the monthly curse but had no knowledge of what they were. She hoped to bump into Chrissie, the only one with the knowledge, but Chrissie was seldom seen these days.

Her steps slowed. Donald Charleston would not mind her lateness. She had noticed the concerned way he watched her as she struggled to hide her weariness from him.

She stopped, rubbed her damp hands down the sides of her skirt and turned towards Chrissie's cottage. There was no anger in her heart now against the other woman. The hurt she had suffered blunted the edges of her jealousy until only a weary acceptance remained. She had to go to her now for there was no one else who could help her.

The barn door stood ajar and she heard a rustle from inside. She pushed gently and it creaked back on its hinges. Weak sunlight streaming into the interior creating a crazy dance among the dust motes. Jack sat on an upturned barrel with a letter in his hand. He shoved it into his pocket and sprang up to face her.

'I'm looking for Chrissie,' she began hesitantly. 'Was that a letter?'

'What business is it of yours,' he snapped. Then more gently, 'why d'ye want Chrissie?'

She glanced again at his harassed face, instinctively believing the letter came from Davie. Why else would he act so guiltily?

'I don't suppose,' she said, 'that yer brother has written to ye?'

'Ye're right in yer supposing.' There was hollowness in the tone of his voice and he avoided her eye.

'I'll go find Chrissie. In the house is she?'

'No. She's off for drift wood.'

'Then tell her I came by. I need to talk to her.'

Isa walked as far as the road when for some reason she turned, surprised when the cottage door opened and Chrissie came out carrying a wash tub. Isa snorted and hurried back, skirting the barn so Jack would be unaware of her return. Chrissie was filling the tub with water when Isa spoke her name. Startled, she spun around, her long hair falling away from her face.

'Isa,' she gasped. Her hand flew to her cheek but not before Isa saw the purple, bruised swelling.

'Jack told me ye weren't in.'

Her brow furrowed for a second. Then her words fell out too quickly. 'I didn't let on I'd come home.' She gave a short, sharp laugh and pointed to her face. 'I slipped in the byre. Daft of me. I'm worse than my granny was – and she in her nineties.' She laughed loudly as if she had said something funny but her eyes remained guarded. 'What can I do for ye?'

Isa hesitated. She licked her lips. 'I'm expecting again.'

'How lovely. Ye're so lucky. I suppose ye want something for the sickness?'

No, Isa wanted to cry out. Davie's gone. I don't want this bairn. However, she had forgotten something that was common knowledge within the Reid family. Chrissie's childless state was a constant heartbreak to her. Now faced with the naked longing in the other woman's eyes, she felt ashamed.

'I . . . thought ye could help me.' Unable to elaborate further, her voice faltered.

'It'll not be easy with Davie gone but every new soul brings its own blessing,' said Chrissie.

'The sickness is bad this time, awful bad. And I've got to

work. I don't know how I'm going to manage.'

'Come on.' With an indication of her head, Chrissie led her into the house and began to take jars from the shelf. She mixed a few herbs together.

'This will help the sickness. Ye *are* very lucky ye know.' The firmness in her voice told Isa she would get nothing more.

'Jack's in the barn. He was reading a letter,' Isa said. 'I thought maybe it was from Davie.'

'A letter?' Chrissie's eyes screwed down. 'Why do ye think it's from Davie?'

'I don't know,' said Isa honestly. She met Chrissie's eyes and saw something that she could not quite put a name to. Was it surprise, shock, fear or hope? 'Did Jack do that to yer face?' she asked.

'I told ye what happened.' Chrissie pulled her shawl across her chest, her eyes dropping towards the floor.

'They're missing you at Scartongarth.'

'Tell them . . . tell them I'm busy.'

'The whole island's talking about the way Jack treats ye. Tyna would take ye in.'

'It's no one's business but mine,' said Chrissie, resolution in her voice. 'Don't worry about me – he would never do me any serious harm.'

'If ye need me . . .,'

'I won't. But thanks.'

'I'm sorry,' Isa whispered and turned to go. Both women had suffered for loving the Reid brothers.

She walked away her despondency greater than before. Jack leant against the door frame of the barn. His arms were folded, hair falling across eyes as cold as the firth in winter.

'Ye found her then,' he shouted.

'Aye, I did.' She made to move on when he spoke again.

'See what she did to her cheek. Clumsy heifer.'

Isa knew she should keep her mouth shut but the sight of his sneering face filled her with a furious fire. In an instant the man before her became the summation of everything that was wrong in her life.

'I'm not believing she fell.'

'What did ye say?' He stepped in front of her.

Her anger peaked. 'Ye hit her,' she shouted. 'And don't think ye'll get away with it. I'll be telling yer mam.'

His eyes narrowed to slits. In two quick strides he reached her. Before she could move he grabbed her by the front of her bodice, yanked her into the barn and slammed her against the wall. The pain shot through her chest and knocked the air from her lungs.

'Chrissie fell. And ye'll tell nobody any different.' His face was inches from hers, his breath tobacco sour. 'Remember, ye're alone at night. Just an old hag and two bairns to help ye. Anything could happen.' He stopped while his meaning sank in. 'And that letter *was* from Davie. He's no coming back – ever. He wanted me to tell ye. He's met another lassie. So ye can go to yer preacher and be damned.'

Isa gasped as he flung her to the floor. She struggled to her feet and backed slowly from the barn, her heartbeat thundering in her ears. Once she put enough distance between them, she stopped.

'Ye're mad,' she shrieked. 'Daft. I don't believe ye.' Then turning, she ran all the way back to Jessie's house. Collapsing behind the haystacks, she gave noisy vent to her grief.

That night she paced the floor for hours suffering the chilling draught that keened under the door and round the window-panes. Unnaturally tense and aware of every tick and click in the house, she found no solace in sleep.

She had truly believed, for a moment at least, Jack had wanted to kill her. She had seen madness in his eyes. Whatever Chrissie said, there was something very wrong with him. There had always been anger in him but now it was more pronounced. And although she could not let herself believe what he had told her about Davie, he had planted a seed of doubt impossible to ignore.

The morning brought little consolation. Although it was already June, an angry wind whipped the firth to a frenzy of white and the shrill cries of sea-maws ripped the air. She cleaned the ashes from the fire and set it before starting her day's chores.

There would be extra work to do at the manse since she had not been there yesterday. Most of the time Donald went out leaving the door unlocked for her. She hoped today would be no different for the tears that bubbled within her heart, burst forth often and without warning.

Chapter 49

As the weeks ran into months, Isa's fear of Jack and her suspicion about the letter did not lessen. She saw Chrissie now and then but she had become remote, with only polite smiles and vague assurances that she was fine. Isa was sure this was not so, but there was little she could do.

The days were hot and the wells were almost dry when the first of the summer storms broke across the land. Isa breathed in the cool air thankfully. Once the drought took hold, the long walk to the crystal-clear spring in the hill of Laighan was not something she relished at the best of times. And especially not now with another bairn on the way.

Once her morning's work was over, she entered the kitchen of Scartongarth and sank into a chair. Overcome by the heat she half-closed her eyes. It was too warm for a fire but Tyna still had to cook.

Christabel, lying on the bed sucking her thumb and clutching a scrap of blanket turned large solemn eyes on Isa and grinned. Tear-washed streaks ran down her grubby cheeks. Her brother lifted the wooden spoon from a now empty baking-bowl, gave it a final lick then ran at Isa's legs, and wrapped his arms around her.

'Where's Danny?' Wee Jimmy demanded.

'He'll come over in the morn.' Isa rumpled his hair. Stocky built and tall for his age, he was already so like his father it hurt.

Mary-Jane's hands stilled and rested on the handle of the butter churn. She gave Isa a tired but welcoming smile. 'I'll just get the tea,' She rubbed her arms as if to ease the stiffness in them.

'It's later and later yer getting,' complained Tyna, tossing a bier scone to the dog that sat by the hearth watching her every move. The voice, once strong and decisive, had become weary whine. It struck Isa how much her mother-in-law had aged this last year.

'There's been no word then, of Davie?' Tyna asked.

The bubble in Isa's chest expanded and the most she could manage was an out rushing of air and a shake of the head.

Tyna blinked and studied her daughter-in-law. For a moment Isa thought she was going to say something kind, but no. 'The cow's been bellowing for half an hour or more,' Tyna sniffed and turned back to the stove.

'Maybe I could manage the milking the day,' said Mary-Jane.

'No. I'll do it.' Isa pulled herself to her feet. 'It was me who took on the extra work.' She wanted to hug Mary-Jane but that was not the island way. Davie might return but Jamsie never would. Isa went to the pantry for the buckets.

In the byre she settled herself on the milking stool. Daisy the cow gave a mournful bellow, swishing her tail as if in protestation for Isa's lateness.

'I'm sorry girl.' Isa rubbed the bloated udder and gently squeezed the teats, easing them downwards. The milk spurted out, hitting the pail in a steady tinny resonance. As she worked she laid her head against the cow's heaving belly and breathed in the scent of warm milk, straw and dung.

When the pail was half full, she brought it to the young calf, set it below his nose and offered him her fingers. He immediately began to suck on them. She lowered her hand into the milk. Once the calf got the taste of the warm liquid, she lifted her hand away and watched him as he confidently drank the milk himself. He had been a weak calf, born late in the season and had needed weeks of careful nursing. As he sucked up the milk, he stared at her with deep brown, trusting eyes. And something snapped within her.

She suddenly knew that she wanted her baby more than anything. Guilt and relief simultaneously flooded through her. With her free hand she rubbed her stomach in a silent apology.

Once she was convinced the calf could manage on his own,

she returned to Daisy's side. Using the clean bucket, she resumed the milking until the cow's udder was empty.

'Ye'll feel better of that, girl,' she said. In the porch, she emptied the milk into the cream separator and turned the handle. The cream, which always settled on top, ran into a jug.

'Davie'll be back.' Mary-Jane came up behind her.

'My father was always away,' Isa said. 'I remember when he came home. Mam got us all dressed up in our Sunday best and took us to the quay.'

'That's the way it'll be for you and Davie.'

'He hasn't written.'

'If he's at sea it mightn't be all that easy.'

'I suppose so.' Isa remembered how her mother would run to meet her dad. He would pick her up and swing her round before turning to his daughters who were almost wetting themselves with excitement. And he always brought gifts. Bolts of cloth for dresses, food, pencils, a book, and once, a sewing machine. For the first time she realised how hard it must have been for her mother. Had being left alone for long periods turned her into the embittered woman she had become? Was history repeating itself? In a way she hoped it was, for that would mean Davie would return.

'Can ye finish this?' she asked Mary-Jane, a lot more brightly than she felt. 'I'll need to get back to Jessie's.' This was post day and Sanny the post with his constantly blinking eyes would be coming up the road about now.

Chapter 50

Ensconced in her armchair by the peat fire, Jessie took a long draw at her clay pipe and scratched her armpit. Sober now that her wee tottie was harder to come by, she seemed lost in a world of her own a lot of the time.

'Come away ben and have a cup of tea,' she said when Isa came into the kitchen. 'Old I may be, but I can still mind how sore a lost love can be.'

'It wouldn't take much for Davie to put a pen to paper,' said Isa. 'Surely he owes me that much.'

'I'm fond of the lad ma' self. But I always said he's bit weak, not nearly good enough for a strong lassie like yersel. But I wouldn't have believed this of him. It's been nigh on four months with ner' a word.'

Isa said nothing. Why did she still feel the need to defend him? 'Where's Danny?' She looked around. Wherever he was playing, he seemed to sense that his mother was home and would usually be by her side within minutes.

'Danny?' Jessie started. 'Was I looking after him? Oh, lord.' She turned her head as if in panic. 'He was here a minute ago,'

'Jessie – when did ye last see him?'

Anxiety filled Jessie's eyes. 'I . . . I don't know

'He's not outside and it'll be dark soon.'

'He's maybe in the barn. He'll not be far.' Jessie's hands clutched at the arms of her chair. Her mouth wobbled.

'Danny,' Isa called, and ran to the door. 'Where is he, Jessie? Oh, just stay with Annie. I'm going to the beach.'

'He'll not have gone there,' Jessie called. 'I've told him about what otters do to wee laddies they find near the sea. I'll look in the well.'

As Jessie walked along the narrow path between the house

and the well, she spoke aloud although Isa was too far away to hear her. 'My wee Matthew was frightened of the otters too. He used to hide whenever I gave him a row or I had a tottie too much. Yet he never went near the shore. He's taking a wee bit longer to come home this time – that's all it'll be.' She clutched at her chest and stopped. After taking a few deep breaths she started walking again, still speaking to herself. 'It can't be my fault. I've not been at the whisky or skelped him, have I? Oh God, when did I last see him? Why can't I remember?'

She touched the flagstone covering the well. 'Thank God I put it back on – he'll no have fallen in.' Straightening up she looked around her, then staggered sideways almost falling over. She put her hands to her head and looked at the well then at the ground by her feet. 'I've no pail. I've forgotten the pail. I'm losing my mind. Coming to the well with no pail. I'll have to go back for it.' And with that she waddled back towards the house.

Isa ran the length of the bay calling Danny's name, stopping now and again to listen. Every sound she heard might have been a seagull, a seal or even a child. In the gloaming, every humped rock and every bush took on a different shape. She could not lose Danny too. A vision of Jack's crazed eyes the day he threatened her flashed before her. But he would not hurt a child, would he?

'What is it?' Her father-in-law came hobbling down the brae.

'Danny, he's . . . he's lost.'

'Ye'll need to calm yersel.' Dan held the lantern high as she babbled out the story. 'Run and get a search party organised, Angus.' He waved at the boy behind him. Then turned back to the sobbing Isa.

Against the lighter surf she thought she saw a shape move. 'Danny,' she screamed, tearing herself free and running over the flat rock towards the sea. Her foot, coming down on green weed, slipped and she pitched forward landing on her stomach. Excruciating agony shot through her body. For a moment she lay dazed waiting for the pain to subside enough for her to rise and continue her search. She limped towards the shadows cast by the new pier. Twisted ankle, bleeding hands and knees, pain like a hot wire around her stomach, all forgotten in the desperate attempt to find her son.

'Are you all right?' Dan picked his way across the stones. His lantern swung and creatures of the night scurried and hid.

"I thought . . . I thought . . .,' she sobbed, seeing nothing before her but swirling foam and jutting rocks.

'Ye get back to Jessie's in case he turns up.' Dan's voice was soft but firm.

'I can't – I can't' she cried, 'I've got to find him. He might need me.'

'We'll find him,' said Dan. 'We'll have every able bodied man on the island looking. Ye'd be better getting a warm bed ready.'

Her teeth chattered and her whole body shook. There was no more power in her legs. She sank into the strong arms of Mary-Jane's brother, Charlie, who had joined them. 'If I lose him too I want to die,' she moaned.

'Ye're not to worry. I was always going missing as a lad. Come on now, I'll get ye home,' he said and half carried her back to Jessie's cottage. The old woman was asleep in her chair her breath coming in short laboured gasps. Annie woke and screamed. Isa gathered the baby up and rocked her back and forth, clinging too fiercely.

'Leave me. Go find Danny,' she moaned to Charlie. 'Please find him.'

She could feel her son, sense his cold and fear. As she cuddled Annie, she willed him to communicate his whereabouts as she had so often for his father. Before her lay the comatose figure of Jessie. She had trusted this woman with all that was precious to her and she could not even stay awake to keep an eye on the baby.

Time and time again Isa walked to the window. Her eyes searched the dimness of a summer night for approaching lights. At long last she saw them materialise out of the amber mists of dawn. A small group of dark figures making their way towards the house.

With a cry, she lifted her skirt a little and ran towards the men. Charlie came first, his face strained and streaked with dirt, a bundle in his arms.

She stopped breathing. Her nails dug into the flesh of her hands. Her stomach clenched. She wanted to vomit.

Charlie sank to his knees. The bundle slipped to the ground.

Like a miracle the bundle stood upright and ran towards her. Danny flung himself to her arms almost knocking her off balance.

'I was frightened,' he sobbed. 'I was picking flowers for ye and when I looked I couldn't see the hoose and I thought I heard an otter coming to get me.'

'It's all right,' Isa crushed him against her. She lifted her eyes in silent question.

'We found him huddled in the corner of Bill Monks's barn, terrified half out of his wits. We'll leave ye now for we're all dead beat,' someone told her.

'Thank God, thank God,' she repeated through her tears. The pain she had been barely aware of since she fell, hit her with a new force. The weight of the little boy clinging to her neck made the pain worse as she carried him home.

Jessie, awake now, absently poked the embers in the fire.

'They found him,' Isa said. 'Ye'll not be watching him again, I'll tell ye that.'

Slowly the old woman turned her face, screwing down vacant eyes. 'Who did ye find?'

For the first time Isa noticed Jessie's grey and distant expression. 'Danny, of course.'

'Was he lost, then?'

'Jessie, what's wrong?'

'I wasn't' mad at him – it was the other boys – they torment him. It's not my fault. What could I do? That bugger went off and left the pair of us. And me without a ring on my finger.'

'What are ye on about?' Isa stared at Jessie in horror.

Jessie was no longer listening. She had a haunted, faraway look in her eyes. 'They were always tormenting him just because he didn't have a dad. That's why he was aye running away.

That's why he went to London.' She reached out and grabbed Isa's arm. Her eyes were unnaturally bright but not focused. 'He'll come back. He will – don't worry yersel.

'What are ye talking about? Jessie stop it.'

Jessie's eyes blanked over and she stared at Isa, her mouth slack.

'He left, left me with a bairn. With no money. And ye know, they blamed me – blamed me for the drink – but what could I do? All these good folks who go to the kirk on a Sunday. Aye, an I could tell ye a thing or two about more than one man on this island. I'd nobody – ma folks all dead.'

She was babbling now; spit flying from her lips, her head bobbing from side to side as if she had taken leave of her senses.

'Ye've been at the whisky again,' accused Isa, disturbed, because drink or no she had never seen Jessie like this. The shock of Danny going missing had obviously been too much for her. Something was very wrong but there was no time to cope with it now. Isa's body pained her badly and Danny was dirty and cold. She changed his clothes. She gave both children their milk, took them in bed beside her, and sank into an exhausted but disturbed slumber that skated along the surface of sleep.

A more powerful and well-remembered pain ripped through her, bringing her to full wakefulness. She looked down at the head of a sleepy Danny. His little body was sprawled across her. Easing him away she struggled to her feet. Her legs shook like saplings in the wind. As the sudden gush of liquid soaked her thighs, she acknowledged what she had been trying hard to deny. Her efforts to save one child had resulted in the loss of another.

'Jessie,' she called, ' help me.'

There was only silence.

Holding onto the wall for support, she made her way to the kitchen and stopped in horror. Jessie lay in the same position as she had the night before, but she was still, and her head hung low on her chest. Isa limped forward and grabbed her shoulders. The grey head lolled backwards exposing a twisted face and cold staring eyes.

Isa hobbled to the kist in the bedroom. She found the white sheet, took it outside and spread it over the peat-stack. Someone would come before long. Someone would have to. No sooner did she return to the cottage than all her strength left her and she lay sobbing on the floor.

Chrissie heard the shouts of a neighbour from the road and, wiping her floury hands on her apron, ran to the door. 'There's a sheet on Jessie's peat-stack,' the woman wheezed through lungs corrupted by a lifetime of hay-dust and dampness.

Chrissie remained just long enough to collect her bag. She ran down the sloping field of hummocky grass. Once at the cottage she tried to open the door but something stopped it from opening fully. Chrissie squeezed through the narrow gap to find Isa collapsed behind it, blood pooling on the flagstone beneath her.

'Thank God ye've come,' Isa moaned, pointing towards the kitchen. 'Jessie.'

Chrissie took a quick look into the kitchen and knew immediately there was nothing she could do. 'Let's get ye sorted then I'll see to Jessie.' She half carried Isa to her bed. 'Just lie back, ye'll be fine.'

'I've lost the bairn, haven't I?' Isa whispered.

Chrissie wrapped up the bloody clothes. Knowing what lay among them and unable to speak, only nodded.

'Jessie?'

'Jessie was an old woman,' said Chrissie softly. 'Ye rest now and I'd do what needs to be done.'

Isa rolled away turning her face to the wall. Her whole body appeared to fold in upon itself.

'I'll take the bairns to Scartongarth then I'll come back and make ye a drink to help ye sleep.' Chrissie tucked the blankets around her patient.

Chapter 51

They buried Jessie in a pauper's grave for there was no money for anything else, and in her arms, they placed the tiny but perfectly formed body of Isa's stillborn daughter.

All through the wake Isa sat in silence. The noise around her seemed to come from far away. As if driven by an inner force, she rose to her feet and reached for her shawl.

'Are ye going out?' asked her mother-in-law who had spent the day serving tea and bread to the mourners.

'I want to go to the grave.' In truth, she wanted to run away from the claustrophobic confines of the tiny kitchen and press of well-meaning bodies.

'Then I'll come wi' ye.'

Tyna's words registered little impact. Isa shrugged her shoulders. It made no difference to her.

Even the weather seemed appropriate. Rain had fallen in the night and the sky was dull and grey. A sea mist started to roll in and the mournful sound of foghorns echoed round the bay.

Together they walked in silence over the brow of the hill towards the cemetery. A flock of sheep ran wildly in front of them before scattering inland, bleating in angry protestation. Isa barely noticed them. She lifted the latch on the iron gate of the graveyard. It groaned and swung open. The two women walked in silence to the newly turned mound of earth each lost in her own thoughts.

'They have to have a stone,' said Isa at last.

'There's no money for it.'

'What about Jessie's son?'

'It'll be weeks before we get news to him. And what did he ever care?' Tyna snorted.

'What happened to her man?'

'Jessie never married.'

Without surprise, Isa lifted her head. 'Who was Matthew's dad?'

'There was an excise man who paid her a lot of visits although he had a wife and six wee ones of his own.'

'Ye all looked down on her, didn't ye?'

'She didn't keep the rules of the good book and I didn't agree with that, but it's not for me to judge. I aye liked her. She wasn't afraid to be different and she did have a heart of gold.' Tyna's voice trembled. 'I mind her as a young lassie. She was as bad as the lads for getting into mischief. We aye had a laugh with Jessie. She'll take good care of yer bairn.' She covered her face with the end of her shawl. Her shoulders shook and Isa realised the woman was crying.

Without any further words they turned as one, their steps taking them away from the grave.

Two seagulls appearing from nowhere, rose into the air, dark against the lighter grey of the sky. Isa watched them, squinting her eyes against the suffused brightness. For a moment they seemed to hover above her head, smooth breasts gleaming white. Then they wheeled away and dissolved into the mist until they were lost from sight. All that remained was their farewell cry, the barking of the seals and the plaintive moan of foghorns.

'Will ye come back to Scartongarth?' asked Tyna

Isa shook her head. 'Jessie's is the only home I know.'

'I'll be here if ye need me.' Tyna's voice was tinged with regret.

I'll never need ye, thought Isa, but nodded her head and said, 'Thank ye.' She turned by her own gate and bade Tyna farewell. All she wanted now was to be left alone with her memories.

Day after day, she washed, fed and tended her children automatically, moving through her chores as if in a daze. Friends came and went but she barely acknowledged them and had she been asked an hour later who had called and what they had talked about, she would have forgotten.

Each night she felt so tired she could hardly move, yet she always knew sleep would evade her. She would stand for hours staring through the open curtains from where she could see the lights of ships that glided through the Firth. Davie could be on any one of them, ready to send a flare so a boat would collect him. How she needed him now. Desperately she would try to reach him with her mind, hoping that somehow he would hear her silent pleas.

Finally, she would curl up in Jessie's bed and lie staring at the oblong of faded moonlit blue of the window until she sank into a shallow and troubled sleep.

The amber light of dawn filled the room and Isa stretched, her feet landing in a cold place where no body heat had penetrated. She jumped slightly and curled herself back into a tight ball.

Her bones were heavy as if she had had no sleep at all. She poked her head from under the covers trying to remember what day it was, knowing there was a reason why she was so cold. It was not until she struggled to sit up that reality struck her, and with it, the knowledge that nothing in the dark depths of sleep could be as bad as her waking nightmares. Her arms ached with the need to hold a little warm body. Martha – she had named the child for her mother. She had lost her best friend and her baby all in one day. And Davie was still gone.

In the distance she heard a cockerel crow, a dog bark, the clink of a milking pail and she shrank from the normality of it all. She pulled herself out of bed, arranged her shawl around her shoulders and prepared to face another day.

Shivering, she poked the dead ash in the fireplace – it was too early to light a fire. And there would be no milk unless she went to Scartongarth and got it herself. The dog began to bark, the sound echoing round the tiny cottage.

'Quiet,' she hushed, pulling open the door allowing the animal to go hurtling into the outside where he almost collided with the legs of the minister.

'What are ye doing here so early?' she asked in surprise.

'I couldn't sleep. I thought I could help.'

'Well, ye've made it harder. The dog's wakened the bairns. I'll have to take them to the milking with me now.' In truth, she had not been near Scartongarth since the funeral but she needed to take her anger out on someone.

'I could do the milking for you.'

In spite of herself she laughed. 'A minister milking a cow?'

'I've seen it done. It doesn't look hard.'

She shook her head. 'There's a knack to it.' Both children were now awake and demanding attention. Suddenly everything was too much. Covering her face with her hands she crumpled forward, her breath hiccupping in her throat. Donald's strong hands were on her arms and it was as if his touch melted something inside her making it possible for all the pain to surface. Her face pressed against his breast, her tears sinking into the rough fabric of his coat. She sobbed until her body ached with the force of it. As the cruel wave of grief subsided, she became aware of the pressure of his arms around her, of his heartbeat against her face, of the faint smell of mothballs and shaving soap. It felt so good to be held again that she never wanted him to let her go.

Embarrassed by her own surge of emotion she backed away and he dropped his arms. They stood in silence for a minute and he cleared his throat. He did not look at her when he spoke. 'You don't have to hurry back to the manse. I'll carry on paying you till you're ready.'

'I'll not take money for nothing.'

'You're due it. You've worked hard.'

'It wouldn't be right.'

'You're physically and emotionally exhausted.'

'I've not had a mind to do much,' she said. 'But I'll get to it.' She knew she should go back indoors and leave him there but was unable to move.

'Isn't there anything I can do?'

Their eyes met and she saw his concern. She saw something else too; something she recognised yet could not put a name to.

'Can ye get Davie back?' she asked, as if the mention of his name would break the gathering spell.

He sighed. 'If only I could.'

'Then no, there's nothing.' Lacing her fingers together she stared at them.

He turned his hat around in his hands. 'I'll be here any time you need me.'

'I'll remember that.' Turning from him, she fled indoors.

She would have to go back to the manse for she needed the money, but in the last few minutes she realised there were things she needed more. She needed a man to hold her, to make her alive again. And the knowledge scared her.

Davie had to return. She needed him here *now*!

She heard the children, but the sound seemed to come from a distance, as if a bubble encased her, which the outside world could not touch. Everything was too much and she started to cry aloud and without control.

She was unaware someone had entered the house until Chrissie knelt before her. 'I met the minister. He's worried. I feel guilty for not coming sooner.'

'I'm fine.' Isa stood up. 'I've been so tired.'

'Of course ye are,' Chrissie said. 'Ye've just lost a bairn and Jessie. Don't worry about the house. I've seen much worse. Come on, I'll give ye a hand to clean up.' She discarded her shawl.

Isa pushed her fingers through her hair finding it tangled and knotted. For the first time in days she realised how her house must appear to an outsider; the sour smell of old food and urine, plates and spoons lying on the table encrusted with dried porridge, pots and pans sitting on the hearth unwashed and the floor looking like it hadn't been swept in ages. She picked up Annie whose face was smeared with dirt and tears, the rags round her bottom soggy and stinking. The hiccupping child clung to her neck with a grip tight enough to choke.

As Chrissie rolled up her sleeves and bent down to set the fire, Isa noticed a bruise on her forearm extending from elbow to wrist, but chose to say nothing. When the water was warm, Isa bathed and dressed the children. Chrissie scoured the pots and dishes and put the dirty rags to soak with some ammonia. Together they scrubbed the table and the floor. Once they were finished the place looked and smelled a lot better. Only then did Isa fill the tin bath and climb into it herself. Chrissie sat in Jessie's chair playing with the bairns, hugging and kissing each in turn.

Isa dressed, tied her wet hair back in a bun, emptied and put away the bath. 'Now we'll *all* go to Scartongarth,' she said to Chrissie.

Chrissie shook her head. 'I've got to get back. Tell them I'll be to see them soon.' Nervously she glanced at the clock.

'Ye're scared of him,' said Isa.

'I'm fine. Ye go. And . . . I *will* be back.'

'Please come with me.' Isa grabbed her sister-in-law's hand.

'Ye don't understand. Jack needs me.'

'And ye don't need to be black and blue.'

'Isa, please don't ask me – not now.' She spoke abruptly, effectively ending the conversation.

Isa hesitated, helplessness washing over her. She needed all her energy now for her own survival. Together they walked to the door and along the road.

'Are ye sure . . . ' Isa began when they reached the crossroads.

'Don't say anything. Go now.' Chrissie picked up the hem of her skirt and crossed into the field below her own house.

'Mind what I said. I want to help,' Isa called after the retreating figure.

Without looking round, Chrissie lifted her hand in a wave.

Chapter 52

Dan was working in the low field. The muscles stood out on his arms like thick ropes, yet he lowered the spade as if he had no strength dig further. Isa understood how he held himself in check, as if admitting to his loss would crack him wide open but now, in this unguarded moment, she saw the raw pain etched in the lines of his face. He started, as if surprised at the sight of her and raised his hand to his eyes, too late to hide the tears.

'It's grand to see ye up and about lassie,' he said. He beckoned to Danny who ran to him through a group of protesting hens. The child laughed and Isa's heart lurched. It was the first time she'd heard him laugh in a long while.

She looked at the few feet of corn Dan had managed to cut. She looked at the impossible amount of crops waiting to be harvested, at the dwindling stack of peats and the rows of potatoes still in the ground. The neighbours would rally round but only after they had finished their own work. And it was no answer. They could not live their lives depending on charity.

Dan followed her eyes. 'Aye,' he sighed. 'It's a sad day to see the croft like this.'

'We can bring it back Dan. It's good land.'

'It needs good hands to work it. Even so a croft isn't much without the fishing.'

'Where are the lads?' she asked of Mary-Jane's brothers.

'I sent them off to shoot some birds, for we've little for the pot.'

'Could Jack not help out?'

'We see nothing of Jack or Chrissie these days. They've got their own lives now.'

'How much is a boat?' she asked, knowing that if she used the money she had in the bank her dream of seeing her parents again would be crushed for ever.

'Ah lassie,' Dan indicated towards his crippled leg. The hopelessness in his eyes tore her heart. 'Even if we had the boat, who would sail her?'

'What about the boys?'

'What's the use in dreaming?'

'We have nothing but our dreams,' answered Isa. Without another word she walked towards the house and into the kitchen. Tyna was at her usual stance, bending low over the stove stirring something in a pan.

'My, but it's grand to see ye.' Mary-Jane looked up from the dough she was pounding and smiled.

Around the table sat two elderly neighbours. Maggie from two crofts down had a grin that showed one brown tooth protruding like a tombstone. Her skeletal face was crinkled and as tanned as old leather. 'Ah, Isa lassie, it's not an easy life this,' she sighed.

The other was as obese as her friend was thin. Her pendulous breasts bulging over her stomach. 'Awe, Tyna, at least ye have four bonny grand-bairns.'

Tyna smiled thinly. She rubbed one misshapen knuckle with the other and winced.

'Are yer hands sore?' asked her buxom friend.

'It's nothing to the pain in my heart.'

'We were just saying none of us have seen hide nor hair of Chrissie for a long while.' Maggie eyed Isa who shook her head.

She won't come because she doesn't want ye to see the bruises, Isa wanted to scream but the words stuck in her throat.

'I don't know what's wrong with the woman. She never even came to the funeral,' said Tyna, turning to look at Isa as if she would have the answer.

'Well.' Maggie leaned across the table, her pale blue eyes darting this way and that, her voice dropping to a whisper, 'Lottie from the shop says she not been in there either, but when her sister's lassie had the bairn, they'd to get Chrissie out of her bed – and it the middle of the day! And when she came her arm was bandaged and she held it against her like this.' She demonstrated. '*Said* the cow kicked her.'

'If that's what she said, that's what happened.' Tyna banged a couple of mugs on the table. 'Mary Jane, see if there's a bit of bannock left to give them wi' their tea.'

'Well my Gussie says he saw Chrissie the day of the floating shop but she stayed well clear of everyone. And have ye seen how thin she's getting? I'd say there's something dealing with that lassie.'

'D'ye think she's expecting?' asked the buxom neighbour. 'Sometimes it can do queer things to the brain. D'ye remember that excise man's wife . . .'

'I'd be the first to know if it was that,' Tyna snapped. 'They've got their own life. They've little time to come visiting. That's all it is. She's a hard worker and so is our Jack. And I'd thank ye kindly not to go gossiping about my family.'

'Ach, we were only concerned. And we're not the only ones on this island.' Maggie settled back and sniffed loudly.

Isa set her baby on the ground and the child crawled over to play with her cousins. In spite of the normality of the scene she felt strangely apart. Anger had replaced her grief, and she was not sure where to direct it. She had been too scared of Jack to say anything – but what did it matter now? Nothing he could do was worse than what had already happened.

'Do ye honestly not know what's going on?' Isa looked from one face to the other.

Tyna shot her a look of ice. 'Jack would be here if he had the time. And if it's true Chrissie's not that well, he'll not be wanting to give us any more worries.'

'Stop sticking up for him,' Isa cried, before the daggers from Tyna's eyes shut her up. She already knew what she had to do.

'If ye're feeling up to it, maybe ye'd go and look for the eggs. I don't know where the hens are laying these days. I don't have the strength to find them myself.'

Isa realised that her mother-in-law wanted her away lest she said anything else. She picked up the bucket.

Chapter 53

Isa stood on the shore, icy prickles of panic creeping over her skin. She took first one step and then another towards the beach where Jack was mending his nets.

'What the hell do ye want?' he said.

'Yer folks need help and ye are one man on a boat.'

He straightened up, coiling the thick rope in his hand. He repositioned the wad of tobacco he was chewing in his cheek. 'What's it to ye?'

'Ye could take young Charlie and give him a share of the fish to bring home.'

'Why would I want Mary-Jane's brother?'

'At least he's helping yer folks.'

He studied her for a long moment. 'What are ye up to?'

'I just want enough food for us all come winter. Ye're the only son left. Ye should be bringing in the fish.'

'And what have my folks ever done for me?' He spat out the words. 'It's always been Jamsie – or Davie. So now they need me, do they?' He laughed, and she stepped back at the wildness in his eyes. If Scartongarth was to survive, however, she could not give up.

'Ye can't just abandon them.'

'I thought I warned ye to stay out of my business.'

She took another step back and hoping her voice would not waver, spoke again. 'Then I'll ask every man on this island if they've a berth for Charlie. They'll be wondering why Jamsie's own brother won't help. There's more I could tell them an all. How's Chrissie these days?'

Jack threw down the rope and stepped towards her. 'Ye think ye can threaten me?'

She stuck out her chin. 'I'm not scared of ye!'

'Then ye should be.' He stopped and cracked his knuckles, his black eyes boring into hers.

She tossed her head and walked away. Once she had put sufficient distance between them, she faced him and screamed, 'Ye're daft Jack Reid. It's ye who should be dead, not Jamsie! Scartongarth did fine before and can again, with no help from ye.' She spun around and ran as if the devil himself was after her.

'I'll take on Charlie if it's so important,' Jack yelled after her. 'But ye ever threaten me again and ye'll be the sorry one.'

Chrissie roasted the last of the pork and served it with potatoes and cabbage, followed by stewed rhubarb. If Jack had a good meal inside him his temper was seldom as bad. She thought Davie's leaving would have improved things between them, but Jack was changing for the worse. He was growing increasingly melancholy and his temper always seemed to be on the boil. The few tender moment they shared were becoming less and less. Even the fire of his passion that had once bound her to him, left her feeling empty and used. If only she could give him the child he so desperately wanted, if only she had been a virgin when they wed, then things might have been different.

Other things worried her as well. He would come back from the mainland with a new coat, boots, and a bolt of cloth for her. All over and above their budget, but she dared not question him.

He stared at the food without comment and Chrissie held her breath. What could be wrong now?

'That bitch of Davie's has been at me,' he exploded at last.

'Isa . . . why?'

'Isa . . . Why?' he mimicked her. 'She wants me to take Mary-Jane's brothers to sea so they can put fish on the table at Scartongarth – that's why.'

Chrissie pushed her food around her plate. She had eaten little all day. In spite of her hunger, her throat closed. Weighing her words, she spoke. 'Ye could do with a hand on the boat. Ye work too hard.'

'What? I know what she's up to. She wants Scartongarth.' He

banged his fork down. 'It's bad enough the way things are. If the twins hadn't been born the farm would have been mine.'

Chrissie gasped.

'With this place too, we could have been as big as the mains. And what right has Isa to tell me what to do?'

Chrissie moistened her lips. 'I'm sure she didn't mean anything by it.'

'The croft is still Dad's. He can make a will in favour of whoever he chooses.'

'It'll be young Jimmy's.'

'Or Danny with Isa pushing the bairn on Dad. I'll be nowhere as usual. The only son not to produce an heir.'

The remark cut like paper. He had no way of knowing how badly her inability to conceive hurt her. And if he did, would he care?

'She'll not be in favour once the family find out what she's been up to,' he continued.

'What are ye on about?'

'I saw her first thing this morning with the minister. Arms round each other they were and it looked like he was just leaving the house.'

'I don't believe it. Ye can't go spreading that about, Jack.'

He rose and she stepped back, her body tense and ready for flight if he should raise a hand. Instead, he picked up his jacket and stared at her.

'Maybe it's as well she lost that bairn. Do ye really believe it was Davie's? She falls easy enough.' He gave a cruel laugh as he swung out of the door, and then shouted over his shoulder. 'I'll take Charlie on, if only to keep an eye on what they're up to.'

Chapter 54

Meanwhile, in the streets of Yarmouth, Don and Davie were making their way from the shop to the harbour. Every minute away from the boat Davie was restless and ill at ease. He refused to go drinking with the other men, preferring to walk along the coast until he was so tired he knew sleep would finally claim him.

'I've never seen any man work as hard as ye. What's driving ye?' asked Don.

Davie looked across the water as the moon stared through a hole in the ragged clouds but did not answer.

'Our Lizzie's fair taken with ye Davie. I hope ye've not got a lassie waiting back in Raumsey.'

Davie still did not speak. He couldn't. A lassie yes, a wife and bairns. Yet she hadn't answered his letters although he had sent her Don's address. The only forwarded mail had been from Jack and the latest ripped his heart out.

'There is somebody,' he answered, 'But I don't think I'll be welcome back.'

'Then decide, man.' Don's voice was sharp. 'Ye're a good seaman and I don't want to lose ye, but I'll not have our Lizzie mucked about.'

'I'll not muck her about Don, for I've done that too often already. Anyway, we're miles apart.'

'No, yer not. Lizzie came down to Yarmouth with the other fisher lassies yesterday to work the season.'

Davie's heart skipped a beat. He missed Isa and the bairns more than he had imagined but if Jack was to be believed, she'd taken up with the minister and wanted no more to do with him. She had been getting the letters and the money he sent but she'd asked *Jack* to write as she'd nothing left to say. He did not trust

Jack but the fact Isa had not replied herself spoke volumes. Once he got to thinking about it she had always been a bit too friendly with that minister.

'Are ye coming to the pub?' Don's voice cut through his thoughts.

Davie shook his head. He still couldn't believe Isa would do this. Yet she was a strong-willed lassie. She cared little for the opinion of others and once her mind was made up there was little use trying to change it. Still, hoping against hope, he decided to write to his mother. Whatever she thought of Isa she was an honest woman. He would get the truth out of her.

Back on Raumsey, Isa was standing on the doorstep staring at the grieve from the mains farm who handed her five guineas.

'Like I said, Mr Adams is sorry it's a bit late. Jessie didn't mind. She knew he always sent it in the end. It'll be ye who takes it now I suppose.'

'But what's it for?'

'Ye don't know? Jessie rent's her land and barns to the Mains. Pays her once a year – give or take a week or two.

'I knew they kept feed in the barn, but I never thought . . . ye mean Jessie owned land?'

'Aye, from here all the way to the high rise.' He waved his hand towards the west, where the fields rolled upwards, ending at the main road which ran through the island.

Isa shook her head and took the money. 'No, I didn't know, but thank ye,' she breathed. She had wished for a miracle and the miracle had happened.

The last floating shop of the year would be here in a week and now she could stock up for the winter. She clasped the money to her chest. Maybe, just maybe, her fortune was changing. 'Come on bairns,' she shouted we're going to buy something good for the tea.'

Meanwhile Reverent Donald Charlton folded a telegram which he pushed under his bible. It had been the right thing to do, informing Jessie's son of her death. Yet what implications this would have for Isa he had no idea. He had expected her son, Matthew, to come to the funeral but it seemed he had more pressing matters. Now he was returning, *to settle his mother's estate*, so the letter said.

Donald Charlton glanced at the clock on the wall. About this time he usually went to visit his parishioners, leaving the door open for Isa. Since he'd held her and seen the answering longing in her eyes, he thought it best they avoid each other. Today, however, he would have to tell her about Matthew MacKenzie's imminent arrival.

Isa was earlier than he expected and she brought with her a blast of fresh autumnal air, rich with the smell of the fields and the sea. The baby, slung on her back, sucked her thumb and stared at him. Wee Danny held onto her skirt, burying his face in the folds. Isa herself, with her tanned skin, and eyes lit with at least some of the old sparkle, looked a lot better than when he had last seen her.

'I hope ye don't mind me bringing the bairns,' she said hurriedly. 'They'll not keep me back from my work.'

Donald flapped his hand at her, dismissing the apologies. 'I've something to tell you.' He walked to the window where he stared at the dark ribbon of the rip tide dividing the firth.

'It sounds serious.' Isa set Annie on the floor and removed her shawl.

'I've had word from Jessie's son. He's coming to the island.'

'Who contacted him?'

'I had to Isa. It was my duty.'

'Why . . . why should he care? He wants the house and croft, doesn't he?' Her voice rose.

'He didn't say.' The reverent was afraid she might be right. If the man had not been in touch with his mother for forty years and did not even turn up for her funeral, it hardly seemed likely that his intentions were anything other than financially motivated.

'All these years she waited . . .' Isa's voice wavered. 'He'll not want to stay, will he? I'll have no home if he turns me out.'

'He won't want to stay. And I can't say he'll be able to sell

Jessie's. Folk are leaving the island. There's no one I know of looking for a house.'

'But there's the land. The rent's the only thing keeping us going.'

'It's his rent, not yours Isa.'

Her hand flew to her mouth. 'His? I didn't think. I spent a fair bit of it.'

Oh Isa, he thought, closing his eyes briefly. 'He might be reasonable,' he said aloud, with more resolution than he felt.

'I'll get on now.' Turning her face from him she lifted the kettle. Her fingers closed around the handle, her knuckles showing white through the tanned skin, and there was nothing else he could do but leave her to her cleaning. She did not look at him again as he left the room.

Once the day's work was over and her children asleep, Isa imagined Jessie in her empty chair. 'He's coming at last and only because he thinks there's money in it,' she said aloud as another thought struck her with the force of lightening. 'Oh my goodness, maybe he'll want to lodge in this house.'

She did not think he would. Yet how could she be sure. Whoever he was, whatever he was like, she could not sleep under the same roof. Her mind raced in circles, desperate to find a way of making certain it did not happen. Suddenly she gave a loud 'hah,' and rising to her feet she ran along the shore road to Scartongarth.

'Have ye killed the pig yet?' she asked, bursting through the door.

Mary-Jane glanced up from the pot of soup she was preparing and smiled in that slow way she had. 'The boys slit its throat this morning. Why?'

'And where's he hanging?'

'In the barn.'

'Could ye let him hang in my ben end?'

'Ye want a dead pig hanging in your ben end for a week or more?'

'Yes. Please Mary-Jane. Jessie's son is coming and how better to greet him.'

'What . . . Matthew? He'll not put ye out will he?'

'I don't know. But I hate him already for how he treated Jessie. I'll not be able to keep my tongue if he stays any length of time. And he can put me out – he can.'

'But why the pig?'

'In case he wants to stay in that room. Jessie always kept it nice for him and I've made it really bonnie.'

Mary-Jane laughed and wiped her hands. 'I'll away and call the boys,' she said. 'Oh, and Isa, I'd dry some fish indoors too, if I was ye.'

Chapter 55

The tall thin man who descended from the cart and dusted his posh clothes was as different from Jessie as was humanly possible. He was all angles and hard edges with eyes that glittered icily above empty pouches of skin sagging onto sharp cheekbones. Where Jessie's smile had been benevolent, he wore no smile at all. Even beneath his full beard, Isa could see the downward turn of his mouth. Had she not known who he was she still would have disliked him immediately. The crofter in whose cart he had travelled clicked his tongue at his horse, then turning to catch Isa's eye, spat on the ground.

Jessie's son rested both hands on the top of his cane and stared at Isa.

'Can I help ye?' she asked.

'I am Matthew MacKenzie, and this,' he gestured at the cottage, 'was my mother's house. And you are?' his voice had none of the soft island lilt about it but was harsh and without accent.

'I'm Isa Reid. I cared for your mother when she was sick.'

His gaze fell on the children where they played on the dusty flagstone path and he wrinkled his nose as if the very sight of them offended him.

'I assume you are here to make the house ready for my arrival.'

'I live here.' The heat rushed to her face.

'Live here? Then I suggest you find somewhere else and quickly. Have you a man?' The tone of his voice indicated she was a dreg of society to whom his mother had given shelter.

'I have. But he's away working. I got the ben end ready in case ye wanted to stay. But ye'll not mind the slaughtered pig hanging there, for I've nowhere else.'

'What — God in heaven! Why would you hang a pig in a bedroom?'

'The barn's been rented out.'

'Rent?' He screwed down his eyes and looked at the cows on the pasture. 'And the land?'

Her breath caught in her throat as she realised her error. She had hoped he would not find out about the rent and now she herself, tongue loose with nerves, had let it slip. 'But it's only enough to keep the house going,' she gasped.

Impatiently he indicated she move out of his way. He walked into the kitchen and gagged at the stink of drying fish.

'Don't you do that outside?' he demanded, his face reddening and spit forming at the corners of his mouth.

'Only when it's not raining, and anyway, the outside racks are full. I need to store food for the winter.'

He pushed past her and through the narrow passageway to the bedroom, stifling an oath when he saw the pig.

'Damn you woman! This place is even worse than I remember. I'm sure the minister will see it as his Christian duty to give me a room. I'll go through my mother's things now. I trust you haven't touched anything.'

'I've not had the heart to,' Isa said, looking at her feet. 'There's not much. Only what's in the kist in the corner.'

'Then I'm sure you have something else to do. I would thank you to leave me now.'

She went outside and attacked the weeds in the vegetable garden with a surge of temper-fuelled energy.

Several minutes later he called her. 'There's nothing here of any use to me.' He appeared agitated and in worse humour than before. 'Do what you want with her clothes.'

Isa followed him down the path. 'What are ye going to do with the croft?' she asked.

'I'll be selling it of course. And I'd like to know when the rent is due.'

Unable to stop herself, Isa covered her face with her apron and started to cry. 'I'm sorry. I didn't think. I spent it on the bairns.'

'What?' He turned to face her, words appearing to stick in his throat. Finally he exploded. 'A thief. You come here and worm your way into my mother's affection and get God knows what from her.' Small beads of spittle flew from his mouth. 'I'll have that money back or I'll go to the law.'

Steadying herself against the solidity of the stone wall behind her, Isa watched him pick his way along the path towards the road. She sank down on the step, burying her head in her hands. Somewhere from over the hill accordion music drifted on the breeze and a burst of youthful laugher rang out. Young folk enjoying themselves and some of them older than her. Yet she felt aged compared to them, her carefree years far behind her.

The next morning, Isa stood in the kitchen of Scartongarth facing her mother-in-law.

'Ye'll have to move back here, although I don't know where ye're going to sleep. I'll not have Davie's bairns out in the cold.' Tyna said, as she wiped her hands on the dishcloth and hung it on the rod over the stove.

'She can share my bed. We'll make up pallets for the bairns,' said Mary-Jane.

Isa nodded her thanks, but the thought of moving back to Scartongarth filled her with dread. And where would they all go once Davie came home?

'What's wrong with ye?' snapped Tyna. 'Is my place not good enough for ye, now ye've been used to that fine house of Jessie's?'

Isa ignored the sarcasm. 'It's not just that. Her son's going to have the law on me for stealing the rent money.'

'He never is!' Tyna's hands clasped the top of a chair as her body shot forward. 'That long skinny dreep. Who does he think he is? We took care of his mother all these years! Charlie, ye and yer brother get Isa's things over here, and if the law comes let's see them get past me.' The old woman could be like a wildcat if anyone threatened her family. If any good came out of this, it was that Isa finally felt included in the circle.

A few hens strutted through the open door, into the kitchen, heads bobbing up and down. Bess the dog jumped from the blanket by the fireside, barking enough to raise the devil, and the hens, in their haste to be outside, flapped their wings and squawked. One jumped onto the table. Bess made to jump after her, and in doing so upset the oil lamp. The lamp rocked precariously for a few moments before righting itself. Another hen flapped onto the dresser, knocking plates and cups from their hooks, sending feathers into the air. Tyna grabbed Bess's collar, ordering her lie down.

Mary-Jane started to laugh. She laughed so hard that she had to hold onto the edge of the box bed for support. And, in spite of herself, Isa had to join in.

'I'll swear that dog's going to be the death of me,' Tyna said, before her sour mouth jerked up at the edges and she too joined in the laughter.

After the melee had settled, the hens shooed outside, the feathers and droppings cleaned up, all three sat round the table drinking tea. Isa felt more relaxed in her mother-in-law's company than she had ever done. It had been good to laugh again.

Chapter 56

Filled with a grim determination, Isa marched back to Jessie's croft. Once inside she pulled out the kist she brought with her from Kirkwall. Memories of her first night in this house and of how much she had hated it then, swept over her. Yet now the thought of leaving pierced her like a knife.

'The post's been – there's a letter for ye,' Angus shouted through the open door. She sprung to her feet snatching it from his hand, her disappointment almost tangible when she saw the Canadian postmark. Much as she looked forward to a letter from her parents, she had hoped that Davie . . . but what was the point? Why did she go on hoping? She tore the envelope open.

Her father had suffered a heart attack and although he had recovered well, he was not expected to see another summer. He wanted to see her. The briefness of the note, coupled with the scraped painful writing, told Isa her mother was not coping well. She pressed the letter to her heart, emotions of grief, loss and longing surfacing, one after another.

'Och, ye look a bonny sight for somebody who's just had word from the other side of the world. What ails ye?' Charlie's voice startled her. She had forgotten Mary-Jane's brothers were there.

'My dad . . .' She stopped, unable to go on. She stared at the letter now hanging loose in her hand. The money her father had left with her would not be enough to pay the passage for both her and the children. Unless she left them behind, she would never see her dad again.

Charlie put an awkward hand on her shoulder. 'I'm sorry. I didn't' mean . . .' Looking into the soft grey-green eyes, for once devoid of mischief, she saw compassion, or was it pity? She shrugged him off.

'Matthew MacKenzie'll not say I left the house dirty – and the devil take him,' she declared and dropped to her knees by the fireplace. 'Get me some kindling. I'll need to heat the water.'

'What the . . .' she started, confused. The curled remains of blackened paper lay in the grate she had cleaned only this morning. MacKenzie had burnt something. Why or what it had been she would never know. With a puzzled sigh, she rolled up her sleeves.

'Is there anything I can do?' asked Charlie.

'Ye'd best go back to Scartongarth. I'll be here for the rest of the day.'

The lad left, his shoulders slumped, his walk slow. Isa had forgotten how tired he must be. Since Jack had hired him, he'd been rising before the sun and not resting till well after it had set. Sometime during the last few weeks, the boy had taken on a new maturity without her having noticed.

She was on her knees, venting her anger and frustration in the frantic sweeps of her scrubbing-brush when she heard the voice behind her.

'You'll be through the flagstones if you don't watch out.'

She turned her head as Donald Charlton spoke. He held his hat in his hands, fingering the rim. 'I came to tell you, MacKenzie has decided to stay until the croft is sold.'

'And ye couldn't turn him away?' She rose to her feet.

'It wouldn't make any difference. He'd have found somewhere.'

'This place'll not be much to him, but everything to me and my bairns.'

'Still no word from Davie?'

Isa drew the backs of her fingers across her brow and sighed. 'None.'

Suddenly it was all too much. In spite of her earlier resolution, her whole body trembled and her eyes leaked. 'It's one thing after another. Now my dad's dying.'

Reverent Charlton reached for her hands.

'I'm so sorry. If Davie loved you he would have never left you like this.'

'But he did and there's nothing I can do.'

'There *is* something you can do.'

'What?' She snatched her hands away. 'Charlie and Angus . . . where are they?'

'There was no one here when I arrived.'

Her mouth was dry. She wrapped her arms around herself, afraid of what his next words might be.

'You know how I feel about you – You must know, though no words have been said.'

'What do ye mean?' she stammered. She knew what he meant and it was her own fault. She had never really discouraged him. 'I'm a married woman Donald.' Her voice lacked conviction.

'A married woman without a man! Davie could have someone else for all you know.'

Jack had implied as much but hearing it from another's mouth sent a chill through her. 'What would ye have me do? Ye a minister of the kirk.' Her eyes flitted to the horizon, to the haystacks and finally her feet.

'I'm only too aware of what I am.' He sucked some air. 'If you were happy I would never have spoken. I would give up the ministry if you said the word. We could go away from this place to where no one would know us. We could go to Canada.'

Canada. He had said the one word that might make up her mind for her. Tumbling emotions overcame her. Hope, fear, guilt, all fighting for supremacy.

'I talked ye into staying. I'll not be the cause of yer leaving,' she declared.

He turned and paced the length of the room. 'Actually I have no choice in the matter.'

'What . . . Why?'

'There have been rumours about you and me. I've had a warning from the kirk session.'

'What rumours?'

'Someone reported seeing me leave your house in the early

hours of the morning. I denied it of course, but I've been given a choice. Either I agree to be posted elsewhere or I give up the ministry.'

'Who would say such a thing?'

'I don't know, but there's gossip all round the Island. The kirk was never as empty as last Sunday. Don't feel responsible for me leaving. That's going to happen anyway.'

'Tyna never said a word.'

'One thing I can say about your mother-in-law, she's not one to listen to idle gossip.'

'I'm so sorry Donald.'

'Maybe it was meant to be. Everything that's happened – can't you see. What choice do we have?'

'I don't know. I need to think.' Her head spun. He was about to lose everything because of her. 'I wish I'd never come to Raumsey. Go now – just go.' She flapped her hands at him.

'Please think about it. I'll be back, Isa.'

As she watched him stride down the path she trembled inside, but whether with anger or emotion or both she could not tell.

That night she tossed and turned until dawn. Over and over she asked herself whether Donald was right and this was their destiny. She imagined what it would feel like to have his hands on her body, to feel his lips against her own. Life would be easy with Donald. She did feel drawn to his strength and goodness. With his help, she could take her children to see her parents and lift herself from this trap of poverty. Donald Charleston would never have left her to fend on her own with a bairn not even born. As for Davie, he had changed so much. He was not the boy she had fallen in love with. Deep in her heart she believed she had already lost him.

Then there was MacKenzie. What if he carried out his threats? She could not risk jail, for what would happen to her children then? Her only option was to give him the money her father left her and lose any hope of joining her parents forever. Her eyes remained dry for there had been enough tears shed already and crying solved nothing.

Yet if she went with Donald, could she ever fully return his love?

For no matter what, her heart remained with Davie, the way he had been before the accident. She thought again of his vivid blue eyes, his slow sleepy smile, his strong weather-tanned hands stroking her body and again the excitement rose in the pit of her stomach. Pressing her face into the blanket, she searched desperately for any scent of him that might linger but found nothing. He had gone, and she was young, full-blooded, and very, very lonely.

Chapter 57

The day dawned slate grey and ominous. Isa rose as weary as she had lain down. With her mind still in a turmoil she took her anguish out on the house, scrubbing and cleaning already clean surfaces until her body ached.

She looked around, knowing she would never blacken this hearthstone again, never scrub the flags and buff them with milk, never again do anything in this cottage she had grown to love. The pig had been returned and the fish taken down and put outside. Matthew MacKenzie would have no cause to complain. Opening her small moneybox, she took out all she had left of the rent. She picked up Annie and grabbed Danny's hand. 'Come on bairns,' she said. 'We'll not go to Scartongarth empty handed.'

The shop was crowded, mostly with elderly women no longer able to work the land. Several had grandchildren in tow. A sudden hush fell over the occupants as she entered.

'Seen much of the minister lately?' The question sounded more like an accusation.

'No more than usual.' Isa sensed all eyes on her. She took a deep breath, banged her basket on the counter and spun round to face her accusers. 'I've heard what ye're all saying,' she shouted. 'And it's not true – not a word of it.' Her eyes flitted from one face to the other. 'Ye all thought the world of Donald Charleston, yet the minute some cruel, vindictive person says a wrong word, ye're all against him. Well, I'll not be doing my shopping here. I'd rather starve.' She made to lift her basket.

'Don't mind her, lassie.' Lottie grabbed Isa's wrist. 'This is my shop and ye're as welcome as any. There's few who would say a wrong word about ye or the minister.'

'Is that why the kirk was near empty last Sunday?'

'Aye, how do ye know that then? Ye who never goes over a

kirk door,' said a triumphant voice.

With flaming cheeks, Isa faced the woman she knew only as Veeda.

'I hope ye all like the new minister as much when ye've driven Donald out with yer vile tongues.' She tore away from Lottie's grasp and almost ran towards the door, dragging her children behind her. 'I'm sick of this place and I can't wait to be gone,' she shouted, at that moment meaning every word.

'Did ye hear what they're saying about me and the minister?' she asked as she stormed through the door of Scartongarth.

Tyna looked up, and then licked pale bloodless lips. 'Aye, I've heard what Jack's saying but I pray to God it's not true.'

'Jack! I might have known. How can ye believe him?'

'It's not just that,' said Mary-Jane. 'Folk have noticed how much time ye spend with the minister.'

'But . . . there's nothing between us.' Not Mary-Jane too. In this island where she had felt so accepted, the people who had been so supportive were now turning against her. Was this how Jessie had felt when she had had a child with no ring on her finger? She could never stay here now to let her life become a mirror of the old woman's.

'I didn't say I believed it. We don't, do we, Tyna?' Mary-Jane said.

'What I think matters little. Ye are the mother of my granbairns, and I'll no see ye homeless.'

'Then I'd rather be homeless than stay where I'm thought to be a whore.' Isa turned and ran out the door.

'Isa, come back,' Mary-Jane called after her, but Isa carried on, dragging her confused children behind her.

If she needed another reason to accept Donald's offer it was this. When they left, the tongues would wag until they fell out, but she would be gone, far away to where no one knew her. Now she understood how her mother felt when she had reported Davie to the excise men. She was leaving, so she cared little for the opinion of others.

Except, when the heat of anger had cooled, Isa realised she did care. She cared very much.

The day had grown unseasonably warm, the air heady with the scent of clover, heather and wild flower. Little puffs of dust rose where her feet struck the road. The water whispered over the sandy beach and rattled gently when it hit the pebbles. The gulls circled overhead sliding on the air currents. Isa no longer saw the beauty. She did not see the women in the fields wave to her as she went past. She did not see anything but her own dismal future.

'We've filled the cart. Will we take it to Scartongarth for ye now?' asked Charlie, when she drew alongside.

'Do what ye like,' she snapped, ignoring the boy's confusion. She sank down on the stone seat and buried her head in her hands. And that is where Mary-Jane found her.

'We want ye over at Scartongarth.' Her sister-in-law lowered herself down by her side.

'With ye all thinking I'm a hussy?'

'I don't think that. I wouldn't blame ye even if it were true. Davie treated ye bad and the minister is a fine looking man.'

Isa lifted her head and stared at her friend. How could she claim that nothing had happened when Donald had spoken so freely the night before? How could she justify her words when she was considering leaving with him as her only option? The person she least wanted to lie to was this woman before her. Mary-Jane watched her as if she desperately needed a denial.

'What Jack saw – Donald was comforting me and he'd just arrived,' Isa whispered honestly.

'Don't ye worry about what folks say.' Mary-Jane spoke more freely now, her voice lighter. 'The morn' they'll have something else to talk about.'

'Thank ye, Mary.' Isa stood up. Mary-Jane believed her – it was a start. 'I'll stay here for the next couple of days. MacKenzie gave me 'til the end of the week. Whatever happens, I want ye to know, ye are the last person in the world I want to hurt.'

Sunday morning found Donald standing at the manse window looking over the firth. He had been wrestling with his sermon for the last four hours. There had been many times his faith had been tested, but none as much as now. There was nothing holy about the feeling Isa stirred in him. Davie might not come back but unless he was dead, Isa would never be free to marry and to live a lie went against everything he believed in.

The day before, he spoke rashly with his heart instead of his head. But then his temper had been fired; both by what he saw as total injustice from the presbytery, and also at the wagging tongues of folk he regarded as friends. On top of that, he had been faced by Isa's distress.

He walked through the kirk, breathing in the scent that had become part of his life, of old books and waxed wood. He wanted to remain a minister very much. Was he really prepared to give it all up for the love of a woman, knowing he would never be at peace within himself? Dropping into the front pew, he covered his face with his hands.

Throughout the night he had prayed, hoping for some divine answer, but none had come. The sermon he started to write had been based on the text, *let him who be without sin, cast the first stone.* Everything he wrote came out wrong and all he had for his efforts was a full waste-paper basket. It was Sunday morning and it was imperative he deliver something, albeit to an almost empty church as tales of his indiscretions flourished and grew.

He rose and went to the vestry where he stared through the window. Whatever happened, his life was about to change in ways he had never envisaged.

It was a surprise therefore, that when he returned to the kirk every pew was full. Astonished, he looked around at the congregation noting faces he had seldom seen in church before. His stomach somersaulted as his eyes fell on Isa, sitting discreetly in the back row. She smiled and lowered her head.

Instead of the hell fire and brimstone sermon he had intended to give, the words, which sprang to his lips that day, were of joy and hope.

Chapter 58

Early Monday morning Isa marched into Lottie's shop. 'I'll buy my messages now if I may,' she announced. She had nothing to be ashamed of and knew she should have stayed and brazened it out before.

'I'm sorry about yon wee bit of bother,' said Lottie with a sniff. ' Veeda doesn't know when to stop.'

'Is it not what ye all were saying?'

The other occupants had the decency to lower their eyes and look anywhere except at Isa. 'Chrissie told us the truth of it,' someone muttered.

'Did she now?' asked Isa, raising her eyebrows. Good for Chrissie. Maybe at last she was beginning to stick up for herself.

'We heard about that son of Jessie's,' Lottie said, and her words hung in the silence.

Another woman laughed with a high-pitched cackle. 'Tyna told us about the pig. I wish I could have seen Mackenzie's face. He was an evil wee bugger himself when he lived here.' The tension dissolved.

'Aye well, pig or not it's him who has the last laugh,' said Isa. 'I've to move out.'

'Oh but no,' said Minnie, who appeared older than the island itself and was almost a permanent fixture in the shop, 'Jessie wanted ye to have the house. That lassie's been more like my own kin than my son has ever been. That's the very words she said to me.'

'But I'm not kin, am I? And I have no rights.'

'The house is yours lass. She willed it to ye,' said Lottie.

'Will – what will?'

'I saw it. Did she not write it out in this very shop and get myself and Minnie here to sign it.'

Remembering the burnt papers in the grate, the blood drained from Isa's face. The door opened and shut but she did not turn to see who entered. She was not interested.

'He must have found the will – and he's burnt it,' Isa said.

'Oh my.'

'The dirty devil!'

'He can't get off with that.'

Words echoed round the shop.

'What can I do?' Isa brought her fists down on the counter, then shook her head so her hair fell across her cheeks. 'It's been destroyed and Jessie's wishes count for nothing.'

'Ye can tell him I've got a copy.' Lottie folded her arms on her chest and stuck her chin out.

'Have ye?' Isa lifted her eyes in hope.

Lottie shook her head. 'Na – more's the pity. But *he* disna know that.'

'What if he asks to see it? He's already threatened me with the law.'

'I'm sorry lass. It's the best I can do.'

'It may be worth a try,' said a soft male voice from the back. Donald stepped into view, his face grim. A hush descended in the room. Only the ticking of the clock filled the air.

'I know what you've all been saying and shame on you for it.' He looked at each guilty face in turn.

'There's been gossip. I'll no deny it,' said Lottie, 'but it's not for us to judge, although there's many who do.'

There was a chorus of 'ayes,' and a nodding of heads.

'Whatever the rights and wrongs of it,' continued Lottie, the most important thing is for this lassie to stay in her rightful home.'

'Aye,' agreed Minnie, 'And don't worry about the law. We'll write out a new will if we need to. My Jemima is awfully good with her pen.'

Tears sprung once more into Isa's eyes, but this time because of the solidarity of islanders who, only days ago, she thought had abandoned her. 'It's no use. Ye'll only bring trouble on yerself.'

'Just say the word,' said Minnie. 'Many an excise man we've put on the run. A constable will not be any different.'

Another murmur of agreement trickled round the shop.

She turned to Donald who nodded slightly and said, 'As far as I'm concerned, I've not heard a word of this.'

'Oh, the minister, we never saw him the day, did we?' Lottie grinned and the other customers shook their heads. All of them burst out laughing.

Isa ran to Jessie's where Charlie and Angus were loading her kist on the cart. 'Ye can put that back in the house,' she announced. 'I'm staying.'

Chapter 59

Less than an hour later, Matthew MacKenzie turned up, his face as dark as night over the Skerries when he discovered Isa gathering vegetables from the garden.

'What are you doing in my vegetable patch?' he roared. 'And have you got the rent money for me?'

Isa shook her head.

'Then I have no choice but to go to the mainland and fetch the constable.'

'I don't think so,' said Isa, breathing deeply to quell the fluttering in her stomach. 'What did you do with the will ye found?'

'Will . . .what . . . what will? There was no will.'

'Aye there was, for it was signed by good friends of mine who'll swear to it, and not only that,' she added, 'Lottie at the shop has a copy as well.'

'I found no will,' he blustered. 'And I wouldn't believe a word that old woman says. Fraud as well as theft. You'll rot in jail, girl.'

Donald stepped out of the cottage.

'I couldn't help overhearing,' he said. 'I have studied a bit of law myself, Mr MacKenzie, before joining the ministry.'

'Then you will know, even if there is a copy, which I doubt, I have every right to contest it.' Matthew MacKenzie glared at the minister.

Isa's heart quivered. She pushed her hands into the folds of her skirt to stop their trembling. The bluff she had devised with her friends was not going to work. Now she had angered MacKenzie he would definitely have the law on her.

Donald turned his hat in his hands and ran his tongue over his lips. 'I also hold a copy,' he said. 'And Isa has shown me the paper she rescued from the fire. She has proof you tried to burn it. I would advise you, for your own sake, to go back to London and say no more about this.'

'Never! If you had a copy you'd have mentioned it sooner.'

'I didn't know there was any need until I found out what you'd done.'

Matthew MacKenzie's face paled. 'The house and the croft are mine,' he shouted. 'It's my right.'

Isa found her voice. 'What right has a son who leaves his mother to starve? Who doesn't even visit her grave. Ye cared nothing for her. And there's not one in this island who will disagree with me.'

MacKenzie stared, his eyes popping, sweat running down his face. 'Have you any idea what it was like growing up here without a father? If I've done well for myself it's no thanks to *her*! She owed me.'

Isa looked at Donald and bit her lip while her heart beat like a trapped bird. 'Ye'll see I get a lawyer to represent me,' she said.

'I have personal friends who will be glad to.' He turned to MacKenzie. 'You'll have heard of Dangwood and Son from Glasgow. Their name is well known – as far as London I believe.'

MacKenzie bristled. ' Dangwood and Son? Of course I've heard of them.' His face had gone from beetroot red to putty. 'Just get me off this bloody island.'

'I will be happy to,' said Donald. He shouted to Charlie and Angus. 'I believe Jack is with the mail boat today, so could you boys kindly take the *Christina* and see the fine gentleman back to the mainland. '

'You'll hear more about this.' MacKenzie yelled at Isa, before following the two lads with his stiff, long-legged gait.

'Ye don't have a copy of the will, do ye?' Isa asked Donald when they were alone.

'God forgive me for my lies,' he said, 'but I believe it would be a greater sin to allow him to turn you out.' They laughed, suddenly easy together.

'What if he does get the constable?' Isa's laughter died.

Donald immediately put his arms around her and held her until she stopped trembling. She felt small and fragile against him and his whole being longed to hold onto her forever. 'I think we've seen the last of him,' he whispered, allowing his hand to stray upwards and stroke her hair.

She jerked away and wiped her eyes. 'Don't let's give them more to talk about.'

'What is there to talk about?' He drew in a sharp breath and straightened his back. 'Still no word from Davie?'

She shook her head. The knowledge should have cheered him, but it didn't. He hated to see her so hurt. 'My offer still stands,' he said gently.

'It wouldn't work,' she whispered. 'I could never forget Davie and ye could never forget God.'

He did not answer her. He could not, for he knew the truth of her words, even as those words tore his heart.

After he left, Isa washed and fed the children and damped down the fire to preserve fuel. She had made herself a cup of tea when she heard the laughter of Charlie and Angus outside.

'Did ye get himself over in one piece then?' she asked as the boys tumbled through the door.

'We did an' all,' laughed Charlie. 'And he'll not be back again.'

'Surely ye didn't do anything daft?'

'Us? Not a thing.' Angus spread his hands and put on such an expression of innocence that Isa fought to keep her face stern.

'We took the boat round the edges of the Boars. The man was green.'

'Oh, ye never! The Boars are dangerous waters. Ye could have all been swamped.'

'An then . . . an then . . . ' Charlie doubled up.

'What?' She couldn't help but be swept along by their merriment.

'Well, he was like this.' Angus set one foot on the rug and the other on a stool. 'Charlie here was steadying the yole . . . he . . . '

The lad burst into another fit of laughter.

His brother Charlie carried on. 'Ye have to imagine it, one foot on the jetty and one on the boat when Angus here shouts, 'Watch for the swell.' Well, that gives me an idea, so I. . . make out I've lost control, and the boat . . .floats away . . . well . . . the big man . . . his legs go like . . . ' Charlie pushed the stool over with his foot. Angus fell on the ground.

'Ow, no need for that.' Angus yelled, struggled upright and rubbed his backside. 'But it was funny.'

'You should have heard the splash,' finished Charlie wiping his eyes. 'Ye should have been there Isa.'

'Poor man, I hope ye helped him out.' Isa pressed her hands together, her whole body shaking with mirth.

'Oh, yes, we couldn't tell him how sorry we were. We took him to the big house at Huna and the family there wrapped him in a blanket.'

Unable to contain herself any longer the laughter exploded through her until her sides ached and tears ran down her face. It was good to laugh again.

Chapter 60

It was the first free time the crew of the *Girl Georgina* had had for three weeks, and the crew stood at the corner of Yarmouth Harbour not yet decided how they would spend Saturday night. Just then a group of fisher lassies from the north came by. With slight surprise, Davie recognised Lizzie.

'We're going to the music hall. Why don't ye lads come along?' one of the girls shouted. Giggling and laughing, they waited for an answer.

'There's an idea now. Ye'll surely come to the show with us Davie. Ye'll not see anything like this in Raumsey,' said Don.

His first instinct was to decline, but the alternative meant sitting alone on the boat. He had no desire to be seen in the company of ladies since there were other Raumsey lads in the port. He met a couple of them earlier in the week, but they had been away from the island longer than himself and had little news of home. However, he might never get a chance to visit one of these shows again.

And it was a grand show. By the time Davie left the music hall, his head was full of the magical images. Isa would have loved it. One day he would take her there. Please God, let me have the chance, he thought.

The others were pairing off and drifting away, laughing and chatting. The prospect of returning alone to the boat was not an attractive one.

'It's a bonny night,' said a voice from behind him. He turned around to find Lizzie by his elbow. She had a sparkle in her eyes, and her lips curved upwards at the corners. Still high from the excitement of the show, he smiled down at her. All he wanted was a bit of company, he told himself.

'D'ye want to go back to yer lodgings or will we take a walk?' he asked.

'I'd like to see a bit of the town.' She glanced at him from under her lashes.

'Ye've not got a lad, then?' he asked.

She shook her head and slipped her hand into his. They walked the length of the sea front and along the streets chatting about their different lives, about their hopes and dreams, and he found himself enjoying her company. Without fully understanding why, he did not mention Isa or the bairns. Outside the door of her lodgings, he dropped her hand and immediately missed the warmth. He curled his fingers into his palm.

'Goodnight, then,' he said.

She did not move and the air between them grew thick with anticipation. They drew together simultaneously and it seemed the most natural thing in the world to put his arms around her. She fell against him, her face tilted. Their lips barely touched.

By God, he thought, jerking away. What was he thinking? Overcome by the conflicting emotions of guilt and longing, he gripped her arms. 'I'm sorry, I can't do this.'

'I . . . I don't mean to be forward.' Even in the semi-light he could see the heat rise in her cheeks.

'No, no, ye weren't.' He traced her jaw line with his finger. 'Ye're a bonnie lassie but there's things ye don't know.' His words did not placate her. She whipped away and ran into her lodgings.

Mentally berating himself, he walked down the road. If he did not watch out he would hurt yet another lassie who didn't deserve it. Once on the boat he decided to write to his mother at once. There would not be time to post it in the morning but as soon as his feet touched dry land again he would find a post office. If only he got a second chance, he would never again do anything to hurt Isa. Maybe he had already left it too late, maybe Jack had told him the truth, maybe his life with Isa was over. He walked towards the harbour dragging his feet.

He had difficulty writing the letter by the flickering light of the oil lamp as the boat steamed towards the fishing grounds. Committing his suspicions to paper seemed like a betrayal. Repeatedly he bunched up a page, throwing it away. Eventually he wrote a brief note asking after everyone and saying he would be home soon. With the envelope in his back pocket, he lay on his bunk and stared at the boards above his head. The memory of Lizzie's warm body against him was fresh in his mind and his longing for a woman was strong. He had been alone too long.

When the bell rang summoning them onto the deck, he had not slept at all. Lightening flickered across the sea. Thunder rumbled in the distance. In the sky, clouds gathered one on top of another, bruised black and grey. The boat lurched from side to side as the sea flung itself over the bulwark, flooding the deck and running into the hold. The storm was building up its fury.

'We've got to get the nets in,' yelled Don.

The boat lurched and several tons of water reared beside her. The men staggered along the deck, grabbing onto anything that would give them stability.

'It's too rough. Cut the nets loose,' shouted Andra, the oldest and most canny member of the crew.

The straining of the capstan as it laboured to reel in the thick tarry rope attached to the net, could hardly be heard above the noise of the storm. Without fear, Davie leaned forward. He scrabbled at the ropes along with the other men. They'd had many close scrapes on this trip, but Don was an excellent seaman, as were most of his crew.

Tonight Davie's mind was not on his work. His head was full of Isa and his Children. What happened with Lizzie made him realise how close he'd come to throwing everything away. Money or no, he had to get back to Isa. He had to put things right. And if she wanted no more of him, he needed to hear the words from her own lips.

The men fought to get a handhold on the tightly packed net. The shouted instructions to each other faded in the roar of the storm. The boat righted herself and rolled the other way.

'For god's sake, Don,' shouted Andra, 'the catch is too heavy. The hold is filling – we'll be down in a minute.'

The boat tipped further and further until the deck slipped

beneath the water. There were shouts and curses from the men as she struggled to right herself.

White froth swirled around Davie's legs before Don gave the order. 'Let the catch go.' With a primeval yell he raised the ever-ready axe above his head and brought it down on the messenger. Once, twice, three times. The net began to fall away.

The thunder roll was loud, sudden, and right above their heads. As loud as an explosion. Davie stiffened and stopped. Suddenly he was back in the cold tomb on Raumsey. Only when felt himself jerked forward over the gunwale did he realise that his fingers were still enmeshed in the retreating net.

A wave hit him in the face, the force and density of it choking the breath from him. Lifting him off his feet, it flung him backwards. His arm felt as if it was separating from his body. Then his hand tore free. The strength of the water carried him where it chose. He was cold, so cold. His mouth and nose were full of water. When there was no more breath left in him, a strange calm overtook him. He opened his eyes and saw only the tattered sky and the bobbing carbide light. Another thunder roll rumbled through the air and then he knew no more.

Chapter 61

At the end of the season the men who chased the herring returned home tired and weary, walking unsteadily as they fought to regain their land legs, and without the promised fortune in their pockets. Isa waited on the shore alongside the other women. With every man that climbed ashore her heart sank further, Davie had not come back.

She ran along the quay, interrupting family reunions with her frantic questioning. There was only a shaking of heads. Then someone said, 'Davie Reid? Didn't I see him with Lizzie Swanson?' the speaker saw Isa, stopped and shuffled his feet. 'What I meant was, he was on the boat with her bother.'

'Was that not the *Girl Georgina*?' someone else said.

'God, was he on that boat?'

A silence descended on the group. Throats cleared, eyes turned away.

'What's wrong?' Isa grabbed the arm of the man who had spoken.

'The *Girl Georgina* did not return home with the others,' he muttered, not looking at her.

'Ye mean – he might be a bit late?' A terrified hope teetered on the brink of her consciousness.

'It was a bad storm. We waited as long as we could. I didn't know Davie was with them.'

'And it's only hearsay that he was,' said yet another voice.

'And no one knows for sure that the boat went down.'

The words hit her like gunfire. She could not be sure who was saying what, but she wanted them to stop. Stop saying these terrible things. The worst nightmare in any fishing community was a boat not returning. Her legs weakened beneath her and her gorge rose.

She ran. Up the hill and across the fields until her legs ached and folded beneath her. She sank to her knees. She should have guessed.

All season he had not written because he had someone else – someone called Lizzie Swanson. Now his boat had gone down. A hot sweat broke across her forehead and trickled down her cheeks. With no power in her, she collapsed face forward into the grass. Davie gone, really gone. This could not be real. She sobbed and sobbed until she had no tears left.

All night Isa lay staring at the ceiling, her eyes fixed on a spider spinning a web across the corner. When morning came, she dragged herself to the fire, fed and coaxed it to life. Then she swung the kettle on the iron hook over the flame. All she had to live for now was her bairns and for their sake, she knew what she had to do.

With Donald's help, she would withdraw the money he had banked for her. Then she would sell the land. Whether or not she would find a buyer for the house she did not know, for the exodus of the island had already begun. Winter was already on them, with its buffeting winds and angry seas. If she sold up now she would get a poor price. Her best options for both money and travel was to wait until spring.

Clasping her hands, she bowed her head. 'If there is a god,' she whispered, 'Please get me to Canada in time to see me dad.'

The days grew cold. Just before Christmas, the snow fell in great flakes that came silently in the night, covering the land with an unsullied blanket of whiteness. With the emphasis on church and family, Isa had little time for this season.

It was only for Danny's sake that she agreed to go with Mary-Jane and the twins to the seasonal dance. The children were excited, grabbing handfuls of snow and throwing them at each other. Their laughter pierced the air. Once in the hayloft, over-warm after the chill of the outside, the bairns ran and slid on the slippery floor, their happiness like a glow of sunshine in Isa's anxious world.

The music struck up – a trio of elderly men, an accordion, a fiddle and a mouthorgan; in spite of herself, Isa's foot began to tap. She clapped her hands in time with the rhythm.

'Here comes Chrissie.' Mary-Jane grasped Isa's arm. 'And Jack.' She stood up and waved, dodging this way and that, trying to catch the eye of one or both of them. It was difficult as islanders, chatting and laughing, continued to fill the hall, blocking her vision.

Finally, Chrissie came over and although it was not the island way, Isa could not resist throwing her arms around her. The hug was brief and Chrissie winced, drawing back immediately.

Isa let her hands drop. 'I'm that pleased to see ye,' she said.

'And me, Chrissie,' agreed Mary-Jane, but made no move to touch her.

Tears gathered in the corners of Chrissie's eyes. She reached out and placed a hand on both Mary-Jane's and Isa's arms. 'And I am glad to see ye too,' she said. 'And where's the bairns,' she looked around.

The twins and Danny appeared from nowhere, dodging legs of disgruntled dancers. Chrissie hugged all three, kissing their heads in turn.

'Where have ye been, Auntie Chrissie,' asked Jimmy, gazing up at her.

'I'm been very busy. But I will come and see ye soon.' She tousled his hair.

'And me, and me,' shrieked Danny and Christabel in unison.

'I will. Soon. I promise.'

Jack came up behind Chrissie, nodded briefly at Isa and Mary-Jane and took his wife's arm. 'Did ye not promise me this dance?' he said.

'It's been lovely to see ye both.' Chrissie looked from Isa to Mary-Jane. 'We'll talk more a wee bit later.'

Jack put his arm round his wife and waltzed her onto the floor, his cheek pressed against hers. The picture of a loving couple.

Isa wanted to spit. 'Did ye see that?' she asked Mary-Jane.

'I'm worried too, but Chrissie's a strong lass. When she needs help she'll ask for it.'

Jack did not leave Chrissie's side for the rest of the night and, when they left early, all Isa's hopes of talking to her alone died.

Dragging a sleepy Danny home at the end of the night, the music still rang in Isa's head. In spite of everything, she had enjoyed the dance. A few hours laughter to chase away the shadows. Maybe she was beginning to live again.

Chapter 62

By the time the waters of the firth had calmed enough for a safe passage, Isa had sold the land to the mains farm for a fair price. There had been no offers for the cottage.

On a soft April evening, Isa leaned back against the cold stone of the house and pulled the black wool shawl tighter around her shoulders. Indoors, what little she owned was packed and ready. Her children slept soundly.

With no wind to stir the ocean, the moonlight laid a gleaming path which stretched as far as the horizon; the low mournful cries of the seals punctuated the air, the incoming tide rattled the shingle, the beam from the lighthouse slowly swept across the firth and over the land, a solitary gull glided across the moon. These were some of the things she would miss.

Something pushed at her leg. She reached down, recognising the thrust of Jessie's cat, Rusty. Picking him up she rubbed her cheek against the soft marmalade fur. The customary deep rumble began in the animal's throat.

'Ye'll be okay with Mary-Jane,' she whispered.

In the distance, she fancied she saw a hunched figure. As she watched, the shape swayed slightly. Her heart quickened – someone was coming. She soon realised her senses were playing tricks with her, for the shape moved no closer. It might be a bush or a stack of corn but not a man.

Why did she still do this to herself? Why did she still cling to the hope that he might return with a plausible excuse even now? She stood up, lowering the cat to the ground. A few hours' sleep, then the long journey into the unknown.

Sanny the post with his horse and cart came for her at dawn. One kist for the three of them. She had debated whether to travel steerage for she would need her money once she got to Canada, but Donald had dissuaded her.

'I have heard tales about the journey and about diseases that can spread throughout the ship. For the children's sake buy the privacy of a cabin,' he had said.

She had not been able to sell the house, but the land brought in enough.

This was the last morning she would greet on Raumsey. The sun painted the sky and sea with amber and gave the islands to the north a warm, smoky hue. A large ship glided soundlessly though the firth. This was the land she had made her home; familiar, safe and wearisome, a place of backbreaking work. It was here she had experienced some of the happiest moments of her life and some of the saddest. Yet she had grown to love so much. The early mornings when a silver film of dew covered the meadows and the air was fresh and virgin. The soft grass undulating in the evening light as the breeze whispered across it, the sunsets turning both sky and sea to fire.

And the sounds – the sea birds and seals constantly mourning, the first lamb of spring crying to its mother, the golden corn-heads rustling against each other in the blowy air, the accordion music drifting over the hill on a summer evening.

Most of all, she would miss the people.

Tyna, Mary-Jane, Dan, Chrissie and the twins came together along the beach track.

'Are ye all tight?' she asked Chrissie.

Chrissie nodded. 'I've started visiting Scartongarth again – I'll be fine.'

Tyna hugged the children and cried. Mary-Jane clasped Isa's hands.

'Ye'll write?' she whispered. Isa nodded, too choked up to do more. Most likely she would never see any of them again.

'Oh,' she cried, 'I nearly forgot.' She ran inside and lifted the picture of the dove from where it hung above the fireplace, edged up the lid of her kist and pushed it inside. Maybe someday, she thought, the dove might bring her peace.

The cart made its way towards the south quay and as they drew alongside the Kirk, Isa touched Sanny's arm. 'Give me a minute.'

'The tide'll no wait,' he grumbled. Isa jumped down and ran up the drive to the manse.

Donald met her at the door, dressed in his coat and hat. The weary lines on his face proclaimed he had not slept all night. 'I'm coming with you,' he said.

'What?'

'I don't mean to Canada, though I wish I did. No, I'll see you to the train. I've sent word to my brother. He'll meet you in Glasgow and get you safely to Liverpool and aboard the ship.' He raised his hand as she started to protest. 'You have never even seen a train, let alone been on one.'

She swallowed hard. In truth, she would welcome his company, for although she would not admit it, she was terrified.

He clasped her hands in his. 'You were right. My place is here in the ministry. You made me see that.'

'I hope the presbytery let ye stay.'

He smiled – a hard grim smile. Putting his hand under her elbow, he led her back to the cart. Sanny did not appear surprised when the minister climbed up beside them. 'Ye'll be going too, then?' he said.

'Yes, but I'll be coming back.'

Sanny clicked his tongue and slapped the reins against the horse's side. They travelled the rest of the way without words. The only sounds were the clomp of the horse's hooves, the crying of the sea-maws and the distant roar of waves against the beach.

Once away from the shore, the sea rose gently beneath them, smooth as oil with the bright spots of reflected light on its surface. A shoal of porpoises appeared beside the yole their bodies arching and diving as if chaperoning her on her way. A sudden rogue wave rocked the boat and a shower of spray hit the sail, rattling like hail. Isa sat on an overturned fish box covered with a tarp to protect her clothing. She stared ahead at the misty greens and purples of the mainland, knowing that to watch Raumsey grow smaller with distance was more than she could bear.

Chapter 63

There was little difference between the countryside and cottages on the mainland to those on the islands. The vast distances along the winding road, however, were foreign to her. She fell silent, lost in thoughts of the past and imaginings of the future. Donald amused the children with stories and simple games for she had no heart for their grumbling. Finally, the town of Wick lay before them.

'How much time have we got?' she asked.

Donald pulled his watch from his pocket. 'Another hour. There'll be time to buy some more bread and cheese for the journey.'

Isa leaned forward and tapped the driver on the shoulder. 'I want to go to the harbour. There's something I have to do.'

The wheels rattled over the cobbles. Children with hoops ran out of their way. Everywhere were large colourful billboards advertising various wares. They drew near the sea. Isa looked around in wonder and for a long moment lost the ability to speak. Never before had she seen so many boats all together. They filled the harbour, side to side, keel to prow, stretching from one quay to the other. The towering brown sails reached up into the sky, more than twice the height of the two-storied buildings along the sea-front. Rows of herring barrels were stacked on their sides along the quay, several layers high. More women that she could count at a glance bent over the gutting troughs, their hands flying so fast she could not see what the knife did. And they were singing and laughing, their voices flowing through other sounds of the melee. A dog barked, gulls screeched and dived, hammers clanged against metal as the coopers constructed the barrels, men shouted to each other. A little girl ran past them screaming, a lad chasing her with a fish head in his outstretched hand. Even when the entire fleet had been in port, the harbours of Kirkwall and Stromness had been nothing like this. For the first time she understood some of Davie's enthusiasm.

'What a rare sight,' she whispered.

'You're going to see many rare sights from now on. I only wish I could share them with you,' Donald said.

Some of the boats had been hauled up for necessary maintenance. Men tarred the undersides, scrubbed the woodwork, mended the nets and painted cabins and decks.

'Wait here,' she instructed the silent, morose driver who only nodded.

Donald followed her, carrying the baby and allowing an energetic Danny to swing on his free arm. The children had been still too long and were now fidgety and fractious, Danny full of questions for which she had no answers.

Isa approached the nearest man who was rolling a sail. He looked up, blue eyes crinkling in a leathered face. Tufts of white hair grew from his cheeks.

'I'm looking for any relations of the man who owned the *Girl Georgina*,' she said.

'The *Girl Georgina*? She's up on the dry dock.' He pointed with the stem of his pipe. 'Limped back to port well after the others. Don himself should be around somewhere.'

Isa gasped. 'Ye mean she didn't go down?'

'Na. There were rumours, but she turned up.'

'And the men, were any lost?'

'A few broken bones I believe. Don's sister, Lizzie should be over there somewhere.' Once more he used his pipe to indicate the direction.

Isa walked to where the group of women worked.

I'm looking for Lizzie Swanson,' she said.

The woman looked over her shoulder. 'Lizzie,' she yelled in a voice loud enough to make horses jump and seagulls forget their food for a second. One girl, smaller and slimmer than the others, deposited the barrel she held beside the gutting trough. She wiped her hands on her dress, lifted her head and pushed a strand of hair under her headscarf. 'What?' she yelled back.

'There's a lassie here wants 'ee,'

Lizzie walked over, screwed down her eyes and studied Isa.

Isa moved towards her, studying the contours of her face as she did so. Her cheeks were round and rosy as apples, her lips perfect little bows, eyelashes long, framing large dark eyes.

'Can I help ye?' Lizzie asked.

This was the girl who had stolen Davie's heart.

'I believe your brother owns the *Girl Georgina*.' said Isa.

'Aye.' She raised her eye-brows as if in question.

'I'm looking for Davie Reid.'

'Davie?'

'Ye know him?'

'Aye, he bides in our house. '

'And . . . and he's fine?' A sudden chilling cold claimed her upper body and shot its tendrils down into her legs.

'Who are *ye*?'

'I'm his wife.'

The girl's face turned to stone. Her bottom lip dropped, her arms fell to her sides like lifeless eels. She stared at Isa. 'He . . . he never said he had a wife.' Her voice quivered.

Isa could hardly speak. When she did, the words sounded thick and foreign to her own ears. 'No, I'm sure he didn't. Well just ye tell him he doesn't, not any more. Tell him . . . tell him I'm taking the bairns and going to Canada.' A tight band had wrapped itself round her chest. In the last few seconds, hope raged through her and just as quickly crashed at her feet. Thinking him dead, she believed herself numbed beyond feeling, but this new revelation plummeted her pain into unbelievable depths. He was alive yet chose not to return.

In Don's house, Davie sat in a chair, his arm in a sling and a bandage round his head. Don's mother was serving him soup and a wedge of thick bread. The door flung open and Don marched in, followed by Lizzie. The pair stopped in front of him. 'Ye never told us ye was married,' he said.

Davie shook his head to clear it. His heart began to pound. 'Wha . . .how . . ?'

'I've just this minute finished speaking with yer wife,' said Lizzie.

"Isa – is she here?' Hope sprung in Davie's heart. She had come to him. There must still be a chance.

'She was looking for ye,' said Lizzie.

'Where – where is she?' He struggled to sit upright, dodging from right to left in an effort to see past Lizzie and Don.

'She sent ye a message. Says she's going to Canada and taking the bairns.'

He stared at Lizzie. 'What – what did she say? Ye have to tell me . . . exactly.'

'She said ye don't have a wife anymore.'

Then she had not come in answer to the last letter. 'Was she alone?' he whispered, not sure he wanted to hear the reply.

'No, there was a preacher with her.'

Davie sank back with a sense of dissolving beneath his clothes until there was nothing left of him but bandages and rags. 'That's it then,' he said. 'Jack's right. She's away with the minister.'

He looked up at Lizzie's distraught face. 'I'm sorry. I should have told ye.'

'Ye should have. I thought there was something wrong with me.'

'There's nothing wrong with ye lassie. Nothing at all.' He reached up and touched her hand, unable to speak. It had been the thought of seeing Isa and his bairns again that had kept him going during the long nights when his life had been uncertain. That – and Lizzie's careful nursing.

Chapter 64

'My brother will pick you up at the other end,' said Donald as he helped Isa and the children aboard the train.

'I can't thank ye enough for everything ye've done.' Her eyes were dry and lit with a strange new hardness that concerned him. 'I wish it could have been different.'

'So do I.' He clasped both her hands in his and they gazed sadly at each other before the guard blew the whistle and the train let out a long hiss of steam.

She jumped and gave a nervous laugh. 'Will ye do something for me?'

'Anything.'

'Look after Mary-Jane and Tyna.'

'I'll do that.'

Her hand slipped from his as the train moved away. He watched until the carriage disappeared down the track. When she told him what happened she'd been too calm, too detached. He had the impression she was holding herself together by every sinew and nerve of her body, all of which were fully stretched and ready to snap.

Filled with a surge of anger, he marched back to Don Swanson's house. He could not leave without seeing for himself what manner of man would do this to a woman like Isa.

In spite of his injuries, Davie paced the small kitchen floor, supporting himself against the furniture. The adrenaline twisted inside him like an ever-active eel.

'Settle down man,' said Don. 'There's not much ye can do about it now.'

'Ye should have let me go home,' he snapped. 'Maybe I coulda' stopped her.'

'Ye were in no fit state to go another inch,' declared Don. 'I posted the letter myself, but God help me, I thought Isa Reid was your mother. It's as well I forgot to put the money in, or ye'd be penniless. Why didn't ye tell us, man?'

'I didn't deliberately *not* tell ye. It just wasn't mentioned.'

'Forget about that now,' said Don's mother. 'Can't ye see the lad's exhausted. Sit yersel' back down, Davie. Yer better off without the likes of her. Takin' up with another man the minute ye were off to the fishing.'

'It's not her fault. Not all of it.' Davie dropped into the chair. 'Why did she not just come to the house? Not even to let me see my wee ones . . .'

'Mam's right. Ye're better off without a trollop like her,' Lizzie said.

Davie covered his face with his one good hand. The thought of his family had given him the will to live. Now the will drained out of him. 'She didn't use to be like that,' he moaned. 'I did that to her.'

Donald rapped hard at the door and stood back as the Lizzie Swanson pulled it open.

'I need to speak to Davie Reid,' he said.

'He'll be wanting nothing to do with ye,' replied the girl.

A young man appeared behind her. 'What do *ye* want?' he demanded.

'I need to speak to Davie.' Donald pushed past them. They were not going to stop him until he had said his piece.

'Well ye'd better come in,' said the young man sarcastically, closing the door at his back. 'Yonder's Davie, what's left of him.'

Donald stopped, shocked at the sight before him. Davie had changed almost beyond recognition. He was stick thin and grey skinned. His eyes were red rimmed shimmering with unshed tears. Bandages covered most of his head, and his arm and shoulder were strapped up.

'I had to see what kind of man would deliberately lose a woman like Isa,' he said, the anger in him dying as he spoke.

282

'Lose her? Is it not more a case of ye having stolen her from me when I was sick and laid up? And ye a man of the kirk.'

'What are you talking about? If she wanted me, believe me I would not be here.'

Davie closed his eyes, resting them for a minute. A tear found its way down his cheek. 'She never answered even one of my letters.'

Now it was Donald's turn to feel confusion. 'Letters? She received no letters,' he said.

'I sent letters and money too. Regular as clockwork.'

'I think we'd best go away for a while.' Don indicated that the women should follow him out of the room.

More than an hour later, Davie sat with his head cradled in his one good hand. 'I can't believe it,' he whispered brokenly. 'What she's gone through. And what happened to the letters and the money I sent?'

Donald shook his head. He had no doubt now that Davie was telling the truth. Letters sometimes went astray – one or two maybe but not all of them. Jack. The one who kept in touch with Davie. Donald always sensed something evil about the man. He said, 'she'll be spending a day with my brother in Glasgow. If I send a telegram now . . .'

Davie struggled to his feet. 'No, no more letters or wires. Can you give me the name of the ship and the time and place it's leaving from? I'm going myself.'

Chapter 65

Isa stood on the deck, dry eyed and clutching her children to her, among the crowds of weeping, waving passengers. Handkerchiefs and streamers fluttered in the breeze. Good luck wishes merged and rose from the shore. It seemed every passenger had someone to bid him or her goodbye. As the ship moved away from the land, she fought her way through the press of bodies. Thinking she had paid for a cabin, she was surprised to find that she had one bunk in a room with several other women, and she had to share that bunk with her children. She leaned her head against the wall, and fought the tears. Seeing other husbands and wives together with their families, heightened her sense of loneliness.

She feed her children and tucked them up for the night, telling them stories her father had told her. Annie was too young to understand, but Danny watched her, eyes round with wonderment as she talked about the grand places he was going to see. Eventually, when both their eyelids had drooped and shut, she lay beside them, sensing the rise and fall of the ship as it ploughed its way into deeper waters. She hoped the motion would send her to sleep, but there was to be no such comfort. Feeling nauseous, she rose and went to the outside deck for some air. Only a few passengers stood around now, like her, watching Britain vanish in the mist. She never imagined her heart could feel so heavy. Dry-eyed she clutched the rail. Had done the right thing? In her anger, she had not waited for an explanation – and now, how would she ever know if there was one? Davie could have been hurt or lost his memory. These things happened. Yet her own weakness had stopped her. If she saw him one more time, looked into his eyes, saw again the crooked smile and heard him say he was in love with another woman, it would have broken the fragile thread that held her sanity. Nevertheless, she should have been stronger. She should have taken the risk. Only by hearing the truth from his lips could she ever hope to find any kind of peace. Now each wave carried her further away from him.

In the distance, she thought she heard someone call her name. But no, there must be many women called Isa.

The light faded from the sky and the lights of Liverpool twinkled in the distance. She heard her name again, louder this time. A voice she recognised. Someone was approaching, someone who walked with a slow, limping gate. She was imagining things. She had to be. Several nights without sleep had addled her brain. Slowly she turned and lifted her eyes.

He stood there, thinner than she had ever seen him, bandages around his head and arm, his skin a sickly shade. She drank in his eyes, still brilliant blue, his lop-sided smile, his chipped tooth, the mole beneath his eye. She reached forward and touched his cheek, unable to believe she was awake and this was no cruel dream. He held out his good arm and without another word, she moved to its shelter. Her cheeks were like ice although her tears were hot where they ran into the collar of his jacket.

'I couldn't let you go without seeing you again,' he whispered.

He was here, really here, on the boat coming with them to a big new future. There would be all the time in the world during the voyage for explanations

'We're going to Canada,' she whispered.

He was weeping into her hair. 'I promise ye, I'll never leave ye again.'

She turned her head long enough to look at the misty outline of her native country, this time with more hope in her heart than she'd ever experienced.

Lightning Source UK Ltd.
Milton Keynes UK
UKOW01f1535250917
309848UK00005B/109/P